---- ★ ----

THE BOY LOOKED UP, BELATEDLY AWARE OF THEM

"Do you recognize this knife, Mrs. Dillon? Is it yours?"

"Why, it was in a drawer in the kitchen— Is that blood on it? He gets into things— Is that *blood?*" She suddenly looked terrified, sagged against the wall. "Freddy—"

Mendoza squatted down in front of the boy. "Suppose you let me have that, Freddy," Mendoza said as he reached for the knife.

"No," said Freddy, but he stopped ripping at the stuffed dog.

"Did you leave the little girl in the backyard, Freddy?"

He held on to the knife as Mendoza tried to take it away. Freddy gave them a foolishly sly grin, and he said, "Pretty doll. She cried." Suddenly he let Mendoza take the knife and started tearing at the dog with both hands.

---- ★ ----

Also available from Worldwide Mysteries by
DELL SHANNON

BLOOD COUNT
CHAOS OF CRIME
COLD TRAIL
MURDER MOST STRANGE
THE MOTIVE ON RECORD
EXPLOIT OF DEATH

SHANNON
DELL
Destiny of Death

WORLDWIDE®

TORONTO · NEW YORK · LONDON · PARIS
AMSTERDAM · STOCKHOLM · HAMBURG
ATHENS · MILAN · TOKYO · SYDNEY

This one is for
Martha Webb,
as a welcome to the craft

DESTINY OF DEATH

A Worldwide Mystery/June 1991

First published by William Morrow & Company, Inc.

ISBN 0-373-26073-3

'Tis all a Chequerboard of Nights and Days
Where Destiny with Men for Pieces plays:
Hither and thither moves, and mates, and slays,
And one by one back in the Closet lays.
                    —*The Rubáiyát of Omar Khayyám*

ONE

"HE WAS AN AWFUL polite young fellow," said Mrs. Margaret Grimes mournfully. "Like I told you, I was coming home from the market. I only go to the market about once a week, it's a kind of chore, what with the arthritis and all." She looked up at Hackett plaintively; she was a thin little old woman with sparse gray hair, ill-fitting false teeth. One arm was in a cast, and there were still bruises showing on her face.

The other woman, Mrs. Light, said vigorously, "It's a disgrace! These awful criminals walking around everywhere—honest people aren't safe going to the market—it's just awful! This used to be a good neighborhood— I was just going out to the market myself, for heaven's sake, middle of the afternoon, broad daylight, I come down to the front door, here's Mrs. Grimes layin' there with blood on her face, all beat up, and she says he stole her groceries—just awful—"

"Could you give me any idea what he looked like?" asked Hackett.

Mrs. Grimes said doubtfully, "Oh, I don't know. He was a Negro, but awful light-skinned. A kind of young fellow. See, like I told you, I'd been to the market— I usually just go once a week because it's a kind of a chore for me, the nearest one's up on Beverly and I got to take the bus. I've got my little two-wheeled cart, but it only takes one bag— That's what I usually get, just one bag— But yesterday there was a sale on a few things, so I got more than usual. Sales on soup, and hamburger, and bread. So I had an extra bag." She was lying on the shabby couch in the shabby living room of this old apartment on Benton Way. "Like I told the other officer, I got off the bus on Beverly and I was walkin' home, I was tired and I'd be awful glad to get home, I had that extra bag to carry, when he come up to me, and he said— he was awful polite and had a kind of low soft voice—he says, ma'am, that seems kind of heavy for you, let me carry it—and he took the extra bag and walked along with me, and I just thought it was awful nice of him, you know— You don't run across nice friendly people like that so often—and we come up to the apartment building and I thanked him, I said I can take it up from here, and he said he'd take it to the elevator for me—and we come in and of course there wasn't anybody around, and it was then he started to hit me, he knocked me down and he kicked me, and he grabbed my purse—there was still about a hundred dollars left of the Social Security, since I paid the rent—and he took both the bags of groceries—"

"Just awful!" said Mrs. Light. "I called the doctor, we both go to the same doctor, Dr. Bernbaum, and he said to call an ambulance— You don't get any attention from doctors nowadays, they can't be bothered—and at the hospital they said her arm was broken and she's all beat up, a black eye and I don't know what all—"

"Could you give me any better description?" asked Hackett again patiently.

"Oh, I don't know," said Mrs. Grimes doubtfully. "He was a kind of light-colored Negro like I said. Kind of young. He was sort of thin— Oh, he had on just ordinary clothes, pants and shirt and a sweater— I don't know."

Hackett repressed a sigh. This was the fifth time in three weeks he had listened to a similar tale from counterparts of Mrs. Grimes. The helpful and polite young light-skinned black man had offered to carry parcels for four other elderly women, had accompanied them home—to two apartment buildings and two single houses—and there attacked them, ransacked their handbags, and made off with the parcels, in all cases bags of groceries.

He asked more patient questions. "Well, I don't know as I'd recognize a picture," said Mrs. Grimes. "I didn't really take much notice— I just thought he was a nice polite young fellow—till he did that."

Dead end, thought Hackett resignedly. The odds were they'd never lay hands on the nice helpful polite young fellow. To date he'd got away with around three hundred bucks—and the groceries—from the five elderly women, who were all living alone on Social Security. There were no leads as to who he might be, and probably never would be. It was another case where Robbery-Homicide would file all the paperwork and eventually stash the case in Pending.

He thanked Mrs. Grimes. "I don't know why you cops don't catch these awful criminals," said Mrs. Light.

Hackett could have told her, but it would be a waste of time. He went down to the tiny entrance lobby, belting his trenchcoat. It was a rainy Friday in mid-January; they hadn't had much rain as yet this winter, so any was welcome to fill the reservoirs. He had parked a half block away, and dodged through the drizzle to the Monte Carlo, headed back to Parker Center across downtown Los Angeles.

Robbery-Homicide LAPD had this and that on the agenda to work. He wondered academically if anybody was getting anywhere on any of it: those heisters, and the latest homicide.

It was four-forty when he rode up in the elevator and came in past the switchboard to the Robbery-Homicide office. Sergeant Lake was sitting there staring into space and smoking. "Nothing new down?" asked Hackett.

"Not so far," said Lake. "You ever tried to quit cigarettes, Art?"

"Not seriously," said Hackett. "These medical fads— one year they tell you it's dangerous to eat ice cream, all the cancer-causing additives, and then next year they've changed their minds— I take it with a grain of salt. Remember all the fuss about cholesterol? Now I understand it's naturally produced by the body and necessary for normal good health—. Why?"

"Well, damn it," said Lake, "Caroline's after me to quit. But it's hard enough for me to try to keep on a diet as it is—sedentary job—and you quit smoking, you start to gain weight like crazy." He looked at his cigarette moodily. "I don't suppose it does you any good—not that I seem to be subject to respiratory trouble—but I've got enough of a problem keeping the weight down as it is." A light went up on the switchboard and he plugged in a line. "Robbery-Homicide LAPD, Sergeant Lake."

Hackett went on into the big communal detective office and found Mendoza perching one hip on Higgins' desk. Palliser was hunched over his desk typing a report; Grace was on the phone; everybody else was out somewhere. It was Galeano's day off.

"And where have you been?" asked Mendoza. He was looking annoyed; dapper as usual in a silver-gray suit, snowy shirt, and dark tie, he had been running fingers through his sleek black hair. Hackett told him.

"Nothing there—she wouldn't recognize a mug shot, and we're pretty sure he's not in Records anyway."

"*¡Condenación!*" said Mendoza. "And we've got more of the same on this punk heister."

Higgins sat back and massaged his heavy jaw. "That pharmacist was just in, and gave us damn all. Just a kid, he couldn't begin to give us a description, he thinks dark hair, maybe seventeen or eighteen, he can't say about height or weight, he was worrying about the gun."

"Naturally," said Hackett, sitting down at his desk. "The punk seems to be a little nervous about the gun."

"*¡Claro está!*" said Mendoza sardonically. This was another ongoing thing; the punk with the gun had hit four victims in the last three weeks, two drugstores, a small liquor store, and an all-night dairy store. They knew about the gun; he had taken a shot at one of the druggists and the lab had got the slug out of the wall; it was an S. and W. .32 automatic. The proprietor of the dairy store said the punk had been nervous— "The way he was waving that gun around, I wasn't about to make a wrong move, he was hair-trigger, you know?" But if the estimates about his age were right, he wouldn't be in Records, and there were no leads on him at all. In the natural course of events, Robbery-Homicide usually had the ongoing things to work.

Landers trailed in, looking very wet and discouraged, shed his trenchcoat, sat down at his desk, and lit a cigarette.

"At a guess, you've wasted the afternoon," said Mendoza.

"What else?" said Landers.

"It's a thankless job. She couldn't tell you anything."

"Carbon copy, what we heard from the rest of them." Landers sat back and shut his eyes. He had been out on yet another ongoing case, the rape assaults from the USC campus.

Time was that the University of Southern California had been in a fairly respectable area of the city, but these days the area around it had deteriorated. It was on the edge of Watts and downtown L.A., and the crime rate was up all over the county, not just downtown. In the last six weeks five USC students had been abducted, assaulted, and raped; one girl was still in a coma at Cedars-Sinai from a savage beating. From what the victims could say, they figured it was the same pair of men on the last three attacks, but there was no evidence to lean anywhere else. The first girl had been jumped on her way to the parking lot, just after dark in mid-November, by a lone male described as big and tough; she couldn't offer any description, he'd been wearing a ski mask and dark clothes. She'd been beaten savagely and raped. The next one had been caught as she left the college library just after dark a week later. After that the girls had been warned and nervous, didn't go roaming the campus after dark; but the third one had been abducted from the parking lot in broad daylight, that time by two men, both described as big and burly, both wearing ski masks, so possibly one of them was the X on the first two jobs. She had been beaten and raped in the back of the car, and shoved out—as the first two had been—along Mission Street by the railroad yards. The fourth had been snatched from a bus stop at the corner of Jefferson and Hoover while assorted passersby thought the college kids were playing a practical joke; she had ended up beaten and raped down by the railroad yards too. And yesterday Marion Bauer had been grabbed outside the college library at seven-thirty in the evening, by two men, and a couple of hours later shoved out of a car along North Broadway.

"All she could say," said Landers, "was that she'd been a fool—she'd heard these jokers were around, but she just had to do this research for a paper in her biology class, and she wasn't very late leaving the library after all—my God." He emitted a long stream of blue smoke. "She's got a broken arm, three cracked ribs, and concussion. All she can say is they were both big and strong and mean. And I am beat."

"In fact, more of the same on all counts," said Mendoza. "All up in the air and nowhere to go. *¡Mil rayos!* I think I'm going home." It was twenty minutes to six; he stood up, brushing his narrow moustache in unconscious habitual gesture.

"All we've got on anything this last week," said Higgins, "just more damn paperwork." He hunched his massive shoulders in disgust.

"The way it goes sometimes," said Hackett.

"For God's sake don't be a Pollyanna." Landers got up wearily and stabbed out his cigarette. "Thank God tomorrow is my day off and I can stay home."

"If you ever get there," said Higgins, and Landers snarled at him. Glasser came in and said he was just reporting in at the end of shift, he'd been out chasing heisters all day with no result at all.

"And tomorrow is also a day," said Mendoza philosophically. With the weekend coming up, the chances were that they'd be handed a few more heists to work, possibly other things. Robbery-Homicide was usually busy. He had just gone back to his office for the perennial black Homburg and his coat when a uniformed messenger brought in an official manila envelope from the coroner's office. He slit it open, glanced at the contents, and said, "*Nada*. Nothing we didn't know, that corpse on skid row last Monday—acute alcoholism."

"More paperwork," said Hackett. "And it's supposed to go on raining tomorrow." Mendoza clapped on the Homburg and went out. The rest of them drifted out after him, down to the elevators. At this time of year it was already dark, the great city all around ablaze with lights, the maze of freeways crowded with homebound traffic. Occasionally all of them wondered what the hell they were doing here, on the never-ending thankless job in the middle of the second-largest metropolis in the country, with the crime rate rising month by month. They'd all be glad to get home tonight.

IT WAS SLOW driving in the rain on the freeway and surface streets through Burbank, and when the tall iron gates politely swung open for the Ferrari, Mendoza was abstractedly glad to get home; he was tired, for no good reason. It couldn't be, he thought, age; though now he came to think of it, he had a birthday coming up next month. He couldn't see the green sweeps of pasture on either side; somewhere the Five Graces—the sheep intended to keep the underbrush eaten down—would be reposing. But outside lights were on for him at the house, the big Spanish hacienda at the top of the hill; he garaged the car thankfully and went in the rear door. Their surrogate grandmother, Mairí MacTaggart, was busy in the kitchen and gave him a welcoming smile. "You'll have time for a dram before dinner, then. It's a nasty wet night."

"Good for the pasture," said Mendoza through a yawn, and collected a jigger of rye before going down the hall to the huge living room. "*¿Qué tal, cariña?*"

Alison was ensconced in one of the big armchairs on either side of the hearth, surrounded by cats; the shaggy Old English sheepdog Cedric was curled up at her feet and there was a blazing fire going. "It's been a lovely day, darling," she said. "I didn't have to go anywhere—I do like a nice rainy day when I can stay in and read and do absolutely nothing. You look tired—sit down and relax. Oh, well, I'll have some sherry, but I'll get it—don't bother. And for once we can have a peaceful dinner—the twins are busy with homework—"

"In the first grade?"

"Oh, that Sister Grace is an awful one for homework, according to them." Alison chuckled. "Just as well—get them into the habit. And the baby went off to sleep without any fuss at all. You might put another log on the fire."

Mendoza squinted up at her fondly, the firelight turning her red hair to bronze. "Nice to be home," he said through another yawn. "Sometimes I get fed up with the damn job, *mi vida*."

"Sit down and relax," said Alison. "Dinner's in half an hour."

LANDERS DIDN'T get home until seven-thirty. After the rat race of the freeway, in the pouring rain, he felt more dead than alive when he pulled into the driveway and dodged through the rain to the house. In the kitchen Phil was sitting at the table nursing the baby; he bent to kiss her and she said, "You need a drink. Go in and sit down, I'll get it. And I won't say it again—it's all my fault."

"All right, it is," said Landers. He trailed down to the living room and collapsed in the big armchair; she brought him a highball and sat down opposite him. For once the baby was quiet, nursing. The baby had decided to arrive a couple of weeks early, in mid-December a month ago, and had turned out to be Sara Ellen, a bouncing and vociferous baby with a good deal of black hair and a pair of healthy lungs. Phil—whose parents hadn't known she would turn into a policewoman when they christened her Phillipa Rosemary—would be on maternity leave until June. But it wasn't the baby who had occasioned their current problem.

"Me being the penny pincher," said Phil as she'd said a hundred times before. "You tried to tell me."

Landers said, "Um," and leaned back and shut his eyes. "Azusa. Well, here we are."

Azusa, of course, was just too far away. Real-estate prices being what they were anywhere closer in, Phil had seized on the place as a bargain; it needed a good deal done to it, but she had argued robustly that they could do everything themselves in time. They hadn't been moved in a week before it was evident that it had been a disastrous mistake. Azusa was just too far from everything. It took Landers an hour and a half to get into the office and back, hitting the rush-hour traffic on the freeway coming and going. The house was falling apart. It was two miles to the nearest supermarket and Phil's car was on it last legs.

"We'll just have to hope that that real-estate women can find a buyer in a hurry," she said mournfully. "We could find some sort of apartment for a while until we can locate a possible house."

"Um," said Landers again, sipping his drink gratefully. "You know the place was on the market for a year before we were fools enough to buy it."

"Don't rub it in. I know. We can just hope." The baby uttered a loud belch and suddenly Phil giggled. "I suppose years from now we'll be laughing about it."

"Probably," said Landers. "Right now I'm just glad it's my day off tomorrow. I think I'll stay in bed all day. I also think I'd like another drink before dinner."

IT WAS PIGGOT'S night off. Bob Schenke and Rich Conway came on night watch a few minutes early. The rain had slackened slightly, and the forecast was confused; it might go on raining tomorrow or it might not. Time would tell.

They hadn't settled down for five minutes before they got a call, and surprisingly it wasn't from Communications, which relayed any new calls when their switchboard was shut down, but a straightforward outside call coming through on the phone on Higgins' desk. Schenke took it.

"Robbery-Homicide LAPD, Detective Schenke."

"I thought it'd be simpler to call you direct," said an incisive male voice at the other end. "My name is John Farber—Dr. John Farber. I'm calling to report a homicide, and it looks fairly unusual to me, I think you'll want to do your full routine on it. The man was a patient of mine, and I couldn't say what killed him without an autopsy. But in the circumstances, I think you'd better have a good look at it."

"Yes, sir? Where are you calling from?"

Farber gave him the address crisply, Valentine Street. "Not that I want to tell you your business, but I did a stint in the coroner's office before I opened my own practice, and I know your routine. I really think you'd better turn out the lab and do some looking around in depth on this one. It's got me beat. I've got the scene preserved for you, as they say," and he gave a short laugh. "No point calling the morgue wagon right away, the man's going to stay dead. What happened, the wife

called me when she came home and found him, and I was
late at the office—had an emergency patient. I was so
flabbergasted when I heard what she had to say, I came
right around to have a look. And it damn well looks fishy
to me. I got the wife into my car and came up here to the
nearest public phone to call you. We'll meet you at the
house.''

Dr. Farber sounded as if he knew what he was talking
about, but Schenke thought they'd take a look before
routing out the lab on a civilian's say-so. He said, ''Yes,
sir. There'll be somebody there directly.'' Somebody had
to mind the store, with the weekend coming up they could
expect more heists and other deviltry. Schenke left Conway to wait for possible other calls, and went out to see
what this was.

The address was on an old block mostly of small single houses, a couple of apartment buildings; the number
Farber had given was a single house, an old stucco
cracker box of a place. There was a car sitting in front of
it; when Schenke pulled up beyond it, two people got out
of the car and approached him.

''Farber. You're—?''

''Schenke. What's this all about, Doctor?''

The woman beside Farber was sniffling into a handkerchief. Farber turned to her and said in a gentler voice,
''See here, Mrs. Maulden, you can't do anything right
now. Suppose you sit in the car and let me talk to the detective.''

''All right,'' she said in a muffled voice. It had stopped
raining, but it was very cold in the street, with a sharp
wind. ''It's been an awful shock—he was just like himself when I left for work this morning, he'd had a good
night, no pain at all, and then to find him like that—and
you know he'd never have done it himself, Doctor—it

was an awful shock— Well, whatever you say, whatever you think best.''

Farber took her back to the car and rejoined Schenke on the walk leading up to the little house. He was a short, square, heavy-shouldered man, bulky in a topcoat.

He said, ''I got her keys and locked the place. To give you chapter and verse, Mr. Schenke, his name was Robert Maulden. He was fifty-four. I've had him as a patient for five or six years. He had progressive rheumatoid arthritis and an incipient duodenal ulcer—mild diabetes. He hadn't been able to work for some time—the wife has a job somewhere.'' He unlocked the front door and they went into the small living room. It was furnished with a miscellany of shabby but comfortable furniture; there was a black-and-white TV in one corner by a front window. In a big armchair opposite that, a dead man sprawled sidewise over one arm, head lolling down. He was a fat little man, with a sizable paunch sagging below his waist; he was mostly bald with a ring of reddish-gray hair left around the back of his skull. He was wearing gray pants and a green wool shirt.

''Yes?'' said Schenke. He took in the scene in one comprehensive glance. Beside the armchair was a little square table, and on it was a dirty tumbler and a pint bottle of bourbon, empty except for a few dregs in its bottom. There were also an ashtray full of butts, a package of Pall Mall cigarettes, and a disposable butane lighter. On the floor beside the chair were scattered the sections of, presumably, today's *Times*. The room was neat and clean except for the corpse; it was a typical modest little house for this area.

''I said I don't know what killed him, but I could have a guess.'' Farber had thrown back his coat and taken off his hat, to reveal himself in the light as a man of about forty-five, with a bush of dark hair, cynical dark eyes, and a solid square jaw. "You can see he's had an attack of vomiting. It looks to me like an overdose of some sort, barbiturates or whatever. We'll find out at autopsy. But if so, where in hell did he get it?"

"Well, if the man wasn't able to work, the arthritis getting worse, if he got to feeling despondent—"

Farber barked a short laugh. "A little more and less complicated," he said. "He was he last man in the world to commit suicide, and he couldn't have anyway. You size people up in my job, Mr. Schenke. Maulden was another Micawber—cheerful little bastard, always about to win a million in the sweepstakes or find a miracle cure for what ailed him. It didn't worry him a damn that his wife was supporting him—and to give the devil his due, he was always damned nice to her, grateful for how she looked after him—and it didn't worry her either, she thought the world of the little man, glad to do what she could for him. In the first place"—Farber stabbed a blunt forefinger—"where did he get the whiskey? His diabetes was under control through diet, he wasn't on any medication for it, and he wasn't supposed to have alcohol, and he knew that. She never kept any around—she says there wasn't any whiskey here when she left this morning. And—"

"A neighbor," said Schenke tentatively.

"Doubt it. They don't know any of the neighbors. Most people on a block like this will be out at work all day, and the Mauldens were pretty self-sufficient, didn't go out or entertain—didn't know many people. I asked her that, and she says they don't know a soul around here, people don't neighbor much. He had a prescription for pain—the arthritis pain came and went, you know—poor devil, it'd have got progressively worse as time went on, he wasn't in a wheelchair yet but he'd have ended up there. As it was, he could get around the house, wait on himself, but he couldn't get out or walk far. He'd had to give up driving about the time I first saw him. So, he had a prescription, codeine tablets—trade name's Bancap—he took as he needed them. And he was damned careful of his own skin, Mr. Schenke, I'd warned him never to take more than two at once—the warning's on the label—and he never did. He also knew better than to take them with alcohol. Well, as I say, when I got here, the first thing I thought of was suicide—though that's incredible, given the kind of man he was—and I checked. Mrs. Maulden says he had the last of the codeine tablets on Wednesday, and she got the prescription refilled yesterday, and he hadn't had any of the new lot yet. I checked, and there's the bottle in the medicine cabinet, unopened. Nothing else in the house stronger than aspirin. There's no way he could have got hold of anything—or the whiskey," said Farber. "You see what I mean when I say it's fishy."

"Um—yes," said Schenke. "The wife?"

Farber snorted. "She's not the world's greatest brain, but she's a nice woman—thought the world of the man, as I say. Waited on him hand and foot and happy to do it. If she wanted him dead, and did anything about it, then I don't know a damned thing about human people. And I don't see how she could have anyway. I'm not about to stick my neck out and say how long he's been dead to the quarter hour, but it's at least four hours and probably longer—say between noon and three. And she works all day, she didn't get home until after six. He couldn't have had whatever he did have before she left this morning or it would have got to him sooner. At least that'd be my guess," said Farber, suddenly cautious.

"I see," said Schenke. "Somebody brought him the whiskey and slipped him a Mickey Finn, that's how you read it."

"And just who the hell wanted the little man dead?" asked Farber. "Inoffensive fellow—no great loss, I suppose—but I'd have said the last man I knew to have any serious enemy. They neither of them have any relatives—there's no money, you can see for yourself—" He looked around the shabby room disparagingly. "Little people, living humdrum lives. Why the hell should anybody want to murder a man like Maulden? But that's what it looks like all right."

"Yes," said Schenke. "It's a queer setup, I can see that."

"I thought you'd better rout out your lab men and have a good look around."

"I suppose so," said Schenke. "But Mrs. Maulden—they'll be busy here awhile."

"Let's go talk to her," said Farber. They went out and down to his car and he opened the rear door. The overhead light came on and she looked up at them dully. She might be a few years younger than Maulden, not many. She was a little scraggly woman with mouse-brown hair beginning to gray, a thin face innocent of any makeup, but she was neatly dressed, with some pretension to smartness, in a navy suit and white blouse. There was the shadow of former prettiness in her wide mouth, arched brows, faded blue eyes.

"Mrs. Maulden," said Farber, "the police want to examine the house—look for fingerprints and so on."

She uttered a little gasp, and her eyes went to Schenke behind the doctor. "Do they think—the way you said—somebody did something to Bob?" she asked faintly. "But who'd want to harm Bob anyway? Why? I thought—he'd had a stroke—worse than the little one he'd had before—until you said—"

"Well, the point is, they'll be busy in the house, and he'll have to be taken to the morgue—you understand, there'll have to be an autopsy. Is there anywhere you could go to spend the night?—a friend, or—?"

"Oh," she said. Her hands twisted together in her lap. "Well, I expect I could go to Agnes—Mrs. Asher. She owns the shop where I work—Agnes Fashions—I've worked there for twenty-three years, and I guess you could say she's my closest friend. I suppose I could phone her—"

"I can take you there," said Farber. "Where does she live?"

"Oh, it's Melbourne Street—she stayed there because it's close to the shop, that's on Vermont, you see—I have to take the bus—only I don't know if they'd be running now, I don't even know what time it is, lost track—since I came in and found Bob—it'd be very kind if you would, Doctor, I appreciate it." She was trembling a little but in control of herself.

"That's all right," said Farber gruffly. "We want to find out just what did happen, you know."

"Oh, *yes*," she said. "So terrible—to see him like that—I thought another stroke, and he was all alone. It was terrible enough with my first husband, poor Jack—but he'd been sick a long time and he was in the hospital with the best care, and I was right there when he died. But Bob—I told you, Doctor, he'd never have done anything to himself, you know that, and he couldn't have any-way—"

"Yes, yes," said Farber. "We'll find out what happened. I'll take you to stay with your friend, and the police will be in touch with you."

"What's Mrs. Asher's address?" asked Schenke. She supplied it in a faint voice. "The dress shop?"

"Agnes Fashions, on Vermont like I said. She's always been so kind—so good to me—but I just can't understand what could have happened to Bob—nobody in the world would want to hurt Bob—"

Farber handed Schenke the keys to the house and climbed into the driver's seat. Schenke looked up the block; this was the middle of a quiet old residential area, and the nearest main drag would be eight or ten blocks away. He went back to lock the house, drove up to Glendale Boulevard, and used a public phone to call the lab. This one did look a little offbeat.

Duke and Cheney turned out, arriving twenty minutes later in a mobile lab van. "I guess we want the works on this one," Schenke told them.

"Another stinking corpse," grumbled Duke.

"Well, you picked the job. When you've got photographs and printed the body you can call the morgue wagon." Schenke left them to it and drove back to Parker Center. It was still the shank of the evening, nine-thirty.

He met Conway at the elevator. "Something down?"

"What else?" said Conway. "Ten minutes after you took off, a heist. It was the ape-man again, by what they handed me. A liquor store on Temple, the owner and a clerk there. He got away with a couple of hundred bucks."

"That one," said Schenke. It wasn't all that often they caught up with the heisters; it was the anonymous thing in the big city. They got the vague descriptions, they looked in Records, they brought in men with the right records to question, and now and then they pinned one down on good evidence, but most of the time it was going through the motions. But whether or not the heisters were anonymous, they weren't always unrecognizable: just by descriptions the same ones showed up here and there. The punk kid waving the nervous gun was one they'd been looking for recently; the ape-man was another. They had heard descriptions of him from three liquor-store clerks, two bartenders, and several patrons of a couple of bars he'd held up; everybody said he was a great big black man, looked as big and tough as a real gorilla, nobody was going to get brave and cross one like that. But nobody had recognized any mug shots down in Records, and none of the street snitches—who often solved the little mysteries for them—had blown the whistle on him.

"They're coming in to look at mug shots tomorrow, but I'm not holding my breath," said Conway as they rode up in the elevator together. "What was the homicide?"

Schenke told him about it and he was faintly interested. "A little offbeat all right. The boss ought to be interested." Mendoza always liked the offbeat ones.

They sat in the big communal detective office waiting for another possible call. "I hope to God it stops raining tomorrow," said Conway. "I've got a date to take Marilyn to a movie." He was reconciled to sitting on night watch since he'd been dating a blond nurse on night duty at Cedars-Sinai.

Schenke had the radio on for company, turned to police frequency; they listened desultorily to the Traffic calls, the accidents, street brawls; the Highway Patrol, responsible for the freeways, was busy with a truck jackknifed on the Golden State freeway and a couple of drunk drivers elsewhere.

The didn't get another call until twenty minutes to one; it was a heist with an address on Avenue Twenty. It was getting along toward the end of shift, and they both went out on it.

It was an all-night gas station, and when Conway pulled up beside the black-and-white squad car alongside the pumps, there didn't seem to be a soul around, and then the uniformed man came out of the garage behind the station. It was Bill Moss, and he was laughing. "Listen, you got a blanket or something?"

"What's with a blanket?" asked Schenke.

"Well, I'd have lent him my raincoat but it's turned damned cold. Anyway he's called his father to bring him some clothes. Wait till you hear—" He ushered them into the cavern of the garage. "Meet Johnny Kieran. Tell the detectives all about it, Johnny."

"You're damned right I will!" Kieran was a good-looking young man in the early twenties, with curly blond hair and a ruggedly excellent physique, which they could readily admire because he was standing there stark naked, and shivering with cold. "I never heard of such a thing—Jesus, getting heisted is one thing, but this—Jesus, I only took this damn job because it sounded easy and peaceful—how much business do you get at an all-night station, and I'm a physics major at UCLA, third year, I need the money and I schedule all my classes afternoons so I can work this damn job—it's been just fine up to now—oh, my God, I'm freezing—Dad said he'd come right away, but he was laughing so hard—"

"So what happened?" asked Conway.

"Well, my God, I hadn't had a customer in an hour when this dude drives up—it was an old Ford Fairlane, naturally I didn't get the plate number, he's a guy about my age, friendly, he says fill it up, and it's cash, no credit card, so I fill it up, and nights, naturally the cashbox is in the garage, not out in front, and I didn't think any-

thing when he followed me back there—and then he pulls
the gun and says, I'll take all the cash, buster, and I clean
out the register for him, and then he says, okay, you
strip—and I say, what—and he says, take it all off, buster—and he makes me strip naked—holding the gun on
me—and he walks off with all my clothes, and, Jesus, am
I going to run out naked and try to make his plate number when he takes off? It's just lucky there's a phone in
the garage—thank God, here's Dad with some clothes—
my God, I'm freezing—''

Schenke was still laughing when they headed back for
the office to write up that report. ''Talk about offbeat!
The boss ought to like this one!''

TWO

"JACK THE STRIPPER!" said Mendoza, amused, on Saturday morning. "A very smart little play, discourage the victim from trying to get the plate number." He passed the night report on to Hackett. "And what looks like a very funny little homicide, not much in it, see if the lab turns up anything. We'll have the latest victims in to look at mug shots, but nobody's made this ape-man yet."

"It's a damn waste of time to go looking," said Higgins, "haul in the just possibles to question, but we have to go through the motions."

Hackett said, "I've got to write that report on Mrs. Grimes—the helpful gent offering to carry parcels—and you want to bet we ever catch up to that one? The hell of a thing, poor old ladies going out to the market—and no decent description of him yet, just a nice polite young fellow, light-skinned Negro—he could be anybody, damn it."

Mendoza was rereading Schenke's report. "On second thought, this homicide could be something a little interesting. Pending the autopsy and whatever the lab turns up—I suppose somebody ought to talk to the wife."

They were currently looking as best they could for five different heisters, and there were autopsy reports due in on a couple of recent corpses, nothing very mysterious.

Hackett started to type the report. Higgins and Palliser went out on the legwork on the heisters. Grace came in late with some new snapshots of the baby, the plump little brown boy they'd adopted a few months ago, and

the rest of them had to take time to admire those. It was
Lake's day off; Sergeant Rory Farrell was sitting on the
switchboard. Wanda Larsen came in late, complaining
crossly about getting held up on the freeway. About then
Farrell relayed a call from a squad, a robbery report on
Wallace Avenue, and Palliser got up resignedly to go and
look at it. As he was leaving the office two men were
hesitating in the doorway, a big fat man and a younger
one.

"Say, is this where we're supposed to come? The detective last night said we should come in to make a statement and maybe look at some pictures—I'm John
Ferguson, my store got held up last night—"

Palliser passed them on to Grace and went on down to
the parking lot, glancing again at the scrawled address—
Wallace Avenue, somewhere up around Elysian Park, he
thought.

It was a block of old houses and apartments, and the
squad was sitting in front of one of the apartments, with
Patrolman Zimmerman talking to a civilian on the sidewalk. When Palliser came up, Zimmerman said, "This
is Mr. Novak, he's got a little story to tell you, Sergeant."

Novak was a short spare man about forty, with an ugly
bulldog face, going bald, and he looked at Palliser
uneasily.

"Say," he said, "I feel like a big Goddamned fool, but
the more I thought about it, I thought the cops ought to
know, see? Could be I'm not the only damned fool
around, if you get me."

"Yes, sir," said Palliser. "So what's the story?"

Novak said, "Well, I was at this bar last night—see, I
live alone, I'm divorced, I work at a Sears warehouse
down on Slauson, I got nothing much to do nights and

sometimes I drop in this place, sit and talk with a couple of other guys come in regular, have a couple of drinks—you know. So I'm there last night, it's Bernie's place on Temple—bar and grill—and none of the other regular guys was in. It was maybe about nine-thirty, I'm thinking of ambling on home, when this dame comes up and starts talkin' to me. She's a pretty good-looker and real friendly"—he gave Palliser a sheepish grin—"and, well, you know how it is, I didn't read her as a hooker, just a friendly dame, my God, I wasn't born yesterday, I know a hooker when I see one, but this dame, she was just—uh—"

"Friendly," said Palliser.

"Well, yeah. And I ain't gonna say I didn't think there might be, you know, somethin' to it later on, she says this place is kinda dead and let's go up to Casey's where they got a piano player, I should buy her a couple of drinks and maybe we'd dance some, baby. So I go out with her—Casey's, it's up on Beverly and she says she got a car in the lot next to Bernie's, so I follow her in there, and by God, they jumped me."

"They, who?" asked Palliser.

"Well, her and this other dame, the other one was behind the car, and they jumped me all of a sudden, the other dame had a hammer or something, she knocked me a good one and I fell down—naturally I wasn't expecting nothin' like that—and they both jumped on me and beat me up pretty good, you can see I got a black eye and you can still feel the lump on my head—they knocked me right out. I guess I was out a couple of minutes, and when I come to they was gone, got my billfold and watch—I had about fifty bucks on me, I'd just cashed my pay-check—"

Palliser suppressed a grin. "Could you give me a description of either of them?"

"Well, hell," said Novak plaintively, "I never got a look at the other dame, the one picked me up was blond, maybe about thirty, a pretty good-looker, she had on a red jumpsuit."

"If you'd like to come into the office and make a statement—"

"I don't suppose you'd ever pick them up anyway," said Novak. "I feel like a big damn fool, but, Jesus, you don't expect a dame to do such a thing, my God. I guess I just put it down to experience like they say, but I thought the cops ought to hear about it. I don't suppose you can do anything about it."

Palliser didn't think so either, but he'd have to write a report on it. The paperwork went on forever. Zimmerman went back on tour and he went back to the office. Farrell told him a new homicide had gone down, Galeano and the boss had gone out on it, and Cedars-Sinai had just called to say that the Ericson girl had died an hour ago.

"Oh, my God," said Palliser. "So now we want them for homicide." He went on into the office; Hackett was just unrolling the triplicate report forms from his typewriter. "You heard about the Ericson girl?"

"Yeah, Rory passed it on. A hell of a thing. So now it's homicide."

Michele Ericson had been the third girl abducted, raped, and beaten off the USC campus; she had been in a coma for two weeks, with severe concussion. "Just what we said," said Hackett, sitting back and taking off his glasses. "By all we got from her—the couple of minutes she was conscious after she got to the hospital—she says it was two men—we can guess it's the original on the first two, and he rang in a pal to share the fun. The only description from the first two, he was big and tough—and the ski mask. But that second girl—what was her name?—Mary Kelly, she says she fought him like a tiger, she didn't figure she marked him because he had on a heavy coat and the ski mask, but she put up a battle before he knocked her out. He could have thought it would be easier to grab the next one if he had a little help. But hell, there's nowhere to go on it, John."

"No, damn it. And we've got another handful of nothing just now, but you'll appreciate the story." He told Hackett about Novak, and Hackett laughed.

"He'll think twice about letting another blonde pick him up, won't he? The females have got liberated all right, encroaching on the exclusively male jobs."

Palliser rolled the forms into his typewriter to start the report. "What's the new homicide?"

"I don't know, the squad called in, body in an alley somewhere over in Boyle Heights. Luis went out with Nick to look at it."

IT WAS A NARROW dirty alley like a lot in that old run-down part of the city. The morning was gray and cold, and Mendoza felt depressed, looking at the body. He and Galeano stood waiting for the lab men; they had sent the squad back on tour. Down here no curious neighbors were about to turn out to gawk at the cops, though there were probably eyes on them from the windows of the two old apartment buildings flanking the alley, which was just a throughway for refuse-collection trucks.

The body was the body of a girl, in the late teens at a guess, and she'd been a very pretty girl with neat regular features, a nice olive complexion, a lot of wavy black hair, a nice slim figure. She was lying on her back, legs

twisted at a grotesque angle, and she was wearing navy
wool pants and a light-blue turtleneck sweater. There was
some blood on the front of the sweater, dried and dark.
Galeano said, "Sometime yesterday or last night?"

"Probably," agreed Mendoza. There was a small
clutch purse beside her; they hadn't touched it, waiting
for the lab men. There could be prints on it; it was shiny
blue plastic.

Scarne and Horder showed up in a mobile van, and
without much conversation got busy. When they had
printed the purse Scarne handed it over to Mendoza.
There were a couple of plastic slots for cards, a double-
snap coin compartment; that was empty, and there wasn't
a driver's license or credit cards, but there was a library
card for the main library, made out to Rosa Galluci, an
address on Savannah Street. There wasn't much for the
lab men to do but take pictures and print the corpse; they
called up the morgue wagon. Mendoza and Galeano went
back to the Ferrari up on First Street and started to look
for the address on Savannah.

It was a shabby old apartment building, and by the
mail slots in the lobby, they discovered Galluci occupied
a unit on the second floor. They climbed rickety stairs
and Mendoza pushed the bell. After a moment the door
was opened by a fat dark woman. She stared at the
badges and put both hands to her mouth. "Police.
Mother of God, you come to tell me something bad
about Rosa, I knew it, I knew it—my poor Rosa, I was
so scared—and Lucia said—but I kept hoping—"

"Your daughter's Rosa Galluci? I'm afraid she's dead,
Mrs. Galluci. She's just been found."

"Oh, Mother of God. I was so scared—"

They followed her into a crowded little living room.
They gave her time. She sat in a sagging old armchair and

wept, rocking back and forth. Finally she sat up and asked thickly, "She got killed? Somebody killed her? That terrible boy—I been so scared—but Rosa was a good girl, she told him not to come around no more, she didn't want anything to do with him—"

"Who?" asked Galeano gently. "A boyfriend?"

She said drearily, "That Danny Fielding—he lived around here since he was a little kid, they were in school together—she like him before, but since he got mixed up with this awful gang, got to taking dope and all, the way they do— Rosa was a good girl, he was always after her but when she found out he was mixed up in all that, she didn't want nothing to do with him—there wouldn't be nobody else wanted to hurt Rosa—oh, my God, I got to call Lucia, got to tell her, she didn't want to go to work this morning but she's scared of the boss, got to keep the job, it's all that keeps us going—when Rosa didn't come home yesterday she wanted to call the police then but I kept hoping she'd maybe gone home with Marion, that's her best friend at school, only she'd've called—and Lucia said—"

"That's your other daughter?" asked Mendoza.

"Yes, they're both good girls, I brought them up right, it hasn't been easy since Joe died, my husband, he was killed in an accident four years back— Lucia, she works at a Thrifty Drugstore downtown, I don't know what we'd do without her salary—but Rosa, she'd've graduated from high school in June, she'd get a job too—she wanted to go to college, but not much chance of that— she was going to save what she could and maybe someday—oh, my God, I got to call Lucia—" They gave her more time, and Galeano made the call for her.

"When did you see Rosa last?" asked Mendoza.

"Yesterday morning it was, when she left for school—she goes to Roosevelt High School, she's always got good grades—wanted to go to college and maybe be a teacher—I don't know anybody who'd want to hurt Rosa but that awful boy—we heard he's been mixed up with some awful things, robbing people and dope and all—and Rosa didn't want nothing to do with him, but he came hanging around—"

The other daughter arrived, a pretty dark girl still in her yellow smock uniform from her job, and she did some crying too, setting her mother off again, and she told them the same tale. "Rosa was kind of shy with boys, she didn't go out on regular dates yet, but that Fielding boy, he was nuts about her, he was always hanging around, they knew each other since they were kids but when we found out he'd been arrested for selling dope she was scared of him, we all told him not to come around anymore— Oh, if Papa had still been alive he'd have beat him up good and got rid of him!"

They asked a few more questions, but that was all that emerged. Rosa had left for school at seven-thirty yesterday morning—she hadn't many close friends, Marion Howland was about her best friend, in the same grade at school—she'd have had a couple of dollars in her purse, to buy lunch, and she'd been carrying an umbrella and wearing her only coat, a three-quarter bright-red pants coat.

On the way downstairs Galeano said, "The bastard took what money she had and even her coat. And there won't be anybody at the school on Saturday. I suppose Juvenile might give us a shortcut."

"First place to look," said Mendoza. They went back to Parker Center and rode up to the Juvenile office. There they talked with Sergeant Boyce, who said rumi-

natively, "Fielding. It doesn't ring an immediate bell, but
the crowds of little punks we get in and out of here—we
can have a look at our records." The records on the ju-
veniles couldn't be filed down in R. and I., it wasn't legal to build the records on the underage offenders, but
some records had to be kept. "He was picked up for
pushing?"

"By what we heard," said Galeano.

"Well, let's have a look." Boyce went away, came back
ten minutes later and handed Mendoza a memo sheet
with some notes scrawled on it. "If this is the one you're
looking for he's now over eighteen, since last November.
He was picked up for selling pot a couple of years ago—
got probation, naturally—we've had him in twice since,
gang rumble at Roosevelt High, and possession. The address then was this one here, Cornwell Street. He's in with
the White Knights gang, that's a mean damn bunch if
there's anything to choose between the gangs, they go in
for beating up the Chicanos and blacks, but they're also
into dealing, mostly pot but some of the hard stuff."

"Thank you so much," said Mendoza. They went out
to the elevators.

"You want to go hunting him?" asked Galeano.

"He's probably out roaming the streets with his little
playmates, on a weekend. You can go to check the address—I suppose there's a set of parents, at least one, and
somebody there might know when he'll be home or where
me might find him."

"Check," said Galeano. They got into the elevator and
rode up to the Robbery-Homicide office to see if anything new had gone down.

WHEN HACKETT finished typing the latest report on the
helpful young mugger, everybody else was out some-

where except Wanda Larsen, who was on the phone. She was calling somebody doctor and he deduced that she was talking to the hospital about the Ericson girl. Mendoza had left Schenke's report on his desk and Hackett glanced over it again. Just on the barebones showing so far, that might be a rather offbeat homicide, he thought. It remained to be seen what the lab might have picked up at the house, if anything, but he supposed it ought to be followed up. The wife hadn't been questioned. By what this Dr. Farber had told Schenke, she was out of the running in his opinion; as a veteran Robbery-Homicide detective, Hackett was more cynical. It was an old axiom, husband or wife murdered, you looked first at wife or husband. And at the moment he was at a loose end. He collected his coat and went down to the parking lot. He didn't think the wife would have gone to work today.

The address on Melbourne Street in Hollywood was an old four-family apartment building on a narrow little block. Asher was listed at the downstairs left unit. The door was opened to him by a thin middle-aged woman with mousy hair; she was wrapped in a blue chenille bathrobe several sizes too large for her. She looked at the badge, and at Hackett's impressive bulk, and said, "I suppose you want to talk to me? Yes, I'm Alice Maulden. You'd better come in." Surprisingly, it was a brightly decorated modern living room, with a couple of pleasant seascapes on one wall, comfortable newish furniture.

"Agnes had to go into the shop, of course," she said. "Could you tell me when I can go back to my house?"

"Anytime today, I think." He should have checked with the lab, but there was time. "I'd just like to ask you a few questions."

"Oh, yes," she said dispiritedly. "Have you found out yet what killed Bob?"

"Well, not yet. What time did you leave the house yesterday morning, Mrs. Maulden?"

"Oh, it would have been about eight o'clock, just as usual. The shop opens at nine and I have to take the bus. I fixed our breakfast, Bob always liked a good breakfast, he'd just fix himself a snack at noon, a sandwich or something. I always eat lunch at the little café down the block from the shop."

"You were at the dress shop all day except for having lunch? Was Mrs. Asher there all day?"

"Why, yes, of course. Just as usual." It didn't seem to enter her mind that he was probing for an alibi. "And we closed at five, just as usual, and I got the five-fifteen bus home, it'd have been about a quarter of six when I got home—and—and found Bob—like that. You don't know yet what he died of? I thought right at first—when I found him—a stroke, like the little one he'd had before—but Dr. Farber said it wasn't." She clutched the robe tighter around her. "I just—just at first—didn't know what to do—and I guess I was sort of in shock, I hadn't any more than dialed the doctor's number when I thought, he wouldn't be in his office now—but he was, and he came right away—he's a very kind man. We only started to go to him because his office is handy, right up on Alvarado. And when he looked at Bob—and asked me about that prescription, but Bob hadn't taken any of it and he'd never have done anything to himself, he wasn't that kind of man—the doctor said about calling the police. And I just can't understand what could have happened—"

"I understand you don't know any of your neighbors well?"

"We don't know any of them. People around there, they're out at work all day, like I am, and it isn't the kind of neighborhood where, you know, people neighbor with each other. When Jack and I lived up on Catalina in Hollywood, we knew the people next door each side, we used to play cards sometimes, but Bob and I didn't know a soul on that block." She was twisting her plain gold wedding band, the only jewelry she wore. "I guess you're thinking—the doctor asked about that too—where that bottle of whiskey came from, if maybe somebody brought it—I don't know how else it'd have got there—but there just wasn't anybody who'd have done that."

"How long had you been married to him?"

"Eight years—it'd have been eight years in May. Jack died more than ten years ago—Mrs. Owens I was then—he'd always been poorly, he had asthma and then this emphysema, he was only forty. We'd never had any children. And Bob, he'd lost his first wife—we were both sort of lonely—and we got along just fine most ways. First we lived in the apartment on Catalina, and then about six years ago my aunt died and left me the house on Valentine Street—and of course it made it easier not having to pay rent."

"I see," said Hackett. "And usually your husband would be alone all day—didn't he have any friends to come by and see him? Didn't you have any mutual friends? What did he do with himself? I understand he couldn't get out."

"That's right, the last couple of years it was all he could do to get around the house, the arthritis was getting worse. Before that he could take the bus to the library, get around a little—he hadn't been able to hold a regular job since we were married. Well, how it was—I've just never been one for socializing much, I haven't had

time—and Bob, well, since he'd been in California, not
working a regular job, he hadn't got to know anybody."
She flushed a little under his glance. "I don't want you
to think he didn't try to make a living—he did. He had a
sort of mail-order business—when we were first married—he got this kind of jewelry wholesale from a place
in Arizona, and he put ads in those newspapers you see
at the market, the *Enquirer* and those—they were Indian
good-luck pieces, for five dollars, and he used to get a lot
of orders—it brought in a kind of steady income. But
then the place that made them went out of business, and
by then he'd got so he couldn't get out to go to the post
office."

"He was fifty-four? What had he done before that—
before you were married?"

"Oh, he'd worked all his life for his mother and father. They had a grocery store in some little town back in
Illinois. But when his father got sick they had to sell the
store to pay the hospital bills, and so when his mother
died there wasn't anything left. He'd had a lot of bad
luck—and then the arthritis coming on, and the little
stroke he had the year after we were married—it didn't
paralyze him or anything, he got over it fine, but—" She
was twisting the wedding ring again, unconsciously.
"And that was another thing, you see, why he couldn't
get the Social Security or any disability payments—they'd
never paid into the Social Security for him. I guess now
it's the law that everybody's got to pay in, but back then
they didn't have to. So he wasn't eligible for any kind of
pension, it was bad luck."

"I see," said Hackett.

"But he wasn't ever lonely or depressed at all, he was
always so cheerful—and he kept himself busy. He didn't
like TV much, not what's on in the daytime, we used to

watch it some at night, but he was always entering contests. You know there are so many of these mail-order catalogs now, and they're always running these sweepstakes things, they give away cash and houses and cars—some of them, you have to answer questions or make up slogans or some such, but a lot of them you just have to enter your name. Bob was on the mailing list for every single one and he was always entering for them"—she swallowed painfully—"He used to say, just by the law of averages he'd be bound to win something sooner or later—he never had yet, but he never gave up hoping he would. And he liked to read—I used to go to the library for books for him, since he couldn't get out—he liked books about crime, real crime I mean, not mysteries, and sometimes westerns, and biographies. I'd like to ask you—I mean, I'll have to think about a funeral—"

"Well, you understand there has to be an autopsy—we want to find out just how he did die. You'll be notified when you can claim the body."

She said forlornly, "Oh. I've just been wondering—he wasn't a very religious man, you know. He was a good man but he'd never been a regular churchgoer even when he could get out. Well, I never was either, but it's funny, as a person gets older you sort of get to thinking about things like that. He used to laugh at me because I liked to watch the Reverend Thurlow on TV, you know he's the minister at what they call the Tabernacle of God, he's on every Sunday. It was Agnes got me to watching him, just the last six months or so—and Bob laughed at me, when I turned it on he'd go into the bedroom and shut the door, he didn't put much stock in ministers or religion. But I'll have to arrange for a funeral somehow."

Hackett told her again that she'd be notified. Having had a look at her, he didn't think she knew anything

about Maulden's death. Apparently she had a solid alibi, unless Maulden had had whatever killed him before
she'd left the house. "That bottle of whiskey," he asked.
"It wasn't there when you left?"

"Absolutely not," she said earnestly. "He wasn't
supposed to drink, with the diabetes. He used to like a
little drink now and then, but when he got the diabetes he
wasn't supposed to. The doctor asked about that when he
saw it, if there was anybody who might have brought it
to him—it looked as if Bob had had a drink, there was
that used glass, but the doctor said that couldn't have
killed him—and there just wasn't anybody who could
have done that. We didn't know hardly anybody. I'm at
work all day and the way I say, since he'd been out here
he hadn't made any friends, the arthritis getting worse
and him not able to work. He came out here to get away
from the winters back East, he thought he'd be better in
a warm climate, but it didn't seem to help."

On the way back to the office, Hackett wrote her off
in his mind. Of course it was remotely possible that
Maulden had committed suicide somehow; but if it had
been a homicide, he didn't think she had anything to do
with it. Maulden sounded like something of a slacker,
though with all his ailments you couldn't judge. And
people were surprising: those with the best reasons for
suicide would cling grimly to life, and the actual suicides
often did it for no really valid reason.

He stopped off at the lab and talked to Scarne, who
said vaguely, "Oh, yeah, that place. Duke hadn't finished all the dusting, Marx went out on it again. We
haven't sorted out what got picked up—we'll get to it,
you'll get a report sometime."

"You're finished with it now?"

"When Marx gets back."

"Well, send up the keys when you are. We'll have to see the widow gets them back."

"Will do," said Scarne.

Upstairs in the Robbery-Homicide office he found Mendoza and Higgins talking about the ape-man. The latest two victims were down in R. and I. looking at mug shots, but it was doubtful they'd make any. Hackett brought Mendoza up to date on Maulden. "See what the autopsy shows, but it's a funny shapeless kind of thing, Luis. And what was the new homicide?"

Mendoza told him about Rosa Galluci. "Nick's gone out to check the address. Maybe a little something to show for a morning's work. Let's go have some lunch." Hackett realized with surprise that it was getting on for one o'clock. "We'll see what Nick turns up later on."

WHEN THEY GOT back to the office at two-thirty, Farrell said that Palliser and Grace had fetched in a possible suspect on one of last week's heists and were talking to him. It was Glasser's day off; Wanda Larsen was typing a report on something. There was no sign of Galeano. Another autopsy report came in, nothing to work; another O.D. of a damfool teenager last week.

Galeano drifted in ten minutes later, and Mendoza said, "And where have you been? I take it you haven't located Danny Fielding?"

"I had to stop for lunch," said Galeano reasonably. "Maybe I have, which is the reason I came back to base, to get a little backup. Now I've got a wife and potential offspring I've turned a little more cautious. There wasn't anybody at home at the Cornwall Street address, but a neighbor told me where I'd likely find Mrs. Fielding, at a bar up on Silver Lake Boulevard. I found her there. I gather Danny's papa is long gone somewhere, dead or divorced or whatever. She was three-quarters loaded, and she doesn't like cops, but she doesn't like Danny much either. She cussed him out for bringing cops down on her and getting on the dope—she doesn't approve of dope—and she tells me he hangs out a lot with the rest of his gang at this pool hall over on Brooklyn Avenue. Well, I'm not that big a fool, or that brave, to walk in there alone in the middle of a crowd like that and ask him pretty please come in and answer some questions like a nice boy.''

Mendoza grinned. ''So go see if he's there—maybe we can clean this one up the same day it broke. I wonder if the White Knights go in for the knives—it looked as though she could have been stabbed.''

''You heard about the Ericson girl, by the way?'' asked Galeano. ''Farrell was just telling me when I came in.''

''Yeah, so we want them for homicide now,'' said Hackett, ''and not a smell of any direction to look.''

''Damn all,'' agreed Mendoza. That kind of thing happened oftener than they liked. He lit a new cigarette philosophically. ''However, the bird in the hand—''

''I just thought,'' said Galeano, ''that I'd rather walk into that place with Art and George behind me.''

Palliser and Grace emerged from one of the interrogation rooms down the hall, with a sullen-looking hulk of a young fellow; he went out in a hurry. ''No dice?'' asked Higgins.

Palliser sat down at his desk and said tiredly, ''He had an alibi for last Tuesday, he was in the drunk tank all that night.''

Mendoza laughed. ''Go look for Fielding, boys.''

The pool hall on Brooklyn Avenue was the predictable sleazy, dirty old place. The proprietor looked like a broken-down ex-fighter, with a cauliflower ear and a much-broken nose; he growled at the sight of the badges.

"I dunno all the names of guys come in here."

"I think you know Danny Fielding," said Galeano cheerfully. "He travels with the White Knights—we understand he's a regular in here." There was a little crowd of unsavory-looking young fellows playing and watching a game at one of the tables at the back of the long room, four others at a table a little farther off, sitting over drinks. That kind could smell cop at a distance; in the last thirty seconds the game had stopped and they were all looking this way.

The proprietor said unwillingly, "He's back there sittin' with some other guys. I run a straight place, I can't help who comes in here if they pay up okay, you got nothing on me."

"We never said we had," said Galeano. The three of them walked back and stopped at the occupied table. Three of the men sitting there, all looking to be in the early twenties, had been drinking beer; the fourth one was leaning back in his chair with his eyes shut. A little concerted mutter went up from the erstwhile pool players, but nobody made a move, they just watched the massive, looming bulks of Hackett and Higgins, stocky square Galeano.

"Fielding!" said Higgins sharply.

"That's him." The proprietor had come up behind them, and indicated the fourth man. He looked older than eighteen, a surprisingly handsome young fellow, with regular chiseled features and curly black hair. He didn't move or look up. Higgins reached down and shook his shoulder, and he slithered out of the chair and sprawled prone on the dirty floor.

One of the other men laughed and called them a couple of obscene names. "Stinking cops. He's out cold, been high on the stuff all day. He can't tell you nothin'."

"Not right now," said Galeano. "We'll be taking him in to dry out. What's he strung out on?"

They just came out with more obscenities. Hackett went back to the desk to call an ambulance; they waited until it came and collected Fielding. One of the attendants strapping him on the gurney said, "At a guess he's full of something besides the joy juice. I suppose you'll be calling in on it."

"You suppose right."

They'd come up here in Higgins' Pontiac; they drove back downtown and Hackett got on the phone to the emergency ward at the hospital. Emergency had just admitted the patient and didn't know anything about him. When they did, somebody would inform Robbery-Homicide.

The liquor-store owner, Ferguson, and his clerk came up from R. and I. and said they hadn't recognized any pictures. "I figure," said Ferguson, "if you'd had a picture, we would have known it was him. I mean, he don't look as human as all the guys in those pictures—he looks like he just come down from the trees. He's got to be six five, maybe over a couple a hundred pounds, and he's got a face like King Kong."

"We'd have spotted him," agreed the clerk. "He's not there."

"And I'm damn sorry he's not," said Ferguson. "One like that belongs behind bars. Or in the zoo. If he wasn't such a hell of a big bruiser I'd have taken the chance he wasn't bright enough to know how to fire the gun."

"And you can't say anything about the gun?" asked Palliser resignedly.

"I don't know much about guns, it was just a big one, all I can say. At least, like I told you, he didn't get much—I'd already put most of the night's take in a deposit bag for the bank, we were just about to close up, it was locked in the trunk of my car. He only got what I'd left in the register to start making change in the morning, about fifteen bucks."

And since the ape-man had made two hits that they knew about before that, without much more profit, that made it all the likelier that they'd be hearing more of him fairly soon.

"And that juvenile with the automatic," said Higgins when the pair had gone out, "is something else. The next time he may end up killing somebody." An automatic in inexperienced hands could be a dangerous gun. But there were no leads on that one either.

Wanda Larsen came over and accepted a cigarette from Galeano. "The coroner's office has just got the Ericson girl's body. Not that there'll be anything in the autopsy—we know it was a depressed skull fracture. She was the first one who told us it was two men, wasn't she? I had a thought about it—that the one who did the first two brought in a pal. Because they were all USC students, it's the same area."

"Bingo," said Higgins. "And that's all she did say, the few minutes she was conscious, that there were two of them. But it's a waste of time talking about it, there's not one damn lead."

Mendoza came in from his office, hat in hand, and said, "I'm going home early. Nothing's moving anyway. Tomorrow is also a day."

"Well, there's still a report to type on Rosa," said Galeano. "I'll get to it sometime."

IT HAD BEGUN to drizzle again gently when the night watch came on. Piggott had picked up a late edition of the *Times* and settled down to read the real-estate ads. "Wishful thinking," Schenke told him. "You'll never find anything under a hundred and fifty thousand in reasonable driving distance. Look how Landers got burned."

"Well, we can look," said Piggott peaceably. "We should have bought a place when we got married, but now, you can't bring up a baby in an apartment."

"I understand some people do. Thank God I'm a carefree bachelor," said Conway devoutly, and the phone rang on Hackett's desk. "Robbery-Homicide LAPD, Detective Conway."

It was a nurse at Emergency at Cedars-Sinai, and she told him that the police had wanted information about the patient Daniel Fielding. It was news to Conway, but he took it down efficiently. Fielding had apparently been strung out on a combination of liquor and heroin, which made it something of a miracle that he was still alive, whoever he was. Emergency anticipated that he might be conscious and able to answer questions sometime tomorrow. Conway expressed thanks and left the note propped up in Hackett's typewriter.

Five minutes later they had their first call, to a heist at a twenty-four-hour convenience store on Hoover. Saturday night was generally busy, and not only for the squad cars roaming the streets on the Central beat.

THE TRAFFIC day watch came on at eight A.M. Dave Turner had been riding swing watch for the last nine months, and was of two minds about doing the eight to four stint. He had rather liked swing watch; he was night people, and liked to sleep in the morning. On the other hand, it did leave the evenings free, and he was just beginning to feel pretty serious about Rena Fuller, a nice girl and a pretty girl, and she worked at a Penney's store as a clerk. Now he had evenings free to take her places, a movie or dancing somewhere. He hadn't figured on getting married just yet, but she was a nice girl, he liked her a lot; maybe he was in love with her.

He sat in on the briefing by the watch commander, and took over the gassed-up squad at three minutes of eight. As he made the light and turned down to San Pedro out of the parking lot, he was also thinking about Don Dubois, and smiling to himself. He'd gone to see Don last night. Dubois had got shot up pretty bad last September, for a while they hadn't thought he'd make it, but he was just fine now. He was due to come back and start riding a squad again in a couple of weeks. It was funny, thought Turner, just since Dubois had got shot up they'd come to be pretty close friends; before, they'd just been acquaintances, both LAPD men, both black, both young, but now it was different.

It wasn't raining, but it was cold and overcast. And he hadn't been out on tour ten minutes before he got a call, to an address on Leeward Avenue. He wasn't far off; he got there in five minutes, and found two frantic people, a little bunch of concerned neighbors.

"My baby—my baby, she's gone— It wasn't ten minutes, she wanted to play in the sandbox in the backyard—I say it's too cold, but she's fussing and begging, I let her—I say just a little while, we're getting ready to go to Mass at eight o'clock, we had breakfast, and I washed the dishes—I think, too cold, I go to bring her in, she's gone—Joe, my husband, we look—we look—"

Turner got the names, Mr. and Mrs. Hernandez, and the little girl Stephanie was three. "Not ten minutes she's out there, I go to bring her in, I'm afraid she'll catch cold, and we look—I asked the Lopezes next door, we all look and call—but she's gone—and Joe says we better call the police—"

In the end, about a half an hour later, four squads turned up and they all started to look, helped by the concerned neighbors, all up and down that block and the next. By then it had started to rain halfheartedly, and it was turning colder. A three-year-old couldn't have got far on her own. They went looking on foot in backyards, a couple of vacant lots, for several blocks around. But it wasn't until after eleven o'clock that they found little Stephanie Hernandez. And then Turner, grim and shocked and feeling sick, went back to the squad to call Robbery-Homicide.

THREE

SUNDAY WAS supposed to be Mendoza's day off, but he usually dropped into the office briefly to see what was going on. He'd just come in when Turner's call went down, and he went out on it with Hackett and Palliser. It wasn't anything good to look at. One of the Traffic men, Turner, said, "This is the worst thing I ever saw on this damned job."

They had finally found the missing three-year-old girl under some bushes behind a single garage at a house down the block and across the street from where she'd lived.

They looked at her, and it wasn't pretty. She'd been stabbed and mutilated, her clothes ripped off and scattered around the body; she'd been crudely disemboweled and pink intestines were spilled out over the little body. She'd been partly shielded by the shrubbery, but the body was wet with rain, the blood remained liquid in puddles all around her.

Mendoza said in a muted voice, *"¡Condenable!"* Hackett just uttered a wordless growl.

"By what we've got," said Turner, "nobody saw anything. It must have been about eight o'clock she was snatched, we don't know if she wandered out of her own yard or got picked up right there. Sunday morning, and cold, nobody was out. Say, the sweater's missing. I just noticed—the mother said she had on a pink sweater. They say she wasn't out there ten minutes before the mother went to get her and found her gone. This is a backwater, a quiet block, how the hell could it have happened?''

A couple of the other uniformed men were with the parents; the lab had been called. There were little groups of people standing around on the street out there; some neighbors had turned out to help in the hunt, and as the word spread others had come out to stare.

Mendoza looked around this bare backyard. On this block the houses were small and old, and it wasn't the kind of neighborhood where people went in for lawns and gardens. There was some straggly grass in patches here, a few thin bushes against a ramshackle picket fence at one side, and a rank growth of bushes behind the single garage. This house was on the corner, a block and a half away from the Hernandez house. It was an old frame place, about five rooms, long unpainted, and its rear windows showed blank curtained faces to the yard.

''Have you talked to the people here yet?''

''No, sir, we waited for you to show, we only found her about twenty minutes ago.''

''Neighbors out up the block,'' said Hackett. ''Anybody from here?''

''I don't know, sir,'' said Turner.

They went back to the street. The mobile lab van had just pulled up behind one of the squads. Palliser waited to brief the lab men; Mendoza and Hackett walked up the cracked strip of cement to the meager front porch of the corner house. It was an ugly little house, square and neglected-looking, with a narrow porch and no screen door. Mendoza shoved the doorbell four times without response, and they were just turning away when the door opened a reluctant crack. ''What is it?'' asked a peevish voice. She peered out at them through the crack. ''I can't talk to nobody, I'm sick.''

Hackett brought out the badge. "Police, ma'am. Lieutenant Mendoza, Sergeant Hackett. We'd like to ask you a few questions."

The door opened a little wider, to show them a thin woman with ruffled graying brown hair, a sallow face, and curiously pale gray eyes. She was holding a man's ancient faded bathrobe around her. "What do the police want?" she asked fretfully.

"Have you noticed anybody in your backyard this morning, Mrs.—?"

"Dillon, I'm Mrs. Dillon, no, I've been in bed and my husband's at work. Why?"

"Is there anybody else here, Mrs. Dillon?"

"Well, just my son, he couldn't tell you nothing, what's it about?" Hackett told her briefly, and she lost what little color she had and said, "Oh, my, that's awful. We don't know any of the people around here, we just moved in last month. That's awful."

"What time did your husband leave for work?" asked Mendoza.

"Oh, I guess about eight o'clock, I've had a sick headache, migraine they call it, I had it since I was a kid, I stayed in bed, I haven't seen nothing. You mean, it was right in the backyard here?"

"I think we'd like to talk to your son," said Mendoza.

"He wouldn't know nothing, he's been in his room." But she gave way reluctantly and they went into a sparsely furnished little living room looking dusty and neglected, with the inevitable TV set in one corner.

"How old is he?" asked Hackett.

She looked at them with a mulish expression. She said reluctantly, "Well, he's twelve—but I guess I got to explain—he's what they call retarded, he hasn't got much brain, he couldn't tell you nothing. Oh, well, if you got to—'' They followed her down a narrow hall past a small front bedroom to a tinier back bedroom. She said, ''Freddy, you being a good boy?''

The room held only a single bed, a straight chair, a painted chest of drawers. There was a boy sitting on the floor at the foot of the bed. He looked big enough to be sixteen or seventeen, a fat pasty-faced boy with dirty-blond hair and a foolish blank face, a slack wet mouth. He was bent over a big stuffed toy dog, busily disemboweling it with a long knife. ''Oh, you shouldn't be playing with that,'' and she reached a hand to take it away from him.

Mendoza said sharply, ''Don't touch that,'' and pulled her back. ''I think we'll take a closer look here.'' The knife had a serrated edge about nine inches long, and there was blood on the blade, blood that had run down to the plastic handle and dried, probably not long ago. Hackett said, ''My God, Luis—''

The boy looked up, belatedly aware of them. ''Do you recognize this knife, Mrs. Dillon, is it yours?''

''Why, it was in the drawer in the kitchen— Is that blood on it? He gets into things— Is that *blood?*'' She looked suddenly terrified, sagged against the wall. ''Freddy—''

Mendoza squatted down in front of the boy. ''Suppose you let me have that, Freddy,'' and he reached for the knife.

''No,'' said Freddy, but he stopped ripping at the stuffed dog.

''Did you leave the little girl in the backyard, Freddy?''

He held onto the knife as Mendoza tried to take it away. He gave them a foolish sly grin, and he said,

"Pretty doll. She cried." Suddenly he let Mendoza take the knife and started tearing at the dog with both hands.

"Christ," said Hackett.

Mrs. Dillon collapsed onto the bed. "You don't mean—you think he did—what you said, a little girl—oh, my God, no, he couldn't have—"

"Has he ever been violent?" asked Mendoza coldly.

She said faintly, "He's always tearing things up—his toys and things."

The boy suddenly threw the dog across the room and said through a drooling smile, "Pretty doll, I made her stop crying. Then she's all red. Pretty color."

"Christ," said Hackett again.

Mendoza stood up. "So now we know," he said remotely. The boy got to his feet and lumbered across to pick up the dog, and where he'd been sitting was a little scrap of something pink, a child's diminutive pink sweater, and it was ripped half apart and there was blood all over it.

"Mrs. Dillon, you'd better get dressed and call your husband, we'll be taking Freddy in."

She fell back against the pillow and began to moan. "I don't believe it, he wouldn't do a thing like that, oh, my God, he's been enough trouble but I can't believe— I don't know where Doug is, I can't get hold of him— I don't believe this is happening, I've been half crazy with my head—"

Mendoza left Hackett there and went out to the street. The lab truck was still there, and the morgue wagon was waiting. It was raining harder and most of the people had gone in, a few still standing out on front porches. All the squads but Turner's had left; Turner was talking to some of the neighbors on the porch across the street. Mendoza used the radio in the squad to call in. They would need some personnel from Juvenile, and eventually they'd need a psychiatrist to help question the boy, if they could get anything relevant out of him. This was going to occupy time and paperwork. He was still holding the knife in his left hand; he looked at it and thought savagely, one bloody damned mess. And an unnecessary mess; if that woman hadn't been such a damned fool as to leave one like that unsupervised— Scarne was just coming up to the van from the backyard; Mendoza went over and handed him the knife, told him about Freddy.

"Jesus God," said Scarne. "What a hell of a thing."

"We'll be taking him into Juvenile, somebody had better get his prints, there'll probably be some on that." He had held the knife by the tip of the handle, carefully; Scarne produced an evidence bag and slid it in.

"Just call us when you're ready. Christ, that poor kid. I'll tell the morgue boys they can take her, and you can break the news to the parents."

Palliser came up the block, head down against the rain, spotted Mendoza; they got into the Ferrari out of the drizzle, and he said, "I've been talking to people on this side of the block, nobody saw a damn thing."

"*Se acaba,*" said Mendoza. "It doesn't matter, it's finished and now we know." Palliser heard about Freddy and said all the expectable things.

"But my God, they must have known he was capable of violence, he'd have shown some signs before, and they just leave him loose to wander around? My God."

"We'll have to tell the Hernandezes."

Palliser looked sick. "I can do that. They've got some neighbors with them, and somebody called their priest, I think. You'll want to brief Juvenile." He got out and started back up the block.

The two officers from Juvenile were both female, Ruth Gordon and Myra Taylor; they were both experienced and fairly tough, but they looked a little shaken at what Mendoza had to tell them about Freddy. They all went back to the house and the girls bullied Mrs. Dillon into getting dressed. They put Freddy in Turner's squad and Hackett rode in with him; Ruth and Myra took Mrs. Dillon in. She was all to pieces then, but by the time Mendoza and Palliser got back to headquarters, down in Juvenile, she'd had some aspirin and was sipping black coffee and she'd stopped crying. Eventually she answered questions in a dull voice. Freddy had never done anything real violent before. He'd torn up his toys and things like that, and once awhile ago he got hold of a kitten—but she didn't like cats and it hadn't really mattered—she couldn't watch him every minute, and she hadn't thought he'd go out of the house, she told him to stay in his room, and she had this terrible sick headache. She didn't know where her husband was, he'd been out of work, he'd put an ad in the paper to do odd jobs, and he got a job doing some painting for a lady and she wanted it done right away so he'd gone to start it today, she didn't know the address, it was somewhere up in Hollywood. He'd probably be home late this afternoon. She still couldn't believe Freddy had done anything like that, he was an awful trial but he'd never done anything real bad. They didn't have a regular doctor, they'd taken Freddy to a Dr. Hansen when they lived in Inglewood, and he'd wanted him to go to a special school but they couldn't afford it, and Freddy'd never be able to learn much anyway.

They didn't try to talk anymore to Freddy, just stashed him in a detention room under the eye of a male officer. About four o'clock Mendoza dispatched a squad back to the house to look for Dillon. He showed up half an hour later, bewildered and indignant and belligerent, a big man with thin red hair and an incipient paunch. He said Freddy had been in his room when he left, maybe a quarter of eight, and he'd never done anything bad before, how could they know he'd do an awful thing like that, if he had done it and the police weren't just saying so. And if he did it wasn't their fault anyway, you couldn't keep an eye on him all the time. He didn't remember what all the doctors had said about Freddy, that was awhile ago, they hadn't taken him to a doctor in a long time.

Mendoza let them both go, reflecting that there'd be some paperwork to do on this; they'd have to get hold of any doctors who had seen Freddy, hear what they had to say. Some of that would be for the D.A.'s office. He had talked to one of the staff doctors at the Norwalk mental facility before Dillon came in, and they sent an ambulance up to fetch Freddy. He'd be examined there, eventually they'd get an official psychiatric evaluation, there'd be a court hearing and he'd be committed somewhere—probably not Atascadero on account of his age, but it was to be hoped he'd be shut away safe.

Mendoza went up to his own office to see if anything new had gone down, and met Palliser waiting for the elevator; everybody else had left. "What a mess," said Palliser sourly. "The Hernandezes went to pieces, naturally, the priest was there trying to talk to them but she went into hysterics and I had to call an ambulance. From what I got, nobody along there knew the Dillons, knew they had a retarded boy—they just moved there last month. There was some ugly talk going on among the neighbors already. Did anything else emerge?"

"Nada," said Mendoza, "but we can imagine it for ourselves, John. That damfool woman just left him to his own devices, and he got out to wander. Maybe we'll never know how in hell's name he spotted Stephanie, whether she got out of her own backyard or if he just noticed her there—or what set him off— Did he get her to go with him, or did he just pick her up? He's a big hulk of a kid, he'd be strong enough. Did he already have the knife, or just how the hell did it happen? *¿Quién sabe?—Sabe Dios.*" He shrugged. "It happened. The lab will find his prints on the knife, and the blood will be Stephanie's type. He'll get locked away, and sometime we'll finish the paperwork on it."

"And tomorrow's another day," said Palliser.

Mendoza was late getting home. At least it had stopped raining. Nobody seemed to be downstairs except Cedric, somnolently stretched out on the hearthrug, and the four cats, Bast, Sheba, Nefertite, and El Señor, in a complicated tangle in Alison's armchair. He went upstairs looking, and found Alison putting baby Luisa to bed. Down the hall the twins, Johnny and Terry, could be heard noisily splashing in their baths, with Mairí supervising.

"You're late," said Alison, looking up from the crib, and after surveying him, "and you look as if you had a rough day."

He put his arms around her and kissed her. "Quite a day, *cariña*. I do get tired of all the stupidities." But it was good to be home, and to find his household serene and safe.

IT WAS LATER than usual when Hackett pulled into the driveway of the house in Altadena, at the end of the dead-end street. He went in the back door. Angel was just straightening from the stove with a casserole in her hands. "I heard you drive in—you're late. Rough day, darling?"

"Very," said Hackett, and bent to kiss her. The children came running up, hearing him, and the monstrous mongrel Laddie chased after them barking loudly. Mark was insistent on showing him a new game, and Sheila was hauling along her favorite big stuffed cat. He picked her up and hugged her.

"Not now, Mark," said Angel. "Daddy's tired, and we're going to have dinner."

"And I think," said Hackett, "I need a drink beforehand."

PALLISER CAME in the back door of the house on Hillcrest in Hollywood, and was met in the service porch by the big black shepherd Trina who offered him a polite paw. He shook it gravely and went on into the kitchen. "I know I'm late—we had quite a day. How are you feeling?"

"Oh, I'm fine," said Roberta. "Both of us." He bent to kiss her; he couldn't get his arms very far around her these days, with the baby bulging; it was due at the end of next month, and they both hoped it would be a girl.

Davy came running up shouting. Palliser hugged him and then said, thinking about the baby, "Yes, and if it is a girl, then you start worrying about the creeps and idiots and perverts, my God."

"What?" said Roberta.

"Never mind. Just, we had quite a day."

HIGGINS HAD been out hunting heisters all day with Galeano, but of course they had heard about Stephanie from Sergeant Lake. It had been the usual wasted day, talking to the possible suspects and getting nowhere; the night watch had left them two new ones to work. But as he came in the back door of the big rambling house in Eagle Rock he wasn't thinking about the heisters. Mary and Laura Dwyer were busy in the kitchen, and there was a good warm smell of dinner nearly ready; the little Scottie Brucie was bouncing around under their feet. He kissed them both, grinned at Steve Dwyer in the doorway of the dining room—Steve looked more like Bert all the time, but Bert dead on the bank floor was a fading memory now. "You look tired to death, George," said Mary. "You've got time for a drink before dinner."

And their own Margaret Emily came trotting up, arms lifted to be picked up. She was just about Stephanie Hernandez' age, pink and plump and laughing up at him. He picked her up and hugged her, and she patted his cheek fondly and said, "George!"

Mary said instantly, "No, darling, it's Daddy."

Higgins laughed. "You're fighting a losing battle. With everybody else in the family saying George, how could she know any better?"

"It's not respectful," said Mary. "It doesn't sound right." But her gray eyes were smiling.

"George!" said Margaret Emily obstinately. He hugged her again too tight, and she squealed.

"I'll take you up on that drink," said Higgins.

GALEANO was thinking about Stephanie too, as he came home to the house in Studio City and went in the back door. Marta turned from the table, her cheeks flushed from the heat of the kitchen. "You are late, Nick." She'd never lose her little German accent. Her tawny blond hair was ruffled. She came to kiss him soundly.

"You been minding the baby?" The baby was due in March, and it would be Anthony for his father or Christine for her mother.

She laughed up at him. "We're both fine, yes. And dinner is ready when we want. We will sit and relax a little first." She had, he noticed, got the cat's dinner ready first; the gray tabby cat she'd christened Muff was crouched daintily over her dish beside the stove. "It is just to put everything on the table, and meanwhile we sit down like civilized people and have a glass of wine."

"That sounds fine," said Galeano. It was good to be home, to find his household serene.

THE NIGHT watch came on, and almost at once Conway took a call, from Emergency at Cedars-Sinai. It was the same nurse he'd talked to the night before, and she sounded a little annoyed. "We understood the police wanted to talk to this patient when he was able to answer questions. We called this afternoon to inform you that you can talk to him. May I ask if he's under arrest? He'll be fit to be discharged in the morning, and we'd like to know whether that's all right with you."

"I don't know anything about it," said Conway. "Sometimes it's a little busy here. What's his name?"

"Daniel Fielding," said the nurse patiently. "He was overdosed on heroin, I believe, but he's back to normal now."

"I'll get back to you," said Conway. He figured Hackett would know something about it, and called him at home to ask.

"Oh, hell," said Hackett. "We forgot all about that one, I suppose Jimmy left somebody a note to say the hospital had called, but we had quite a day. For God's sake tell them to hang onto him, somebody'll be over to talk to him in the morning.''

"Okay," said Conway, and called the hospital back.

They didn't get another call until nearly nine, and that would just give them more paperwork; it was a hit-run on Third, with a woman dead. At that hour of night there hadn't been many pedestrians around, just three people waiting for a bus on the corner, and it had been raining again, visibility was bad. One of the pedestrians had called in and a squad had come out. All the witnesses could say was there hadn't been much traffic, and the car had come down Third going pretty fast and hit her and gone on without stopping or slowing down. They'd seen her step off the opposite curb and start across the street against the light, so maybe she'd been drunk or nearsighted or something. Piggott and Schenke had come out on it; they got the witnesses' names. The squad was routing traffic, such as it was, around the body, which was in the middle of the street. They went to look at it; she'd been a middle-aged woman, nondescript in an old raincoat, a dark pantsuit. The raincoat was black, and Schenke said, "Chances are he never saw her until he was on top of her." There was a handbag, and by the identification—a driver's license, credit cards—she'd been Marcia Buckner, of an address on Miramar only a couple of blocks away.

"I hate breaking bad news to people," said Piggott, annoyed. As it turned out there wasn't anybody to break the news to. It was an old apartment building, and nobody answered the door; they tried the next one to it, and the couple there told them that Mrs. Buckner had lived alone, and they didn't know if she had any relatives, she worked at the Broadway downtown. Piggott had brought the handbag, so they found her keys and let themselves into the apartment, looked around and found an address book. There was a Jerome Farbstein listed with the notation, lawyer. They looked up his home number, which was West Hollywood, and called him. He said he barely remembered the woman, he'd drawn a will for her last year and he thought there was a daughter somewhere. He had a copy of the will, he'd check it in the morning and get the relatives' names and addresses.

They went back to the office. The morgue wagon had come and gone by then. And the rest of the night was quiet; they didn't get a single call. Piggott went on looking at real-estate ads, while Schenke and Conway played gin; there was always a pack of cards in Mendoza's desk; he claimed he could think better while he was practicing the crooked poker deals.

HACKETT, HIGGINS, and Landers came in at the same time on Monday morning, and Lake told them the boss wouldn't be in for a while; he was going out to the facility at Norwalk to talk to a psychiatrist about the Dillon kid. "God, what a thing—that poor little girl, and her parents—just damned senseless."

"I just hope," said Hackett, "the head doctors don't decide it'd be bad for his little psyche to shut him up somewhere safe."

Galeano came up behind him and said, "Morning. Say, we got sidetracked yesterday—those new heists— had anybody called the hospital about that Fielding?"

"The hospital called us," said Hackett. "Rich relayed the message last night. We can talk to him anytime."

"Then let's go and do it," said Galeano. "Maybe clear that one away before we get the autopsy report."

The night watch had left them only the hit-run, with the paperwork on that to do, the relatives to contact. "I don't suppose this lawyer'll be in his office until nine-thirty or so," said Higgins. "I've got to be in court by then. Probably get held up there all day, damn it." And there were still the heisters to hunt.

Landers was yawning. "I can't seem to get enough sleep these days, it's all the damn driving. I tried to tell Phil it was too far out, but it wasn't until we actually got there—well, we've got the place up for sale, but we may not get a bite for months," he said morosely. "And then try to find a decent apartment for under four hundred a month and hope the price of houses goes down eventually."

"Hah!" said Galeano. "That's past praying for, Tom. Don't remind me of the monthly payments." He and Hackett started out again, passing Wanda Larsen and Glasser on the way in. They took Hackett's garishly painted Monte Carlo out to the looming pile of Cedars-Sinai. They had to wait a few minutes to get the attention of a nurse at the first station in the Emergency wing.

"Fielding?" she said blankly when she noticed them. This was a busy crowded place. She had to look it up, said finally, "Oh, yes, that's the one the police wanted to talk to when he was conscious."

"We're police," said Hackett.

She looked at the badge interestedly. "He's in one-eight-seven down that hall, sir. He's ready for discharge today, and we always need the beds. If you want us to keep him you'll have to speak to Dr. Petrie about it."

"We'll let you know," said Hackett. They dodged a couple of gurneys, more nurses, a couple of interns on the way down the hall, and found the right room. There were three beds in it, and only two were occupied at the moment. Danny Fielding was in the bed nearest the window. The middle bed held a comatose elderly man with a gray stubble of beard; he wasn't taking any notice of anything. Fielding was looking gray and ill and sorry for himself. He was propped up on a couple of pillows staring out the window at the gray overcast sky. Seeing him conscious for the first time, Hackett realized what a handsome fellow he was, the regular clean-cut features, curly dark hair, wide-spaced dark eyes.

"We'd like to talk to you, Danny," he said. "Police. Sergeant Hackett—Detective Galeano."

He just looked at them once, and away again. "All right," he said dully.

"About Rosa Galluci," said Galeano. "Do you know she's dead, Danny?" He just nodded. "Do you know anything about it? Some people seem to think you might."

For a long moment he just lay staring out the window, then at his hands clasped loosely on the sheet drawn up to his waist. Then he said in a low voice, "I'm awful sorry about it. Awful damn sorry. She was an awful nice girl. I guess I, you know, loved Rosa. I did. But she never had no time for me—when we were kids I guess she liked me okay, but not since. Her and her sister and mother lookin' down their noses at me—like I was a bad smell." He was silent again, and said a little desperately, "Jesus, you got to be in with some gang down here, you got to take sides and sorta belong, or you get robbed and beaten up—you got to belong somewhere just for, you know, protection like." That was one of the facts of street life, accepted by all too many of the kids like Danny, and once in a gang, they couldn't get out if they wanted to. "I'm just awful damn sorry," he said.

"What about Rosa? Do you know what happened to her?"

"She'd never go out with me," he said, looking at his hands. "She told me not to come around there no more, she didn't want nothin' to do with me—account she knew I got picked up by the cops—and the pot, and all like that. Jesus, people don't understand—you got to be in with some bunch, alone down here you're a nothing. Just a nothing. People, they don't know about that—she didn't know it. Talkin' about goin' to college—like she thought she was livin' in Beverly Hills or somethin'! I should have forgot about her, what the hell, but I never could, you know? I guess I was really in love with her. It was crazy, but feelings—I guess you can't help feelings. You know?"

"Did you see her last Friday?" asked Hackett.

He was silent again for a long time and then he said, as if it didn't matter, "Yeah. I did. I saw her. It was crazy, I wasn't lookin' for her, only maybe I was. Maybe. See, it was the stuff—the H. I'd been on pot, who doesn't smoke pot, it's a lift, kind of—and I tried the coke once or twice but it costs a bundle." He'd have been picking up his spending money hand to mouth, probably in on some muggings, shoplifting, with the gang, and dealing in the pot, and whatever else that gang was into. "But that day—that day, Barney had some H, he was going to peddle it, only I snitched it while he was in the john. I never tried none before, it costs, and besides you can get hooked on it, you can get dead. I knew a couple of dudes went to mainlining, one of 'em passed out with an O.D., and the other one got sent up to some bughouse. Only I was feeling kind of mad at everything and I thought, what the hell. You know? Like that. And I picked up the hypo at one of them porn places down Broadway, I guess I gave myself a pretty damn good jolt."

"And then what?" asked Hackett. There weren't any chairs; they just stood over him beside the bed. "Let's get back to Rosa, Danny."

He plucked at the sheet restlessly; he still wasn't looking at them. "Sure," he said remotely.

"When did you get the jolt—sometime Friday?"

"That's right. I guess. I'd borrowed Jim's heap before that. He owed me for some pot since last week. I was just ridin' around. I'd been feelin' sort of mad—just about everything—but I guess it was the stuff got me to feelin' mad about Rosa all over again. How she wouldn't even let me talk to her—wouldn't talk to me. She hadn't no call say I'm no good, just a bum, when she don't understand things—I guess you wouldn't understand either—she just didn't know how things are with a guy like me. It was all sort of goin' around in my head, I can't explain how it was, but I guess it was the H—I couldn't seem to think of nothin' else, goin' round and round. I wasn't payin' no notice much where I was, I sort of remember I seen a squad car and went down some side streets, I thought if I got picked up high I'd get thrown in the slammer—only all of a sudden I was alongside the school. I ain't been to school in a couple years, that's a real drag, but it was the one she went to. She was still goin' to school."

"Roosevelt High," said Galeano gently.

"Yeah. Yeah. The kids were just comin' out, and I spot her—Rosa—it was crazy, it was like the other kids wasn't there, she was the only one I saw—and I was just so damned mad with her, had to make her listen to me, notice me some way—she was with another girl, but I know where she's got to turn off to walk home, you know? Off Soto onto the side street—she'd be alone then and I—I drove up there and waited. It was all just so plain in my mind, what I had to do—just get her alone to talk to her—and she come along, there wasn't nobody else on the street—and I got out and just grabbed her and got her in the car.''

"Did you intend to hurt her, Danny? Rape her?''

"I dunno now,'' he said. "It was all so plain right then, you know? Only she fought me, she screamed and I had to shut her up, I guess I hit her or maybe she fainted. I dunno. Only—only—awhile later''—his voice was dragging—"I don't remember how long only it was dark then—and she was layin' in the seat and I felt her and she was cold—she was all cold and there was blood. She was dead.''

"How did you kill her?''

"It must've been with my knife, I guess. There was blood on that too. And I wasn't so high then and I was scared—I was scared somebody'd see her—and I drove up some alley and pushed her out. Only I keep seein' her. Ever since. I felt so damn bad about it—her in that old alley—she always dressed nice, looked pretty—it wasn't nowhere for her to be. And the only time I stop seein' her there is if I'm stoned on something, you know? I just couldn't stop seein' her, like she's lookin' right at me— and I stole some bread from Ma's purse to get some more H, and then I was all right. Only now you put me here I'm not stoned no more and I just keep seein' her— lookin' at me.'' Incongruously tears began to run down his cheeks. "I'm awful damn sorry she's dead.''

Hackett said, "You'd better get up and get dressed, Danny. The hospital says you can go, and we'll be taking you over to jail. You'll be up for murder two, I suppose you know that.''

He just said dully, "It don't seem to matter much now. I don't know where they put my clothes.''

"We'll find them," said Galeano.

LANDERS AND GRACE had gone out on the legwork, and Glasser was typing a report. Wanda felt rather annoyed with the men, walking out and leaving her with the piddling jobs, but they would do it. Well, at least she had been getting more street experience the last year or so.

At nine-thirty she called that lawyer, Jerome Farbstein, and had to remind him why the police were talking to him. "Oh, the Buckner woman—I haven't had time to have a look for that will, I'll call you back." Wanda prodded at him in her sweetest tone, and to get rid of her he left her hanging on the phone while he looked. There was a daughter mentioned in the will, a Mrs. Phyllis Crane, at an address in Evanston, Illinois. Wanda thanked him and called information. She talked to the daughter, broke the bad news, and waited for her to stop crying. She explained about the autopsy, about claiming the body.

The daughter gulped and sobbed and said, "Oh, she'd want to be buried next to Daddy, right here. She only went out to California to nurse Aunt Edna, but she died last year, Aunt Edna I mean, and we'd been after Mama to come back home—" Wanda explained about arranging that with a funeral home here, looked up a couple of addresses for her. Naturally nobody on the night watch had got around to writing a report on this. Feeling annoyed all over again, she got out the forms and carbon and started to do that. Then she was more annoyed when Lake relayed a call. Glasser had wandered out somewhere while she was on the phone to Evanston, and nobody else was in.

"What is it, Jimmy? I'll be finished with this in ten minutes."

"Well, it's a squad calling in a homicide," said Lake. "I don't know the details, but you may want to turn out the lab."

"Oh, damn," said Wanda. "All right, what's the address?"

"Geneva Street," and he added the number.

It wasn't raining, but looking as if it might start at any minute. Wanda got her raincoat, went hastily down to the ladies' room to powder her nose and renew lipstick, and started out. Of course she ran into Glasser just coming down the hall from the coffee machine. "So suppose you come along and do a little work for a change, Henry."

"What on?"

"Let's go and find out."

SERGEANT LAKE felt a little lonely, sitting there at the switchboard with not a soul in the office, none of the usual voices or rattle of typewriters. Wanda and Glasser had gone out over an hour ago, and nobody else had come back. He hadn't had any calls since then. Usually he brought a paperback along for something to do when business was slow, but he'd overslept this morning and forgotten it. It was an interesting book too, about the First World War; he'd always been something of a history buff.

His stomach rumbled and he thought about lunch. The other men could go out to a restaurant and eat a civilized lunch. On his perennial diet about all he could have was cottage cheese and fruit, and he usually took fifteen minutes to go up to the canteen. Generally the mildest of characters, Sergeant Lake was stirred by his rumbling stomach to resentment of all his colleagues. There wasn't anything fair about it at all; in fact it was damned unjust. There was Mendoza, a year older than Lake, still as

slim and elegant as he'd been twenty years ago; and Tom
Landers as thin as a rail, with his boyish face that made
him look so much younger than he was. There was lean,
tall, handsome Palliser; and even the two big bruisers,
Hackett and Higgins, never had to worry about gaining.
Galeano—he had to watch it a little, Lake admitted to
himself grudgingly; his wife was a good cook; but he
didn't seem to worry about it much, and of course he got
out to get the exercise. All this sitting at a desk all day—
but it just wasn't fair. Lake sat back and thought wist-
fully of a decent lunch: of a tuna sandwich with lots of
mayonnaise, of a hamburger with french fries and onion rings, or breaded veal cutlets with plenty of cream
gravy.

He wondered if there was anything to this reincarna-
tion. If so, he hoped he'd been good enough this time
around so that when he got back here he'd be one of
those people who could eat anything and never gain a
pound. Caroline had been at him to quit smoking—but
it was enough trouble now to keep under a hundred and
seventy, and everybody knew when you quit smoking you
started to gain.

He left the switchboard for fifteen minutes, went up to
the canteen and had some cottage cheese and peach slices.
He was still feeling hungry when he got back. The
switchboard was quiet. Everybody else would be out
having a decent lunch, of course.

Hackett and Galeano came in at a little after one, and
Galeano started to type a report while Hackett got busy
on the phone starting the machinery on a warrant; so
they'd cleaned one up. There hadn't been a glimpse of
Mendoza all day; he'd still be talking to the psychiatrist,
probably. Lake thought again fleetingly of that poor little girl. Hostages to fortune, he thought, and was glad

their two were grown, Jim junior twenty and in college, Linda eighteen and graduating from high school in June. And still the switchboard was quiet. It was usually either feast or famine.

That thought sent him back to his stomach again. Damn it, he was still hungry. And not that Caroline nagged him about it, she wasn't that kind of wife, but she saw he stayed on the diet. Four ounces of lean steak, he thought gloomily, and what the hell was a steak without french-fried onion rings and mushroom gravy?

The switchboard flashed at him and he jerked back to his usual efficiency and plugged in. "Robbery-Homicide LAPD, Sergeant Lake—" A minute later he rushed into the communal office. "You'd both better make time over to the Hall of Justice, Art, there's some kind of gunfight going on and a man shot dead—"

"The Hall of Justice?" said Hackett, startled. "For God's sake, has one of our bleeding-heart judges gone officially off his head?"

"I don't know—it was one of the bailiffs, he was pretty excited."

"For God's sake," said Hackett again. He and Galeano went out in a hurry and Lake was left alone again.

Of course, five minutes later he began to get calls. The first one was from a Traffic man over on Temple, reporting a heist. "There isn't anybody in," said Lake.

"Well, my God," said the patrolman, "I've had to call an ambulance—it's an independent drugstore, the owner was alone, and the guy took a shot at him—he gave me a vague description before he passed out. I don't think he's too bad, he's lost some blood is all—but do I just go back on tour?"

"You'd better try the emergency number on the door." Lake took details; the owner a John Lemoyne, the address. "We'll be on it sometime."

He'd no sooner unplugged that call when he got another. The voice at the other end said doubtfully, "What did you say—Homicide? Well, listen, I just called in, I guess I've been talking to your central desk or whatever, when I said what it was about they put me through to you. Can you tell me, there was a murder or something on Valentine Street the other day? A fellow named Maulden. It's been sort of on the grapevine around the block, know what I mean, my wife was talking to the woman next door—"

"Yes, sir," said Lake, remembering the name. The voice didn't sound like that of the ordinary street snitch calling in anonymously. "What about it? May I have your name?"

"Sure. I'm Floyd Hoffman. I might know something about it, couldn't say if it'd mean anything to the cops, but I figured I ought to come out with it if it might be important. I tell you what it is, I saw something there, it was last Friday by what we heard, I saw—"

"One of the detectives will want to talk to you, Mr. Hoffman. There's no one in right now, but somebody'll get back to you, if you give me your address."

"Oh, well, okay, if that's the way you do it. I just figured I ought to tell the cops if it's anything important— we live right across the street," and he added an address. Lake thanked him; they appreciated the citizens trying to help, even when it turned out to be mistakenly.

He wondered what the hell was going on at the Hall of Justice.

The switchboard flashed again and he plugged in re-signedly. It was another Traffic man, and he was report-ing a body. "None of the detectives are in," said Lake.

"Well, for God's sake, what do I do, stand guard over it? It's on a bench in Westlake Park, looks like an old wino just passed out with the DT's or maybe a heart at-tack, but we're supposed to report to you—"

It didn't sound like anything they'd be calling the lab on for the full scientific treatment. "You'd better just call the morgue wagon," said Lake. He sat back, lit another cigarette, and wondered just where everybody was, on what.

FOUR

THE ADDRESS on Geneva Street was an old stucco house on a narrow lot, on a block of similar old houses. The squad was sitting in front of it, and the uniformed man was talking to a mailman on the sidewalk. The body of a woman was sprawled head down on the shallow front steps of the house. The patrolman was Jim Frawley; he greeted Wanda and Glasser with relief. "Here are the detectives—this is Ben Darby, he's the one called in."

The mailman was a tall young black man, in the light-blue post-office uniform with a trenchcoat over it. "And I'm sorry but I got my route to cover, I'm half an hour late now, I don't know anything about this, I just happened to be passing. I can tell you her name it's Katherine Polachek, she gets the welfare checks regular, nothing else. I don't know how long she'd been laying there, but a block like this, people out at work, probably I was the first one to spot her."

"When?" asked Glasser.

"About half an hour ago, I'm usually along here about that time. Naturally I went and looked at her, thought she was sick or passed out, and my God, she's got a knife in her, so I went back to the nearest public phone and called you cops. And that's all I know, and I'm late on my route—"

They took his address and let him go, and went to look at the body. The woman looked to be forty or around there, with bleached platinum hair tumbled around her shoulders, a mask of too much makeup—too white powder and too dark magenta lipstick; she looked almost obscene, sprawled head down on the cracked cement steps. It was an angular thin body in a black pantsuit and ankle-high boots, some cheap costume jewelry, a fake pearl necklace and big pearl earrings. Death had made her anonymous; it was impossible to say if she'd been good-looking under her makeup mask. There was an ordinary plastic-handled bread knife sticking out of her chest.

Glasser bent and felt her wrist and said, "She hasn't been dead long."

"I don't think there's anybody in the house," said Frawley. "And no car in the garage."

"Well," said Wanda, "I suppose we'd better get the lab out." Now belatedly it appeared that at least one neighbor was at home; a woman had come out on the front porch a couple of houses up and was staring curiously. Glasser got on the radio in the squad, and Wanda went up on the porch past the body. The front door was open and she went in. It was a squalid little living room, no entry hall; there was an old mud-colored sofa, a couple of chairs, a portable TV, a shallow fake hearth on one wall. She went looking for a phone, a possible address book. A mean, narrow hall led her down toward the kitchen at the back, and she nearly jumped out of her skin when there was a sharp rustle of movement from there. "Is anybody here?" she asked sharply, and stepped into the kitchen.

There was a girl standing in front of the sink, a thin dark-haired girl looking about twelve or thirteen. She had a round pale face, rather pretty, with a small straight nose and dark eyes. Wanda stared at her and she stared back silently.

"Is that your mother on the front porch?" asked Wanda abruptly—all she could think of to say immediately. The girl shook her head. "Do you live here?"

The girl said in a thin voice, "Yeah. With her. Is she dead?"

"Do you know anything about it? How she was stabbed?

"I've been scared she isn't dead, just hurt bad, so she'd beat me up again. I just couldn't stand it no more, I never tried to hit her back before but that last time she yelled at me and started to hit me, I just did it."

"You stabbed her?" asked Wanda.

She nodded. "I was peeling the potatoes for lunch, I just stuck the knife in her and she yelled some more and run out. I was scared she'd come back and beat me up." There was a dark bruise on one side of her face, and she had the beginning of a black eye. Wanda heard Glasser come up behind her. She asked, "What's your name?"

"Linda," said the girl, and then, "I'm Linda Kent and I live at Thirty-four Holly Road in Hempstead." That was a rapid singsong as if it were something learned by rote.

Glasser said softly, "My God, have we got another nutty juvenile?" The girl looked at him warily. She was incongruously dressed in a woman's pink summer dress too old for her, too large; her legs and feet were bare.

Wanda felt a little helpless. They went on staring at each other. Finally she asked, "Mrs. Polachek isn't your mother—is she a relative?" The girl looked confused.

"I don't know what you mean. Who are you?" She looked nervously at Glasser. "Is she dead? If she's dead I'm glad. I never knew how easy it'd be, if I knew I'd of hit her before."

"How long have you lived here, Linda?"

"With her, you mean? Forever and ever, I guess. I don't know. If she's dead maybe I can go somewhere else, only I don't know where."

Glasser asked, "She used to beat you up?"

She looked at him nervously. "She gets mad awful easy, if I don't do things right, don't cook things right or forget to make the bed or other things. I never tried to hit her back before."

This was something new to both of them. The girl didn't seem to be stupid, but there was a curious vague innocence about her, the little-girl voice, the lifelessness. She said again, "Who are you?"

"We're police officers, Linda. We're going to take you somewhere else, we want to ask you some questions. How old are you?"

"I don't know. She never said nothing about that."

Wanda looked at Glasser and he shrugged. "Do you go to school?"

"I don't know school," she said blankly. "What's that? I'm not supposed to go out of the house. When she goes away she locks me in the bathroom. But I don't care, when I'm alone I can talk to myself, and sometimes Louise comes and I talk to her."

"Who's Louise?" asked Wanda.

"Just Louise. She's just like me."

"My God," said Glasser under his breath. "Another nut."

It sounded that way. Wanda said, "You'll have to come with us, Linda."

"You goin' to beat me up because I stuck the knife in her?"

"Of course not, we just want you to answer some questions."

"You mean—go somewhere else? Away from the house? I never been away from the house since we come here. I'm not supposed to."

"When did you come here?"

"I don't know," she said vaguely. "Forever. What's your name?"

"My name's Wanda."

"I never heard that name before. It's kind of pretty."

"Have you got a coat, Linda? Go and get it, it's cold outside—and put on some shoes and stockings."

"I haven't got no shoes, hers was too big. She give me her old clothes when I started to grow some but I haven't got no shoes."

My God, what is this, thought Wanda. Well, they'd give her some clothes at Juvenile Hall. The lab would be poking around here. She went and looked in both bedrooms. The rear one was barely furnished with an old cot, nothing else. In the other one she found a pair of old felt slippers on the floor of the closet and made the girl put them on for the ride in. She shepherded her out to the squad.

Glasser said, "I'll see if I can raise some neighbors."

Astonishingly, on the ride downtown in the squad the girl sat up and grew animated, looking out the windows at the streets and the people. "Oh, it's so big—all the people—such pretty clothes! I never knew there was anywhere so big! What's its name, where we are?"

Wanda had nearly stopped feeling surprised. "It's Los Angeles. Didn't you know that?"

The girl repeated the name thoughtfully. "It's a funny name. Is it the same as New York? I only know about New York, and some other place, another funny name—"

"It's California."

"Where's that?" But she was entranced with the crowds and noise and traffic lights. "It's all so pretty!" she said.

Wanda let her stare. At Headquarters she took her up to the Juvenile office and ran into Ruth Gordon right away. They'd been at the Academy together; she liked Ruth, who had married a sergeant at Hollenbeck Division last year. Wanda sat Linda down in a chair and gave Ruth the rundown on this thing.

"My God, what we do see," said Ruth. "She looks about twelve."

"She said the woman beat her up, never let her out of the house. But who is the kid? How did the woman get hold of her?"

"You don't know anything about the Polachek woman yet. She could have been the natural mother and the kid's just batty."

"I don't think so, there's something offbeat about it. Let's see what more we can get out of her."

They took Linda into the office Ruth shared with another officer; it was empty at the moment. They started to talk to her. She said timidly, "I'm awful hungry, we hadn't had no lunch yet, and she always said I ate too much anyways." Ruth went up to the canteen and brought her a sandwich and a glass of milk, and she wolfed it down ravenously. "You're nice. I like you," she said to both of them. "I don't know anybody except her, I talk to myself mostly, she doesn't talk, she just yells at me."

"Is she related to you?" asked Ruth.

That confused her again. "I don't know what that means," and she brought it out again, a litany learned by rote and repeated like a recitation. "My name is Linda Kent and I live at Thirty-four Holly Road, Hempstead."

"When did you live there, Linda?"

"Where? I don't know."

"How long had you lived with Mrs. Polachek? Katherine? What did you call her, Aunt or what? How long have you lived here?"

She said vaguely, "A long time. Forever. I didn't call her anything. We came in a car with a man. Billy." She began to shiver. "He went away a long time ago and I was glad. I was so glad he went away and never came back. He did awful things to me—and he made me watch them do awful things together. He used to hurt me awful bad. I was always scared one of the other ones might do that but they never did, and I was glad."

"What other ones?" asked Wanda.

"The ones come back to the house with her most nights. Different ones. You never said if she's dead."

"Yes, she's dead. You won't see her again."

Linda sat back in the chair and a dreamy peaceful smile stretched her small mouth. "Oh, then I'm glad. Then could I stay with you? I'm real good at cooking things mostly and I know all how to do, dust and clean and iron clothes, I had to do all that for her and I'd be real glad to do it for you. You've been nice to me."

They exchanged glances. "She made you do all that?"

"It had got easier since I began to get bigger, only sometimes I forget things and she yelled and hit me."

"Didn't you ever try to get away, Linda? Didn't you know there'd be people to help you, that she hadn't any right to treat you like that?"

She was confused again. "I don't know what you mean, where'd I go? She wouldn't have let me. When she went out somewhere she locked me in the bathroom. But I kind of liked that, when she was gone I could sit and talk to myself."

"And sometimes Louise came?" asked Wanda cautiously.

She nodded vigorously. "Yes, I liked that. I could talk to her."

"Who is Louise?"

"She's just in my head, kind of, she's somebody just like me and I can talk to her."

"Do you know where Mrs. Polachek went when she left the house?"

She shook her head. "Nights she went, she got all dressed up and went away—and then she'd come back and bring them with her—different ones—and I was always scared they'd want to do the awful things to me— but they never. Not since Billy went away. She'd lock me in the bedroom then but I knew they were doing awful things in her room."

"Do you remember Billy's other name?"

"I don't know. It was a long time ago he went away."

They left her with another glass of milk and went out to the anteroom. Wanda said, "My God, what a tale. Reading between lines. Maybe something else will emerge if we find out more about the woman."

"That girl isn't retarded or stupid," said Ruth, "but apparently she's been kept more or less in solitary confinement for God knows how long. That little piece she came out with, the address—"

"Yes, I wonder about that. On the way in she said something about New York. Have you got an atlas?" Ruth found one and they looked. There was a town called Hempstead on Long Island. "Well, they'll look after her at Juvenile Hall, and the D.A.'s office will decide what to do with her. Just from what we've got, I can't say I blame the poor kid for sticking the knife in that woman.

We'll have to get psychiatric opinion on her. All we can do, maybe.''

"But I'd like to know how the damn woman got hold of her.''

"So would I,'' said Wanda somberly. She took Linda down to Juvenile Hall and talked to a couple of the matrons about her. They'd seen everything there was to see, and didn't turn a hair. Linda was entranced all over again at meeting more new friends, at the tiny cubicle of a room with its neat clean bed and chest of drawers, at the clothes they gave her, the plain tan uniform dress and cotton stockings and moccasins. "We'll be having dinner after a while,'' the matron told her kindly, "and tomorrow there'll be a doctor to see you. You're not afraid of doctors, are you?''

And Linda asked blankly, "What's a doctor?''

Wanda went back to the office and found Glasser just putting down his phone. It was nearly four o'clock. He said sardonically, "Well, we're a little further on. I've been trying to get something out of the Welfare Bureau for the last couple of hours, you know the red tape. I finally got some information. The Polachek woman's been on welfare here for about five years. Claimed she couldn't get a job and her ex-husband wasn't paying alimony. They don't know anything about a dependent child.''

"She was a hooker,'' said Wanda crossly. "Don't they check up on people? Just hand over the money for the asking?''

Glasser said dryly, "They've got too much paperwork to go out checking claims in the field. Did you get any more out of the nut?''

"She's not a nut,'' and Wanda told him about Linda. "Whatever the story is, it's something damnable, Henry.

She's not stupid or retarded, but she's completely illiterate, evidently kept like a prisoner for years, that woman making her do all the housework, not even giving her decent clothes or food. You'd think the neighbors would have noticed something, my God, but on the other hand it never seems to have occurred to her to try and get away, yell for help. God knows how long it's been—if she ever had any kindness from anyone she's forgotten it, probably too scared to trust anybody—all she's known is being shut up in that house, slaving for the woman.''

"And they say we're making progress at civilization all the time," said Glasser. "The only neighbor I raised didn't know anything about the woman, hadn't any idea there was anybody else living in the house. I left the lab there but I don't suppose it matters."

"No," said Wanda. "She can't be more than thirteen. The D.A.'s office'll call it involuntary manslaughter and she'll be held while she's a minor. But there must be some background on it—maybe there are relatives somewhere, if we can turn them up."

"Probably a waste of time," said Glasser. There wasn't anybody else in the office. "I haven't got around to starting an initial report on it, I suppose I'd better, and we can file it and forget it."

Wanda didn't think she'd ever forget Linda. Wearily she sat down at her desk and dialed information. There was a Holly Road in Hempstead, Long Island, and after verifying that she was bona fide police, the operator connected her with that address, 34 Holly Road. But the woman she talked to there was a Mrs. Abbott, and she didn't know anybody named Kent. They had lived at that address for seven years. They owned the house, and she didn't remember the name of the people they'd bought it from. It had been through a realty company.

"Dead end," said Wanda. "Where is everybody?"

"According to Jimmy," said Glasser, rolling forms into his typewriter, "there's been some hijinks going on at the Hall of Justice, of all places. The lieutenant got back about an hour ago and went right out on it with everybody else."

HIGGINS HAD been peacefully talking to one of the bailiffs, waiting outside Courtroom Three at about a quarter of one. He'd been reconciled to wasting the day; now and then all of them had to show up at court, and judges and lawyers always took their own time. There was a hearing scheduled today for a couple of thugs who'd been picked up for armed robbery last November. The courts were backlogged. They'd been arraigned in mid-November and had been sitting in the county jail ever since, waiting for sentencing—Tony Alvarez and Juan Camacho. It wouldn't be a jury trial, just the hearing before a judge, but the court would want the full police evidence and Higgins had been the arresting officer. He'd been hanging around here waiting since nine-thirty, and the hearing hadn't been called yet. Alvarez and Camacho had been waiting too, ferried over from the jail and stashed in one of the detention rooms on the eighth floor.

He was thinking of going out to get some lunch—he probably wouldn't be called until two o'clock or so now—when the uproar started. The first they heard on the ground floor was a fusillade of gunfire from somewhere upstairs, and then a uniformed bailiff came plunging down the stairs at one end of the corridor outside the courtrooms and began punching elevator buttons. He had his gun out. He shouted at the little crowd in the corridor, "Scatter—there's a couple of armed men loose—"

All the other bailiffs within hearing converged on him, Higgins after them. "Somebody call up some cops, for God's sake—it's a couple of thugs out of detention upstairs, they shot Connolly with his own gun, got away to the elevators—"

One of the bailiffs ran for the nearest phone to call in, and Higgins barked questions. It was Alvarez and Camacho and that was a mean pair, both with long and bad pedigrees. Nobody knew how they'd managed to get away, but that could be sorted out later. Higgins said in automatic reaction, "They'll be heading for the underground lot to pick up a car—come on!" He yanked out his own gun, and he and four of the bailiffs piled into the elevator. If the damn thugs didn't have too much of a lead—down in the underground parking lot they'd need twenty more men to cover the area, the rows of hundreds of parked cars, but they did their best, fanning out hunting. In the next half hour more men came out, everybody from Robbery-Homicide and a lot of uniformed men, fanning out along nearby streets in case the thugs hadn't hopped a car. God knew they'd be easy to spot, both wearing the official tan uniforms emblazoned L.A. COUNTY JAIL, but an hour later there'd been no sign of them and the little army started to mount a search of the building in case they'd doubled back. None of the Robbery-Homicide men thought that was likely; they were a fast, experienced pair of pros and they'd want to get away from there, pick up other clothes.

The bailiff Connolly was dead, shot through the heart. Higgins and Hackett talked to the other bailiff who had been stationed in that detention room. His name was Daley, and he was nearly ready to break down and cry.

"Listen, it was all my fault—I just stepped out to the john, a guy's got to go to the john, I wouldn't be gone five minutes—and they'd been sitting there quiet as damned lambs, not even any cussing—I says to Connolly, I'll be right back—he was bigger than me, he's been on the job years, but God, he wasn't as young as he had been and he'd picked up some fat—they must have jumped him while I was in the men's room, I heard the shot when I was just coming out, they were at the end of the hall when I came out the door—I got off six shots, a full load, and they took some at me, but I don't think I winged either of them—" Bailiffs didn't have to keep up the practice on the range.

It had been a stupid senseless accident, just Connolly's bad luck. There hadn't been any other prisoners on that floor, no other bailiffs. The Robbery-Homicide men were ready by three o'clock to quit the search of the building, but of course they had to be thorough. Knowing it was probably futile, they put out an A.P.B. with the official descriptions; it was some comfort to know that the stolen gun was probably empty—there were two slugs in Connolly and Daley thought they'd fired another four at him—but a pair like that would know the ropes, where and how to get resupplied. Alvarez had a wife living in Huntington Park, and Camacho had a girl friend in Hollywood; they dispatched squads to cover those addresses.

Mendoza was there by then, cursing the damn stupidity of the whole thing. "I know, I know," said Hackett, "that's no pair to have on the loose, they've both done time for murder two, they're hair-trigger and mean as they come. But there it is, Luis."

"They'll have picked up a car somewhere," said Mendoza with a vicious snap of his lighter. "They're long gone. They've got better sense than to approach the women openly—if they've got a yen for female company they'll phone and set up a meeting."

"And neither of those females'll come snitching to us about it," said Higgins. "Not so damned much to choose between them, the Alvarez dame's been in for grand theft and the other one's a part-time hooker. We can set up tails on them—all we can do, damn it."

The Hall of Justice was a big building, and they didn't call off the search until five o'clock. "We'll get the word," Mendoza kept insisting. "They've picked up a car, and it's even money they jumped some citizen to get some running money—or they'll pull a heist within twenty-four hours. We'll be hearing."

They drifted away at the end of shift at six o'clock, the night watch just coming in. It was Conway's night off. If any word came through, they'd be alerted.

PIGGOT AND SCHENKE hadn't been settled down ten minutes when Communications relayed a call; it was a squad reporting an assault and rape on Mission Street. Schenke left Piggott holding down the desk and went out to look at it, with a premonition. The premonition was right.

The patrolman was Gibson, and he had the girl in the back of the squad. "She flagged me down ten minutes ago, staggered off the curb at me, I damn near hit her."

Her name was Alicia Johnson and she'd been beaten and raped, she said she thought her arm was broken and she had bruises on her face, the beginning of a black eye. She'd been grabbed from the parking lot at USC about an hour and a half ago. "You're not the first one," said Schenke. "There've been several rapes in that area, all the students have been warned to avoid being alone there after dark. Can you give me any description?"

"Listen," she said, nursing her arm and half crying, "I just got to this town, nobody told me about any rapes." She'd have been a pretty girl normally, with blond hair and a heart-shaped face. "I'm from Lancaster, just starting college next month in the new semester, I got here last week and found an apartment a couple of blocks off the campus. I was at the college registering for classes this afternoon and it was just starting to get dark when I got to the parking lot, nobody around but I never gave a thought to it. Me the small-town girl—and this pair of gorillas jumped me—how could I tell you what they looked like? They were both big, but they had ski masks on—pulled me into a car and drove some place, I don't know, a side street somewhere, I tried to fight but they were just too strong—they beat me up like this and they both raped me and then they drove some more and just shoved me out of the car—they didn't stop, just pushed me out, and I hit my head and scraped both my legs pretty bad—and they got my purse, I had about forty dollars in it and all my identification—I was never so glad in my life when I saw that police car—"

Schenke told her soberly that she was lucky, compared to some of the other girls. They'd all had their bags stolen too; the cash wasn't identifiable and the papers had probably been thrown away. He drove her out to the Emergency wing at the hospital. Somebody would have to get a formal statement from her tomorrow, but this was just more of the same. He wished to God they could get some lead on that damned pair, but she couldn't tell them any more than the other girls had.

When he got back to the office Piggott was on the phone scribbling notes. The word was finally coming through, and Mendoza had hit the target all right. Twenty minutes ago a badly shaken man had called in to Valley division and told the boys there about Alvarez and Camacho. His name was Julian Morley and he was a lawyer with an office downtown. He'd got to the Hall of Justice about a quarter of one, he'd had a client with a divorce hearing scheduled at one-thirty. He'd just been getting out of his car in the underground lot when that pair had jumped him, running from the elevators. He hadn't, of course, any way of knowing that the gun was empty. They'd forced him to drive home, which was an address in North Hollywood, and had held him and his wife hostage until five minutes before he called in. They'd ransacked the house, got his wife to fix dinner for them, and taken off in her car. It was a late-model Chrysler Imperial, and he gave them the plate number. They'd taken all the cash in the place, about two hundred dollars, his wife's jewelry and his watch, and a .32 Colt revolver with some ammo for it; they had also taken four of his suits and some shirts and underwear. Presumably Morley was of similar size and the clothes would fit them.

Piggott called Mendoza to pass on the news, after he put out an A.P.B. on the Chrysler.

"Así," said Mendoza. "But they won't hang onto that car long, Matt. They know it's hot. And they'll both have pals around. The damn funny thing is, a pair like that, they're not always so smart—the logical thing for them to do would be to make tracks across the nearest state line, but they're both native Angelenos and this is home base for them. I've got a hunch they'll hole up somewhere right here."

"You could be right."

"Time will tell, if we're lucky."

AT SEVEN A.M., with the Traffic shift coming to its end, a patrolman on the Burbank force spotted the Chrysler parked in a loading zone on Hollywood Way. There was no telling how long it had been there, and it would be a waste of time to rout out the men to search the area, which included several blocks of warehouses. That report was waiting on Mendoza's desk when he came in on Tuesday morning. He had got out the new County Guide and was brooding over the several detailed maps of that area, ruminating about the idiot boy and the lost horse, when Wanda Larsen came in.

"I'd like to hear what you think about this peculiar new homicide, Lieutenant. There isn't any mystery about it, at least about the homicide, but—"

He listened interestedly, brushing his neat moustache in habitual gesture, while she told him about Linda. "Peculiar you can say. Who's the Polachek woman, and how did she get hold of the girl in the first place, if she's not a relative? I suppose we could trace that address back—you know, that's just the sort of thing you'd coach a child to memorize, in case of getting lost. The name and address."

"I thought about that. I don't know yet what the lab may have come across at the house—it looked fairly bare. Henry wants to canvass the bars around—she evidently didn't have a car—it could be she was known as a regular at some place down there."

"As a hooker. *Possible*. But the girl—"

"She's a little like a ghost," said Wanda. "A lost soul. I've got a meeting set up with the doctor, he'll be seeing her this morning—and I thought I'd ask Dr. Baxter to have a look at her." He nodded. Felicia Baxter was one of the psychiatrists who donated some time to Juvenile Hall. "She seems a little leery of men, and no wonder."

"That's a queer one," he said. "Keep me posted on it, will you?" He looked at his watch as she went out. The first report on Freddy Dillon would be in the D.A.'s office by now; he wondered if anybody had looked at it yet. That was a fairly smart bunch of boys, and usually on the ball. He put his hand on the phone and then sat back. He said, *"¿Qué significa eso?"* There was no hurry about dealing with Freddy Dillon; the court would take its own time.

A LITTLE BELATEDLY, they had got to the couple of new ones that had broken yesterday. Palliser had gone over to the morgue to have a look at the corpse found in Westlake Park. It didn't look like much of anything to work; he'd been an elderly man, and the doctor said it looked like natural causes, maybe alcoholism, a heart attack. There hadn't been any identification on him at all; all he'd had in the pockets of his shabby gray suit were sixty-one cents and a half-empty pack of cigarettes. There'd be an autopsy, and the city would bury him. The lab was busy, but Palliser might chase somebody over to get his prints, see if he could be identified that way.

From there he went out to the Emergency wing to talk to the drugstore owner who'd been held up yesterday afternoon. His name was John Lemoyne, and he gave Palliser a little something. He was dressed, sitting on a bench in the corridor; he was a thin gray-haired man in his sixties. "Oh, they said somebody would want to talk to me. The doctor's letting me go, I'm waiting for my wife to pick me up. I'm just as glad I'll be retiring next year, the crime rate—" He shook his head. "Getting shot—and in broad daylight—I guess I was more surprised than anything else."

"I'm glad to know you weren't seriously hurt," said Palliser conventionally.

"Oh, no, the bullet went through my arm. I really don't have much business lately, not like it used to be—people go to the big cut-rate drugstores for prescriptions. I was alone in the place when he came in."

"Could you give me a description of him?"

"Why, he was just a kid," said Lemoyne, still sounding surprised. "I figured he'd come in to look through the girlie magazines, it's a nuisance, the kids coming in without buying anything—and then he came back to the prescription counter and pulled out the gun. He was about seventeen or eighteen, I'd say, a white kid, kind of a round face and long black hair, he wasn't very big, about five seven or so I'd say. And he was nervous," said Lemoyne. "His hand was shaking when he shoved the gun at me, like he was scared of what he was doing."

So there he was again, the punk kid with the automatic. "How much did he get? You didn't try to resist him?"

"No, no. There wasn't much in the register, business had been slow. I think it'd have been about twenty dollars. No, I think his shooting me was an accident—he didn't mean to. Born to be hanged," said Lemoyne with a tiny grin. "I suppose he could have shot me dead, accident or not. It was when he reached to take the money, I could see the gun shaking in his hand, and all of a sudden it went off. And he turned and ran out. I managed to call the police—"

"Do you know whether the doctors here found the slug—a bullet in your arm?"

"No, they didn't, one of them said it had gone clean through without touching the bone—lucky again. I lost some blood—"

Well, assurance doubly sure, thought Palliser. They'd better look around for that slug to match the one they already had, see if it was the same gun. He asked Lemoyne if he could have the keys of the store. Lemoyne said his wife would have them, so Palliser hung around until she got there, and took them. He started back to base to collect somebody from the lab, and ran into Higgins in the hall. "What are you doing here, George?"

"Came in to see the Johnson girl, the one who got raped last night. All she can tell us, it was that same pair. Big, ski masks, rough and tough."

"I wonder why USC?" said Palliser.

"Does there have to be a reason? It's on the edge of the high-crime-rate area, and there are a lot of pretty girls on any campus."

"Yes," said Palliser. "There aren't often any deep mysteries come our way. It'd be nice to drop on those boys, but there's nowhere to look—the girls can't identify them." He went on out to the parking lot, drove back to headquarters and went up to the lab. Scarne was at loose ends, and went down to that drugstore with him; but they had to look for that slug high and low, trying to estimate where Lemoyne had been standing, which way the heister had been facing. Finally Scarne located it; it had evidently taken a slight upward angle and lodged in the wall just above a row of bottles of vitamins. He dug it out with his knife; it hadn't penetrated very far. "Well, just with the naked eye, I'd make it a thirty-two all right." He started to crawl around the floor in front of the counter and presently found the casing resting against the indented baseboard. "Automatic. It's in pretty good shape, one look through the microscope will say if it's the same gun."

"By the description of the heister, I'll take a bet," said Palliser.

"Let you know in an hour," said Scarne.

MENDOZA HAD BEEN on the phone most of the morning, talking with various divisions, speculating on possible hunting grounds for Alvarez and Camacho. Hackett thought privately that was a waste of time; nobody could figure how thugs like that would think or plan. They'd surface somewhere eventually.

Landers brought in a suspect on a heist, and he sat in on an abortive questioning. They'd just let him go when Lake relayed a call. Hackett talked to the Traffic man and said to Landers, "Damn it to hell, here's our polite helpful parcel carrier again."

"That one. We've got a hope in hell of finding him."

But they had to go through the motions. Hackett went out to talk to the woman. It was the same general area where he'd hit before, this time on San Marino Street. The woman's name was Dorothy Foster; she was nearer seventy than sixty, shaken up and scared. It was the same story, on her way home from the market, the polite light-skinned young black man offering to carry her bags, and knocking her down as soon as they got inside the apartment entrance. She was just lucky she hadn't been hurt worse. He had taken her purse with about ten dollars in it, and the groceries. Adding insult to injury, thought Hackett; none of these old ladies had much for groceries.

He went back to the office intending to write a report on it and get it out of the way, and found Mendoza standing beside the switchboard reading a report. "So *adelante,* Arturo. Eventually we learn things. Here is the autopsy report on that Maulden, and for good measure the lab report. Maybe we'll start to find out some answers on that." He perched a hip on the corner of Hackett's desk while Hackett skimmed the autopsy report.

Robert Maulden had died of an overdose of a Nembutal codeine prescription. It was generally used as a tranquilizer or sleeping aid; it was supplied in capsules of various strengths. It had been in the bourbon; he had had the equivalent of about three strong highballs. The doctor's estimate was that it might have taken a couple of hours to produce death, but he'd have been comatose quite a while before he died. The estimated time of death was between noon and five on Friday afternoon, probably closer to the earlier hour. Hackett grunted, "Say he had the drinks between ten and twelve that morning." There was more, about his general condition, the arthritis, the diabetes, but that was the gist of it. He took up the lab report.

The lab didn't have much to say. There hadn't been any prints in the house except those of the Mauldens, with one exception; they had picked up four clear latents from the paper label of the bourbon bottle. They weren't in L.A.'s records, so they'd been sent to the Feds, who had a lot more records to look at. The only interesting thing the lab had to report was that there had been a thousand dollars in cash, all in twenties, in the pocket of one of Maulden's jackets in the bedroom closet. Hackett grunted again. "This money—"

"*¿Significante?*" said Mendoza.

"A little funny. Where'd he get that kind of cash? A humdrum little fellow like that—well, it all backs up what that doctor said, his own prescription untouched, and he couldn't get out of the house. It looks like deliberate homicide all right." Suddenly he remembered something. "Oh, Jimmy was saying something yesterday, somebody who called in—" He rummaged on the desk, found the note. "Fellow named Hoffman who says he knows something about it. I suppose I'd better go talk to him."

"If the Feds know those prints it'll give us a short-cut."

"Do you want to bet?" said Hackett.

"No bets. But it's a slightly offbeat one, Arturo."

At least the cloudy weather had gone and they were back to normal for winter in southern California: clear blue skies, sunshine, a sharp chilly wind.

THE ADDRESS was on Valentine Street, and it was directly across the street from the Maulden house. Hackett glanced over there as he parked; he wondered if Alice Maulden had gone back to work, and what kind of funeral she'd be arranging. The coroner's office would have notified her by now that she could claim the body.

This house was an old square stucco place, a little newer than its neighbors. A weekday; but somebody here would know where Hoffman worked. He went up on the porch and rang the bell. After a minute the door opened, and he faced a sharp-faced red-haired man about forty. Hackett showed him the badge. "I'm looking for a Mr. Floyd Hoffman, could you tell me—"

"That's me. Say, you a detective? Is it about that fellow across the street? I called in yesterday—"

"Sergeant Hackett. You said you might have some information for us."

"Say, what the hell happened there anyway? Was it a murder or did he commit suicide?" Hoffman was looking avidly interested. "We didn't know them at all, they sort of kept themselves to themselves like the saying goes, but word gets around when something happens, and we saw that van parked there on Saturday with the LAPD sign on it. My wife heard from the people next door that he's dead, their name's something like Mauden or Bauden."

"Maulden," said Hackett. "Yes, he's dead. We're not quite sure what it was. Do you think you know something about it, Mr. Hoffman?"

"Well, maybe. Come in and sit down, I'll tell you. The more I thought about it, the more I thought you might want to hear. I guess you could say it's specialized knowledge." He grinned at Hackett and turned awkwardly toward the living room past this tiny square entry hall, and for the first time Hackett noticed that he was wearing a heavy cast on his right leg. He followed Hoffman into the living room and accepted an armchair. Hoffman shoved an ashtray toward him on the coffee table, sitting down on the couch.

"My wife's gone out to the market," he said irrelevantly. "Well, I'll tell you about it and maybe it'll be some use to you. You can see I got a busted leg. Since three weeks ago, I got knocked down crossing Hoover by a damfool female driver. I'm off work while I got the cast on, and I get damn bored sitting around all day. I don't care a damn for what's on TV daytimes, and you can't read magazines all day—I get bored. And last Friday—I know the day because it was the first hard rain we'd had since November—I was sitting there right where you are feeling damn bored. I wasn't interested in that book my wife gave me, never been much of a one to read, and every so often I was looking out of the window. You can see there's a good view of the house across the street."

"Yes?" Hackett lit a cigarette.

"And how come I happened to notice the car, well, it's a couple reasons. Those people never had anybody come to see them, and they don't own a car. I just happened to be looking out when it came up and parked in front. It was about ten o'clock Friday morning."

Hackett felt slightly more interested. "So?"

"So, a guy gets out and goes up to that house and gets let in." Hoffman shrugged. "I couldn't say much about him, just saw his back, he was just a guy, sort of tall—he had on a raincoat and a hat. But the car I can say something about, Sergeant Hackett." He leaned forward eagerly.

"You don't mean you saw a plate number?"

"For God's sake, no, it was sideways on to me, how could I? But it was a rented car. It was a Hertz car," said Hoffman.

"How do you know that?" asked Hackett skeptically. "They don't wear signs."

Hoffman grinned. "Specialized knowledge like I say, Sergeant. Do I know a rental car when I see one! I've been working for Hertz for fifteen years, I'm in their big garage out on Western, and anybody knows anything at all about rental cars, you can spot one as soon as you lay eyes on it. This one was a Ford Fairlane, light blue, last-year's model. It hadn't been out of the agency long. Rental cars, they get waxed and polished oftener and better than any personal cars, whenever they come back they get the works. I don't figure that one'd been on the street long, in that rain—it was clean as a whistle, see what I mean. And I know it was a Hertz, one of ours, because that's all we buy—Ford products. Avis goes for GM cars. And it was nearly new—you know Hertz never keeps them over two years—and the color."

"What do you mean?"

Hoffman looked at him patiently. "Light blue. Baby blue. All the rental agencies, they'll buy up the dealer's leftovers, to save money, so they get all the unpopular colors, like baby blue and dark tan and yellow or something like that. Who buys a baby-blue car to drive all the time? That was a Hertz rental car, Sergeant, and it hadn't been out of a Hertz garage very long—probably that same day.''

Hackett stared at him.

"Say," said Hoffman, "was it a murder? Was that guy murdered? We didn't know them at all—seemed like ordinary people, quiet, but with the police around—was he murdered?"

FIVE

"OF COURSE it's a completely useless piece of information," said Hackett, and Mendoza and Palliser agreed. "Not a hope of running that down, the number of car rentals in the county on any given day."

"But it's a little more to make it look offbeat, Art—and the time fits. He said it was about ten o'clock he saw it parked there?"

"And he thought it was there almost an hour, an hour and a half—it was gone by around noon. It fits all right, if Maulden got the dose before noon. But who in hell could have had it in for Maulden?"

Palliser said, "Better talk to the wife again."

"I think it'd be a waste of time, she doesn't know anything. If he got the dose after eight that morning, she's clear—she was at work, she's alibied."

They were sitting at a table at Federico's on North Broadway, and had just finished lunch. Mendoza poured himself another cup of coffee, and Palliser sat back to light a cigarette. "At least," he said, "we know it was the same kid, on the daylight heist yesterday—the slug matched the one we had. And a lot of good that does us."

Landers came up to the table and pulled out a chair, sat down and picked up the menu. "Bricks without straw," he said laconically. "I don't know why we bother to go looking and haul in all these suspects, it's once in a blue moon we can pin one down. Nine out of ten witnesses can't identify anybody. I get fed up." He was looking tired. "And adding insult to injury, as if I didn't have to get up an hour earlier to make that drive in, the baby kept us awake most of the night."

Hackett said sympathetically, "We've all been there, Tom. They grow out of it eventually."

"And Nick and Matt will both be finding out about that," said Landers. "Funny how all the wives are producing babies at the same time. I think the Piggotts' is due around the same time as yours, John." The waiter came up and he ordered.

Mendoza stabbed out his cigarette and said lazily, "Something catching going around the office, all the babies. Not that anything's moving, but I suppose we'd better get back to work."

Palliser stayed on to keep Landers company. Back at the office, Lake handed Mendoza a manila envelope: the autopsy report on Rosa Galluci. Mendoza glanced at it and put it down. "That's cleared away at least."

"The D.A.'s office called a couple of hours ago to say Fielding will be arraigned on Friday," said Lake.

"Anything in on the escape artists?"

"Nary a thing," said Lake. "They'll be lying low or over the state line by now."

"I have a hunch they're somewhere around," said Mendoza. "And that two hundred won't last them forever." The description of the Morleys' jewelry was out to all the pawnbrokers, but that was just a gesture; Alvarez and Camacho would know the fences. Morley hadn't known the serial number of the Colt.

Galeano came in and said, "I suppose you've all had lunch? We may have struck a little pay dirt. That pharmacist from one of the Saturday-night heists just made a mug shot, and the guy's got the right pedigree, two counts of armed robbery. Somebody like to come hunting him? I'll run up to the canteen for a sandwich first."

"Sure," said Hackett. They started out together fifteen minutes later, and Mendoza was the only one in when Lake passed on a new call.

"There seems to be a body on a city bus, a squad car just called in."

"*¡Por la gracia de Dios!*" said Mendoza. "Where?"

It was an ordinary big cumbersome yellow city bus, and it was parked at the corner of Olympic and Alvarado obstructing traffic, the black-and-white squad angled in behind it. The squad-car man was talking to the bus driver on the curb, and a fat elderly woman was sitting on the curb beside them. Most of the passengers on the bus were crowded to the street side, staring. A thin old man in a shabby gray suit was arguing with the bus driver as Mendoza came up, leaving the Ferrari in a red zone behind the bus. "This is a most unwarrantable delay," he was saying fussily. "This bus is due at the corner of La Brea at three o'clock, and it is ten minutes of three now. If you are not going to proceed on your normal route, the passengers should be informed so they can catch the next bus, some people have schedules to keep."

The uniformed man said, "I'm sorry, sir, but somebody from the detective office will probably want to talk to the passengers."

Mendoza said, "So what's the story?" He introduced himself.

The Traffic man was hardly more than a rookie, pink-cheeked. "Oh, it's a hell of a thing, sir—it's a baby. In a paper bag. This lady here found it in the seat when she got on the bus, and started to scream—"

"Took ten years off my life," said the bus driver. He was a stout square man with a bald head, in the blue uniform of the transit company. "She went off like a siren, I nearly ran into the car in front of the bus, I thought she was having a heart attack or something—''

The Traffic man, looking a little sick, said, ''Maybe I should have called a backup, there's about ten people on the bus, I told them to keep away, but—'' He should have preserved the scene better, but that couldn't be helped.

''Are you going to proceed on your route?'' asked the elderly man insistently. He took out a large gold watch. ''It is now five minutes of three, this is a disgrace and I intend to complain to the company.''

Mendoza swung up into the bus. ''It's on the last seat on the left,'' said the uniformed man.

There were nine or ten people on the bus, mostly women, crowded at one side and silent. They watched him as he went up the aisle. In the next to the last double seat on the left side of the bus there was a large paper bag standing upright against the back of the seat. It bore the printed name of a large supermarket chain. The top wasn't folded over; he held it open and looked, and in the bottom of the bag was the naked body of a baby looking to be only a couple of days old. *''Por Dios,''* he said to himself. There wasn't anything on the seat or floor looking relevant to the bag, and these buses were kept fairly clean. He left the bag where it was and went out to the street again. The fat woman was still sitting on the curb moaning softly. ''You found it? Can I have your name, please?''

''Oh, oh,'' she said, ''It's terrible—a dead baby—I got such a shock—Holst, my name's Amy Holst, Mrs.—I'd just got in and sat down, right beside it—I thought, somebody's forgot something and I'd better tell the driver when I got off, and I just looked to see what it was—oh, oh, such a terrible thing, a dead baby—''

Mendoza asked the driver, "Did you notice anybody get on carrying a big paper bag?"

The driver spat disgustedly. "I don't notice passengers much, I'm concentrating on traffic, and believe me you've got to concentrate along a city route. They get on and put the fares in, they get off, and sometimes there'll be three or four people get on together—when they get off it's at the back and I don't see them. I couldn't say if anybody got on carrying that damn thing, but I suppose somebody did."

"It wouldn't have been on the bus when you started out on the route?"

He looked at Mendoza witheringly. "Well, God's sake, of course not, it couldn't of been, the buses get cleaned every night. It must of got left since this morning sometime, I take over the route at nine-thirty."

"The hell of a thing," said the Traffic man.

"If you are not going to proceed on your route, would you kindly inform me when the next bus is due?" asked the old man.

Mendoza swore to himself. It could have been on the bus for hours; only a few buses carried the crowds of passengers, and anyone noticing the paper bag would just take another vacant seat—Mrs. Holst was the first one to exercise curiosity. It would be a waste of time to question the passengers on the bus now, and not much chance that there was anything relevant on the bus. He told the Traffic man to call up the morgue wagon. It came in fifteen minutes, and when the attendants had collected the bag he let the driver take the bus back on his route. The elderly man was still fussing and fuming. Mendoza trailed the wagon back to the morgue, and followed the attendants in. One of the doctors from the coroner's office was coming up the front corridor, and he said, "Come and take a look at this."

The doctor lifted the tiny body out of the bag and onto an autopsy table. He said mildly, "My God." The baby was a boy, and quite naked, the only thing in the bag.

"How old would you say?"

"Not more than a couple of days, the navel's not healed. Healthy-looking baby, normal. No sign of any wound—could have been smothered, the easiest thing. My God. Do you want an autopsy?"

Mendoza said irritably, "We do have to go by the rules." They'd never find out anything about this one. Somebody hadn't wanted the baby, so they'd killed it and left it on the bus. Simple and economical. Probably a she. Nobody would ever know any more about it. He drove back to headquarters, feeling frustrated, and asked Lake automatically if there was anything new down.

"Haven't had a call since you left," said Lake.

Galeano and Hackett brought in the suspect heister and took him into an interrogation room. Mendoza roamed around the office smoking, and presently Galeano and Hackett came out looking pleased, with the suspect, who was a thin young black man. "You did some good?" asked Mendoza.

"Once in a while we catch up," said Hackett. "He admitted it when he heard he'd been identified. I'll start the machinery on the warrant." They took him out to ferry him over to the jail, and Mendoza lit a new cigarette. Nobody else was in. There would have to be a report written on the baby, and that would get shoved in Pending right away, nowhere to go on it. He hadn't started to do that when Hackett and Galeano came back. He told them about the baby and Galeano said, "God. The things that happen."

The phone shrilled in Mendoza's office down the hall and he went to answer it in a hurry, half expecting to hear somebody telling him that Alvarez and Camacho had been spotted somewhere. But it was Horder in the lab. "We're sending up a little surprise for you, Lieutenant. I think you'll be interested."

"Oh?" said Mendoza.

"We just got the kickback from the Feds—on those prints on the whiskey bottle at the Maulden house," said Horder. "Little surprise. Marx is on the way up."

Three minutes later Marx came in with a teletype from Washington. Mendoza read it and uttered an outraged yelp. "*Por el amor de Dios,* what the hell is this? What the holy hell? Come and look at this, Art." He handed over the teletype. "Did you say the Maulden thing looked shapeless? This doesn't make it look any better, and what the hell it means—"

Hackett read the teletype and said blankly, "But that's crazy."

The Feds had had those prints in their records. They belonged to one Gilbert Kramer. He had a pedigree with both the police in Newark, New Jersey, and the Feds. He had been charged with fraud in Newark twenty-four years ago, served nine months in the state pen in New Jersey, and been arrested again on the same charge a couple of years later, got probation. Twenty-one years ago he had been charged by the Feds with mail fraud; Uncle Sam was a little tougher than the local courts, and he'd served seven years at the federal pen in Fort Leavenworth. He'd been released over fourteen years ago.

Hackett said, "Of all the Goddamned funny things, Luis. What the hell has one like this got to do with Maulden?"

"Well, by the evidence he's got to be the one who slipped Maulden the spiked whiskey. He handled the bottle. And echo answers why. Fourteen years—apparently nobody has heard of him since, officially so to speak."

"But what the hell could Kramer have to do with Maulden? Maulden hardly knew anybody—just living a quiet dull life, the wife supporting him. This just makes the whole damn thing more shapeless."

"I think we talk to the wife again."

"I don't think she knows anything about it, Luis. Of course there was that cash—I wonder if she knew about that.'

"Wives usually know this and that about husbands," said Mendoza sardonically. "But where a pro con man like this Kramer fits into the picture, I'm damned if I can see. Kramer let loose all that time back—*es cierto,* it's very funny indeed."

IN THE MIDDLE of the week the night watch was usually quiet. They sat around, bored, and listened desultorily to the police frequency on the radio. They only had one call the whole watch, to a mugging in the parking lot of an office building on Wilshire. The victim was a young C.P.A. with an office there, and he'd stayed overtime to do some tax work for a client. He'd been roughed up a little and lost about forty dollars and his watch. "I suppose I was a damned fool to be down here alone at this hour, we know the crime rate's up, I expect I was lucky not to get killed. Some of these jokers, they'd murder anybody without thinking about it."

"Can you give us any description?" asked Schenke.

"Not much—the overhead lights were on, of course— there were two of them, both black, pretty young, I just

got a glimpse before they jumped me. I couldn't be sure
about recognizing a picture, if you want me to look at
mug shots.'' That would be a long chance anyway; there
were a lot of muggers around, loners or mixed up with
the concerted gang activity, who'd never acquired an official record and photographs on file. He said he didn't
need a doctor. They went back to the office and Schenke
typed a brief report. There was enough going on out in
the street for Traffic to deal with, the accidents and bar
brawls and drunks, but nothing went down for Robbery-Homicide the rest of the watch.

HACKETT WAS off on Wednesday. Nothing had been
heard anywhere in the county of Alvarez and Camacho.
Hollywood Division was keeping an eye on Camacho's
girl friend, and headquarters had an eye on Mrs. Alvarez, but apparently neither of them had been contacted yet; they were staying home and not doing
anything unusual.

Mendoza passed that teletype on to Higgins and Palliser, but nobody had any bright ideas about it. "It might
be helpful to know a little more about Kramer than shows
in his pedigree. But would anybody in Newark remember him? Twenty-four years ago—'' He put in a call to
the Newark force and talked to a Sergeant Edwards
who'd never heard of Gilbert Kramer.

"But twenty-four years, hell, I was nine years old. Tell
you what, I'll see if Durand's around, he's a senior officer on the detective force and might remember something.'' After awhile a rough elderly voice came on.
Durand listened to what Mendoza had to say and said
tersely, "It rings a faint sort of bell, Lieutenant, but I
couldn't give you any details.''

"Do you keep records that far back?''

"Yeah, they'll be on microfilm stored somewhere in the basement. You want us to look up the case for you?"

"If it's not too much trouble, Sergeant."

"Well, okay, I'll see what I can turn up and get back to you sometime."

Higgins had been on the phone to Washington. He said, "Such busy, busy boys they always are." He sat back and lit a cigarette. "Damn it, I know they're good, but they always give you the impression they're so damned occupied chasing down the important crooks they can't spare a minute for us dumb locals. Nobody I talked to knew anything about Kramer, but they finally agreed to look up some details and pass them on. God knows when, of course."

"I'll talk to the wife again," said Mendoza, and got up. In the outer office Galeano was talking to Wanda Larsen and Glasser; Jason Grace was hunched over his typewriter.

"Is there anything new on your peculiar homicide?" Mendoza asked Wanda.

"Just the doctor's report. Dr. Baxter's supposed to see the girl sometime today."

And Lake passed him in the entrance and said, "There's a new body, a squad just called."

"No rest for the wicked," said Galeano, and stood up. "So we'd better go look at it."

ALICE MAULDEN said, "You're not the one talked to me before."

"No, that was Sergeant Hackett, he's off duty today. I'm Lieutenant Mendoza. I've got a few more questions for you, Mrs. Maulden."

"Well, all right," she said readily, "but I don't know anything more to tell you. Do you know yet what killed

Bob? Somebody called to say I could have his body, and I've got the funeral arranged, Agnes helped me find a good funeral home. She said I should take a few days off work, the shock of losing him like that."

He had found her at the house on Valentine Street, sitting in the rather shabby-looking living room watching a talk show on TV. She said, "It's lonely without anybody else here. Do you know what he died of?"

"It was an overdose of a Nembutal codeine prescription," said Mendoza. "Sleeping pills. They were in the whiskey." There hadn't been any prints on the used glass except Maulden's.

She looked surprised. "That's queer. There wasn't anything like that in the house. I never heard of that."

"He never took anything to make him sleep?"

"Not that I ever knew, since we were married."

"Do you know anybody named Kramer?"

She looked honestly bewildered. She shook her head. "No, I don't." She might have been vapidly pretty as a girl; now she was just a plain middle-aged mousy-looking woman. She hadn't gotten dressed this morning, was wearing an old cotton housecoat and slippers.

"Did your husband ever mention knowing a Kramer—Gilbert Kramer?"

"Why, not that I remember."

"But you'd only been married eight years—he must have known people, had friends, before you knew each other."

"Well, I suppose so, but he never talked about that. You see, he felt kind of resentful, how his parents' little business had to be sold and there wasn't anything left for him. And how he wasn't eligible for the Social Security or disability because they hadn't paid in. Bob had had a lot of hard luck in his life. He said—when we got married—about making a new start and putting all the past behind."

"He didn't write letters to friends back East? You said he came from Illinois."

"That's right, some little town there. Why, I never knew him to write any letters or get any. The way I say, he wanted to forget the past."

She wasn't a particularly intelligent woman, he thought, and she sounded honest. "Where did you meet him, by the way?"

Unexpectedly she flushed and looked embarrassed. She didn't answer for a moment, and his interest in her quickened. Then she said, "Well, maybe it sounds a little, I don't know, queer. But after Jack died, I was lonely—we had some friends in the neighborhood, from where he worked—he was a clerk in a men's shop when he could work—I've never been much of a one to socialize, but it was lonely. It's not easy for a woman alone. I used to, well, buy these papers at the market, and one of them has what's called a Meet New Friends page. People put in ads telling about themselves and asking people to write them if they're interested in making friends. There isn't anything wrong about it, I mean anything nasty, if you know what I mean. I used to look at what the ads said, but I never answered any until I saw Bob's. And I felt awfully embarrassed about it, it seemed, well, a little unladylike." She brought out the old-fashioned word primly. "But finally I did—he sounded lonely too, he'd just put something like, widower with no family wants companionship—and I wrote to the box number and he answered my letter. We got on fine from the time we met, and after a couple of months we decided to get married." She looked slightly defiant now. "I hadn't much chance to meet anybody any other way. And Bob and I got on fine. We had a happy marriage. He'd just come out to California then, he thought the climate might be better for his arthritis, but he just got worse and finally he had to go to the doctor for it."

Mendoza reflected that she'd lost one invalid husband and deliberately acquired another, but some women seemed to attract unsatisfactory husbands; he thought fleetingly, maternal instinct, or a martyr complex. He didn't think she was a very complicated woman. He asked, "Did you know that he had a thousand dollars tucked away in a jacket in the closet?"

She stared at him. "A thousand—why, that can't be so, where'd Bob get a thousand dollars? He hadn't been able to work in four or five years—"

"Go and look," and Mendoza leaned back and lit a cigarette. The lab had left the cash where it was.

She got up in a hurry and went into the bedroom, and he heard the closet door open. When she came back she was holding the money in both hands, looking stunned. "All this money—I can't get over it—I suppose the police saw it when they were looking for something here. I just can't imagine where he got it, I don't know anything about it. But goodness knows it'll help with the funeral—but where did it come from?"

"Did he ever get any mail? Personal mail, that is—" Remembering all the catalogs and contests.

"I never knew him to, of course I'm gone all day and he could have, but—well, he never mentioned any or showed me any, and he wasn't a secretive man, he wasn't the kind to do anything behind my back, if you see what I mean. I can't get over this, where'd it come from?"

"Did you have a joint bank account?" asked Mendoza. But the bank would only have handed him the cash in person, and he couldn't get out on his own.

"No, we never got around to it, he hadn't earned anything since awhile after we got married. I've got an account at the Bank of America."

"And you're sure he wasn't able to go out on his own?"

That turned her indignant. "You mean, he might have been playacting that he couldn't? He'd never do such a thing, it was an awful trial to him to start getting crippled at his age. The last couple of years he hadn't been able to get out alone at all. The arthritis was getting pretty bad. He could get around the house all right, so far, but when he went to see the doctor I had to help him on and off the bus, and he'd started to use a cane."

And the doctor would have spotted any fakery there, thought Mendoza. Looking at the woman he felt frustrated. A naïve, not too intelligent woman, but probably honest: not enough brain to be anything else. It was a million to one chance that she knew anything about Maulden's death. And just how this Gilbert Kramer came into it—he thanked her and stood up.

Reverting to her first surprise, she said, "Sleeping pills—but who'd want to kill Bob with sleeping pills? I don't understand it at all. I mean, I should think you'd have to know a person pretty well to want to kill them, and we didn't know hardly anybody—just casual like, you know, no real close friends. Just Agnes. Of course she's a close friend, but aside from that, people at the market, the clerks, and the bus drivers I see every day, and the doctor and his nurses—there couldn't be anybody had any reason to kill Bob. I just don't understand it."

She was still standing there with the money in her hands when he left.

"I TELL YOU, it rocked me," said the uniformed man to Galeano and Higgins. His name was Armstrong. "It didn't sound like anything for us, when I got sent out here on unknown trouble."

The other man, a tall thin elderly man with sparse gray hair and steel-rimmed glasses, said, "I didn't know what else to do about it but call the police. He wouldn't let me in, and the people downstairs say there's water coming through the ceiling." They were all standing in the small front lobby of an ancient apartment building on Twelfth Street. "He'd paid the rent on the first, but I hadn't seen anything of him like I usually did, for about a month or so. He usually went out mornings to get a paper, go shopping—they'd go out together. I hadn't seen her in quite a while. I thought he was acting kind of funny, that day he came by to pay the rent." The elderly man was Thomas Trotter, and he managed the building. "And I couldn't get him to let me in to check where the leak was. I called the cops, and he"—he looked at Armstrong— "didn't want to do anything at first."

"Well," said Armstrong reasonably, "it didn't look like a job for us, did it? But when Mr. Trotter said the man had been acting funny and he hadn't seen the woman in a while, I went up with him."

"Her name's Green," said Trotter. "Mabel Green. He's Ed Filer. I don't know if they're maybe brother and sister or what. They've lived here about four years." For the first time he showed a little emotion. "Should have thought he was the last man in the world to do a thing like that, quiet fellow, polite. He told me he'd worked for the city all his life, the Parks and Recreation Department."

"So you got in," said Higgins.

"I didn't have the master key, I'm supposed to keep one but it got lost."

"When I said it was police and we'd have to break the door in," said Armstrong, "he finally unlocked it. Then he tried to jump out the window, but I grabbed him. And then we looked around—my God."

"So let's have a look at it," said Higgins. Trotter didn't come upstairs with them. It was an apartment on the second floor at the back. The door was still open, and Higgins and Galeano sniffed as they went into the living room. It was in wild disorder, newspapers scattered around, one chair overturned; it was an old shabby place with not much furniture. Armstrong gestured toward the adjoining bedroom; there the bed was unmade, with gray sheets half on the floor, and clothes lying around. The bathroom led off that, and they crowded up to the door, Higgins' bulk filling the doorway.

"Sweet Jesus," said Galeano.

The woman's body was in the bathtub, lying in a nearly full tub of water. The doctors could say how long she'd been dead, but it was a long time, probably more than a month. She'd been a fat old woman, and her wild white hair floated on the water; she was naked, grotesquely discolored. There wasn't anything to show how she had died.

"I tell you, it shook me," said Armstrong. "My God. Like you saw, I got him cuffed in the squad."

"And we'll want the lab," said Higgins. "You'd better take him in, Nick. I'll wait till the lab shows."

They called the lab from the squad. Sitting in the backseat, Filer was silent. He was a middle-sized man probably in the late sixties, without much hair left, a thin lined face, a tight narrow mouth. He looked at his handcuffed wrists and was quiet. Galeano got in beside him and Armstrong took them back to headquarters. There they took the cuffs off and Galeano got Landers to sit in on the questioning. Filer wouldn't say anything.

"Did you kill her, Filer?" asked Galeano. "How long has she been dead?" Filer just sat, head down, and was silent.

"Why did you put her in the bathtub?" asked Landers.

He just sat and looked at the floor.

"Come on, you'll have to tell us something about it, Filer. Did you kill her? How?" They couldn't get anything out of him, and finally they gave up and took him over to the jail and booked him in. He opened his mouth then for the first time, asking quietly if he could keep the pack of cigarettes and matches. That was all they let him keep; the jailer took his shoes and belt and the little pocket knife on him; he might be a potential suicide. Maybe later he'd feel like talking; people usually did in the end.

There should be an initial report started on it, but Galeano didn't feel much like doing it. Higgins came back and they all went out for a belated lunch.

WANDA CAUGHT Mendoza when he came in about three o'clock. "You wanted to hear about the doctor's report on Linda."

Lake said, "The D.A.'s office wants you to call— somebody named Duffy."

"I'll get to him," said Mendoza. "What did the doctor have to say, Wanda?"

"Well, she's not a virgin—we could have guessed that, by some of what she said. She's pretty badly undernourished and anemic. When you think of the life she's had—" She grimaced. "Dr. Baxter was supposed to see her sometime today. I'm surprised she didn't try to fight back at that woman before. We still don't know much about Polachek. The house is owned by a big realty company, and all they could tell us was that she paid the rent with a check on a United California bank. Henry's trying to get a court order to look at the account."

"And that wouldn't tell us much, probably."

"Well, you never know. He's going bar-crawling later. He thinks she might have been known as a regular at any of the bars within reasonable distance, because she didn't have a car. The nearest ones, on Third or Sixth or Beverly."

Mendoza smoothed his moustache. "That could be. Looking for the willing game to take home."

"The Welfare Bureau doesn't know one thing about her," said Wanda. "Just handing over the taxpayers' money for the asking. The only other thing we know is that she had rented that house for nearly seven years."

"And according to Linda, they came there in a car with a man named Billy. That long ago? And from where? Hempstead, Long Island?"

"Heavens knows," said Wanda. "I haven't heard if the lab picked up anything in the house, but I doubt it, barring any known prints. I had a look around, it was all pretty bare. She had a lot of cheap flashy clothes and cosmetics, but practically nothing else—there wasn't an address book by the phone, or so much as a newspaper or magazine in the place."

"Well, I'll be interested in what Dr. Baxter thinks about Linda." Mendoza went on into his office, and called the D.A. He talked to the assistant D.A. in that office, Duffy, for quite a while. Duffy wanted to discuss Freddy Dillon. "You know it may be weeks before we get an official report from the head doctors, *amigo*. They'll want to look at him every which way and run all sorts of

tests, and prod at the parents and every doctor who's ever
had a look at Freddy, for his history, before they decide
to commit themselves to any pronouncement. Then
they'll hand us a forty-page report full of the six-dollar
words and it'll all add up to just what we already know
about him. He's got the brain of a two-year-old and the
impulse to violence. If the parents had any brains themselves they'd have suspected that years ago and either put
him away somewhere or kept a closer eye on him.'' Mendoza thought about the kitten Freddy had once got hold
of and lit a new cigarette with a violent snap of his lighter.
''As it is, at least we know about him, we've got him.''

''Hell of a thing,'' said Duffy, ''but straightforward,
Mendoza. We won't bring a formal charge, just get the
court order for committal. It could be he'll stay right
where he is.''

They kicked it around a little, and Mendoza said then,
''We've got another juvenile killer you'll hear about
eventually, but it's a very different kettle of fish. You'll
hear about it sometime—we're still investigating.'' When
he put the phone down he sat and thought about Freddy,
about Bob Maulden and Gilbert Kramer, about Alvarez
and Camacho and the pair of rapists.

At four-thirty he had a call from Sergeant Edwards of
Valley division. ''We're a hundred percent sure Alvarez
just pulled a heist at a liquor store in Van Nuys. The witnesses both made his mug shot.'' They had scattered
copies of both mug shots to every bunch of lawmen in the
county. ''No make on the gun, naturally. He got away
with another couple of hundred bucks.''

''And no make on any car, *naturalmente*. That should
tide them over for a while. I knew they were holed up
somewhere around, and maybe right there on your beat,
pulling a caper in the general area.''

"It looks like it," said Edwards. "If we only had some idea—but something else, Mendoza. They'll have pals around, but there's never much loyal brotherhood among thieves. Could be they're forking over the pay for a safe pad, and just in the nature of things somebody may decide to snitch on them."

"Lucky for us it's a thing that happens," said Mendoza. He swiveled around in the desk chair and looked out at the clear view over the Hollywood hills eight miles away. He was thinking about Maulden and Kramer again. He thought, a rental car. And they had said, hopeless to run that down, but a small glimmer of an impossible idea came to him.

When he went down the hall at twenty to six he heard about Ed Filer from Galeano and Higgins, and said, "*¡Vaya por Dios!* Maybe you can get him to open up when he's thought it over for the night."

It was already dark, and the wind had risen to a gale, but there was a half-moon showing in the clear night sky; as he drove up the hill past the tall iron gates he could see the white shapes of the Five Graces on the green slope. He wondered briefly whether their man of all work, Ken Kearney, had taught himself to shear them; last May it had been an expensive proposition to import a sheep shearer from a hundred miles off.

In the kitchen Alison and Mairí were chatting animatedly over dinner preparations. He kissed Alison and asked, "Good day, *mi vida?*"

"Thank heavens it's cleared up. The twins have been out riding their ponies since they got home from school, working off excess energy."

Johnny and Terry came running to greet him yelling at the tops of their voices. "I got a gold star from Sister Catherine—" "I could get one too if I wanted to—"

"*¡Demonios, qué relajo!* Quiet down, *niños.*" Baby
Luisa, her hair as red as Alison's, was crawling around
under the kitchen table pushing a stuffed bear. "What a
brood," said Mendoza. "Come sit down and have a
drink with me before dinner, *querida.*" He opened the
cupboard to get down the bottle of rye, and of course El
Señor had cat ears and appeared on the scene in five seconds flat, purring and demanding his share. "*¡Señor
Borracho!*" said Mendoza, and poured him half an
ounce in a saucer.

UNEXPECTEDLY IT turned out to be a busy night for
Robbery-Homicide. First they got a call to a body, at
seven-thirty, and it looked as if it might give the day
watch a little work. It was the body of a young woman in,
of all places, the parking lot behind a classy and popular
Japanese restaurant in Little Tokyo. There wasn't a
handbag or any identification on her. She looked about
twenty-five, a pretty blonde, and she was wearing an
anonymous dark pantsuit and coat. There wasn't any
sign of what had killed her, and she hadn't been dead
long. She'd been reported by a couple heading for the
restaurant, a middle-aged doctor and his wife. Piggott
and Conway annoyed the restaurant staff, who weren't all
that busy on a Wednesday night, by asking them to take
a look, but nobody recognized her. There wasn't much to
do but send her in to the morgue and hope the prints
might be on file somewhere.

Piggott, who liked to clear things up as they came
along, had just finished typing a report on that when
Communications relayed a call to a heist at a market on
Olympic. He and Schenke went out on it, and by what
they got from all the witnesses it had been their ape-man
again.

The market had just been about to close, at ten o'clock, and there had been some late customers in. The manager had been in the back stock room bagging the day's take for the night deposit at the bank, and he hadn't seen or heard a thing. But out in front there had been six customers, four of them male and two of those young and husky, four checkout girls, and two box boys. One of the checkout clerks was still in a dead faint on the floor when Piggott and Schenke got there, with the manager anxiously dabbing her face with cold water, and another woman was starting to go into hysterics. Bill Moss, who had answered the first call, calmed her down by suggesting they'd better throw some water over her; she gave him an outraged glare and stopped screaming. But upset as everybody was, they told a straight story and gave graphic descriptions, and it added up.

"I was never so scared in my life," gasped the prettiest checkout clerk. "Ooooh, he looked like something out of one of those old Frankenstein movies! He was about seven feet high—and he had a face just like a great big gorilla—and he had a gun—he was just so big it scared a person to look at him—and he went right up to Lila, that's Lila there, she was at the next checkout stand, and I knew it was a holdup but I was just too scared to scream—"

"He was the hell of a big bruiser all right," said one of the two young and husky men. "Jim and I'd just dropped in to get a six-pack of beer, and we were at that stand over there when he came up with the gun. My God, if he wasn't seven feet he must have been six five at least, and damn near as broad as he was high. Like a big gorilla like the girl says, and black as the ace of spades, and the gun was damn big too—and Goddamn, I was thinking he'd rip off everybody in the place and I've got a couple of hundred on me, I got lucky at poker last night—"

"I never saw anybody so vicious looking," said the woman who'd decided to forgo hysterics. "Oh, my goodness, he was just huge and he looked so mean—I hope I'm not prejudiced, but you hear of so many vicious black criminals—I was just terrified—"

Another of the men said, "Sure looked like an ugly customer. I'm just glad nobody got hurt. Well, who's going to stand up to a gun anyway, but a mean-looking brute like that—"

Whatever else they knew about the ape-man he was both unlucky and stupid. He hadn't taken much of a profit yet, and this time he had really missed the target. All that had been left in any of the registers was tomorrow's starting change, and probably out of stupidity he'd cleaned out only one. It didn't seem to have occurred to him to rob the customers. He'd grabbed the ten bucks or so and left, and of course nobody had followed him to see whether he got into a car.

They were both disciplined and experienced LAPD officers and they did what they had to do: got the witnesses' names and addresses and stories; but on the way back to the office Schenke indulged in some colorful cussing. Piggott the earnest fundamentalist Christian wasn't a swearing man, but he listened without voicing any disapproval. "Goddamn it," said Schenke, calming down a little, "there were four men there, and those two young ones could have jumped him from behind, where they were standing—if they'd acted together— Goddamn it, stand by like sheep and never make a move at that bastard—what the hell's got into people these days? So they were scared of the gun— Good Christ, all those so-called men were behind him, if they'd gone for him in a bunch—"

Piggott sniffed. "It's our training, Bob. I've heard the lieutenant say it's only a born policeman jumps toward trouble instead of away."

Schenke was still growling when they came into the office. Conway was just taking off his coat, and he was laughing. "I got a call just after you left, and it was Jack the Stripper again. He hit an all-night gas station on Beverly. The fellow at the station was another college kid, and he was nearly foaming at the mouth. The guy cleaned out the register and walked off with all his clothes, including a new coat he'd just paid ninety bucks for—he'd come on the job from a date with his girl, no time to change." Conway went on laughing. "He said the guy was really having fun, laughing like crazy to leave him stark naked. He gives us the same description, naturally."

"It's really not so funny," said Piggott. "Ninety bucks is ninety bucks, Rich."

And they'd hardly sat down when they got another call. There seemed to be some wholesale uproar going on over at an address on Elden Street, with three squads out. They all went out on it, and when they got there, they found a little crowd of citizens milling around in the middle of the street, one of the uniformed men holding his gun on them.

"What the hell?" said Conway. They pushed through the crowd in a hurry. "What goes on?" There were two other Traffic men there, looking as if they'd been in a fight, one with his uniform jacket ripped down the front and the other with an ugly knife slash on one cheek.

"I had to pull the gun on this damn crowd," said the third man. "I guess they've quieted down now—it's the corner house—there's one man dead and the others don't look too good— I don't know what the holy hell the citizens were doing out, but they roughed up Carlson here and he had to call a backup— I don't know what the hell it's all about—"

The patrolman with the knife cut said, "The woman up there on the porch says she's the one called in, I just had a look and went back to the squad to call in a homicide when that bunch jumped me—they were all out in the street when I came up—all I got out of her was her name, Hernandez—"

They went up to the porch of the corner house. The woman was a pretty plump dark young woman; she was sitting on the top step crying and when Schenke spoke her name she looked up at them and said wildly, "I tried to stop him—it's the wrong way to think, the priest says— leave vengeance to God—but Joe, he was just crazy, he's been drunk for two days—he's a good man, he never got drunk before—he says, gonna kill those people bring a murderer here, kill our Stephanie—he's been goin' around the neighbors sayin' that—I couldn't stop him—"

And then they remembered the name and last Sunday morning.

In the living room Doug Dillon lay bloodily slashed and dead, and the woman was still alive but only just, stabbed and slashed too. Joe Hernandez had tried to stab himself, his hands still on the knife in his chest, but he still had a pulse.

Conway said, "Christ," and went out at a run to call up an ambulance.

SIX

THAT WAS WAITING for them on Thursday morning.
Mendoza said coldly, "Another stupid bloody mess!"
The Dillon woman had died about an hour after they got
her to the hospital, but Hernandez was still alive. If he
didn't die he'd be charged with murder one, the way it
looked now, and there was another life gone down the
drain all because of stupidity and hatred. And they had
to deal with the new body. Mendoza called the lab and
asked somebody to go over to the morgue and take her
prints. There was also Ed Filer, and that body. It was
Higgins' day off.

Glasser came in late and drifted into Mendoza's office. "I've collected something more on the Polachek
woman. She was known at six or seven of those places I
tried, they're all sleazy fourth-rate dives on Sixth and
Third. She was in one place or the other most nights, and
all the bartenders knew her for a hooker, in business for
herself. You know those joints, live and let live, nobody
gave a damn. They weren't even leery about admitting it,
she'd picked up some man every time she was in one of
those joints."

"And maybe she'd just run out of time, Henry—she
was a cheap hooker, she'd mistreated the girl, who could
be her own daughter, and the girl finally retaliated. *Fi-
nalizar*, conclusion. That girl, she's the little mystery."

"She says Polachek wasn't her mother, but would she
know? We'll probably never know anything more about
it, if you ask me. Wanda's hot on trying to find out who

the girl really is, but it could be just as simple as that." He yawned. "I got home at midnight, and had a bath—those dives made me feel like I needed one." He uncovered his typewriter and started a follow-up report on it.

Galeano came over and said, "I want to go over to the jail to do some prodding at Filer. Anybody inclined to come along as a witness?"

Mendoza went with him for lack of anything else to do. The jailer brought Ed Filer into one of the interrogation rooms and they faced him across the tiny table. He'd been given a tan jail uniform, but hadn't been allowed to shave; gray stubble stained his narrow chin, and his expression was blank but his eyes wary and hard.

"Are you ready to talk to us now, Filer?" asked Galeano. "Tell us something about it?"

Filer said, "I'm out of cigarettes," and Mendoza gave him one. "Thanks." He drew on it strongly. "I guess I better tell you what happened."

"All right," said Mendoza. "Suppose you start at the beginning. Was Mabel Green your sister?"

He gave them a small mirthless grin. "No, she wasn't. We'd just been living together. That was the whole damn trouble. My God, what's the odds, we were old enough to know what we were doing, and it wasn't anybody else's damn business. What the hell difference was it at our age? Mabel was sixty-nine and I'm seventy-two, we're not a pair of wild kids, for God's sake. I guess you could say it's the government's fault."

"How come?" asked Galeano.

He said resentfully, "Well, for God's sake, the damn Social Security. Mabel and I knew each other more than thirty years. I knew her husband, Sam, we worked together in the Parks and Recreation Department. And they knew my wife, we used to visit back and forth, go places together. Sam died five years back and I'd already lost Sally—my wife—she died of cancer six years ago. We never had any kids. Mabel and Sam had a daughter. That damn little prissy bitch.'' He put out his cigarette and Mendoza laid the pack on the table. ''Thanks. So, Mabel had Sam's Social Security, and I had mine, but it don't go far the way prices of everything are sky-high. Mabel and I always liked each other, and my God, the ordinary way we'd of got married, but if we did she'd lose Sam's pension. With that and what I'm getting we could live a lot easier than either of us could alone, and only one rent to pay, but if we got married legal she'd lose the pension, so we just moved in together. We were getting along fine, the rent in that place isn't bad, and we always got along good. Mabel was a pretty good cook and neither of us much for goin' out at our age, just living a nice quiet life and doin' no harm to anybody. Together we had enough money to manage good. But that damned daughter of hers—that Audrey! She kept on with Mabel about living in sin—she's one of these damn born-again Christians and she kept on at Mabel, telling her I was a wicked old man corrupting her—my good God, it wasn't no choice of ours to live in sin if that's what she wants to call it, we didn't have no choice, we needed Mabel's pension—you can see how it was.''

''And what happened to Mabel?'' asked Galeano.

Filer lit another cigarette. ''I didn't have anything to do with her dying,'' he said in a subdued voice. ''That damned Audrey, she kept on and on about it and I'll be damned if she didn't get Mabel convinced she was a wicked woman, and she was going to move out on me. Audrey kept sayin' she should come live with her, hah, Mabel'd be the hell of a lot less comfortable in that place, four kids and a two-bedroom house and Mabel on a cot in the kids' room! And that Audrey bossing her around—but Mabel got it in her head it was the right thing to do. And if I know Audrey, she wasn't thinking so much about Mabel's immortal soul as about the Social Security, and somebody to babysit the kids—her husband's out of a job and they're on welfare.''

"So you wouldn't have Mabel's money anymore," said Galeano.

He said angrily, "Damn it, it was a piddling little amount by itself but with what I had—yeah, that's right, and I argued with her about it, I tried to make her see she was being stupid. But she was stubborn as that damn Audrey." He was silent for a long minute and then he said in a dragging voice, "The way it happened, I'd never hurt Mabel anyway, no matter what she did, but she was packing her clothes to move out, I was arguing at her and I guess I was talking pretty loud and she told me to shut up, and all of a sudden—I'd noticed her face was pretty red—she gave a sort of little gasp and fell down. I thought she'd fainted, I tried to bring her to and then—well, I saw she was dead." He gave a long sigh. "I don't know if it was a stroke or a heart attack or what, but she was dead."

"Why didn't you call a doctor, report it?" asked Mendoza.

And Galeano said softly, "You were thinking of the money, that was it, wasn't it?"

Filer's mouth drew tight. "All right, I was. That I was. There was Mabel gone and out of things, nothing couldn't matter to her anymore. It was only a couple of days before the end of the month and our checks would be coming along, I thought I'd let it go till they come—and I thought, put her in the bathtub, only place I could think of, and maybe if I ran some water into it, it'd stop her, you know, starting to rot for a while. And I—just left it like that.''

"You must have known you couldn't leave her indefinitely," said Galeano. "What did you plan to do about it eventually?"

He made a vague helpless gesture. "I don't know. Her check come and I put her name on the back and the bank give me the money. And when Audrey called on the phone I told her Mabel had changed her mind and we didn't want her to call up again. She'd keep calling, I knew, but I just didn't answer the phone. I knew she couldn't be coming to the place, they live way out in Sherman Oaks and she hasn't got a car, catch that lazy bum of a husband take her anyplace. It just sort of went on like that. I'd had a couple of ideas, I even thought about cutting Mabel up, but I couldn't do that to Mabel—it just sort of went on, and then it was time for the next check to come—" Suddenly he buried his face in his hands. "It just came to me plain—what an awful thing it was—when Trotter came with that cop yesterday, they were going to find her, and I thought I'd be better off dead too, but that cop grabbed me away from the window—"

Mendoza said, "If she died of natural causes there won't be much of a charge on you, Filer."

And he said bitterly, "I'd just as soon you keep me in jail. At least I wouldn't have to worry about the rent."

Mendoza left him the pack of cigarettes and they went out to the corridor. The jailer came up to take him back to his cell. Galeano said seriously, "I think they were wrong about that, you know. About the Social Security. I think she'd have gone on getting it if she remarried."

"I don't know the rules that well, you may be right."

"Well, see what the autopsy says. There's some stat-
ute about concealing a dead body, I think."

"And the Board of Health has rules too. It wouldn't
be much of a charge. He'd probably get probation."

"And then," said Galeano, "start worrying about the
rent again."

PALLISER HAD called the hospital to check on Hernandez. They were now saying he'd live; they'd been pump-
ing blood into him and he'd been briefly conscious.
When he was sitting up and taking notice they'd have to
get a statement from him, but it would be some time before he'd be transferred to jail and it probably wasn't
necessary to put a guard on him, he wasn't going anywhere. But that melee last night—he talked it over with
Hackett and Mendoza. Those citizens attacking patrol-
men—on one hand they ought to be charged with assault, but on the other feeling was running high enough
as it was. Palliser said, "There were already some threats
being made on that block about the Dillons, as soon as
word got out what had happened to Stephanie. And another thing"—he rubbed his handsome straight nose
thoughtfully—"there's the ethnic aspect to it. Most of
the people along there are Hispanic, and the Dillons
aren't."

"These hot-blooded Latins," said Mendoza cyni-
cally. "They were ready to back up Hernandez on taking the vengeance. The one I feel sorry for is Mrs.
Hernandez—she tried to stop him. We'll have to get a
formal statement from her. And I'll talk to the D.A.'s
office about the hot-blooded citizens, but I don't think
there'd be any percentage in bringing a charge, John—
just stir them up all the more. And another thing—what

she said to the boys last night—if Hernandez was drunk that would reduce the charge to murder two.''

"I suppose that's what the court would call it," agreed Hackett. "Incapable of judgment. But damn it, he knew what he was doing all right. These damned technicalities—" He took off his glasses and polished them on his handkerchief.

"What are the odds?" said Palliser. "Would it do any good to make it murder one and put him inside for nine or ten years before he's let loose on parole? He's clean, he hasn't any record—decent productive citizen—if we're talking about technicalities, he was temporarily insane."

Hackett said heavily, "On account of Stephanie. Yes. And we've all got children, we can understand how he was feeling, if none of us would have gone to such lengths. It's just a bloody mess all around."

In the end Mendoza talked to the D.A.'s office and the decision was made not to charge the vengeful citizens. Palliser went out to bring Mrs. Hernandez in to make a statement, and Hackett got hold of the doctor who'd worked over Hernandez last night, to find out if he'd been drunk.

The doctor said dryly, "Well, we weren't worrying about his blood-alcohol rate, we were trying to save the man's life. But if you want a guess, he was probably drunk as a skunk, you could smell him ten feet off. Yes, I could testify to that if I have to."

When they talked to Mrs. Hernandez she confirmed that, he'd been drinking wine all afternoon and evening, she'd begged him to stop but he wouldn't listen, and even drunk he'd been strong as a bull, just pushed her away when she'd tried to stop him from leaving the house. Palliser typed a statement and she signed it in a painful scrawl and he drove her home. A little crowd of relatives had showed up to give her moral support.

One of the lawyers from the public defender's office would be assigned to him; he probably wouldn't spend much time inside.

HACKETT WAS rereading that teletype and thinking unprofitably about Gilbert Kramer when at three-thirty a call came in from a squad: a mugging and an ambulance called. It was another of the ongoing unimportant things they had to handle, unimportant unless somebody was seriously hurt or dead; that sort of thing happened too often in the city jungle. And the city fathers could upgrade this oldest part of the city, tear down the old buildings and put up the clean new high-rise ones, but they were still surrounded by the ancient narrow residential neighborhoods with the comparatively cheap rents, filled with what now had to be called the ethnic minorities, where street gangs roamed and crime was higher than in other places.

It was Coronado Street, and he spotted the squad half a block from where it crossed Wilshire. An ambulance was just pulling away, red lights and siren going. There was a big parking lot along here, behind one of the new high-rise office buildings on Wilshire. He found a slot in there and walked back to the squad. The Traffic man was Zimmerman. There was a citizen talking with him, and on the sidewalk was the body of a big dog with its throat cut, a pool of dark blood all around it.

Both the men were looking very angry. "What's the story?" asked Hackett.

"I've seen a lot of damned things riding a squad in this town," said Zimmerman, "but this is about the damndest. This is Mr. Packer—Sergeant Hackett. It was a blind man, Sergeant—these bastards jumped him and killed his dog. Christ, if that's not as low as you can get—"

Hackett looked at the dog. It was a beautiful big specimen of a yellow Labrador, a female, wearing the regulation guide-dog harness. "Good God Almighty," he said.

"I saw it happen—" Packer was in the thirties, a short spare man with a bush of dark hair, a bulldog face with a prominent jaw. The jaw was very much in evidence, thrust out belligerently. "And I'll tell you what gets me, for Christ's sake. There weren't many people on a side street like this, a couple of women down the block and you can't blame them, I don't, but there were two men right across the street, they had to have seen it too, and they just looked the other way and made tracks toward Wilshire—my God, what's got into people these days? In the name of common humanity—see a blind man attacked—and I was too far away, damn it. I'd just come out to the parking lot, I'd had a dentist's appointment in the professional building there, I'd just got to my car when I heard the commotion, and looked up here—the dog was snapping and snarling—I've got long sight, and they were right opposite the entrance to the lot. I saw it was a blind man, I could see the white cane, and these three black sons-of-bitches roughing him up—the dog was taking after them, and I saw the man go down—I started up here at a run, reflex action, and yelled at them—I don't know what the hell I could have done against three of them, they were all pretty big, but God, I'd have had a damned good try—but by the time I got to the street they were just taking off at a run, down toward Wilshire, and I saw the man was unconscious and bleeding—and the poor damn dog—I figured I'd better see what I could do for him, those bastards were long

gone, I'd never catch up with them. I went back to the
building and called the police. My God, he was just a
young fellow, kind of good-looking—and when the
squad car came the officer called an ambulance—"

"Was he seriously hurt, do you think?" Hackett asked
Zimmerman.

"He was bleeding like a stuck pig, Sergeant—I think
he'd been stabbed—I didn't like to move him, I think
he'd had a knock on the head. There was an empty billfold beside him, looked like they'd stripped it and just
dropped it. If there was identification on it they'll have
it at the hospital, but the dog—my God, those bastards
killing the dog—"

Packer said, "Not that it means much to anybody
thinks anything of a dog, but they're valuable animals,
cost a lot to train—a cousin of mine is blind, she's got a
big shepherd."

"What do we do about the dog?" asked Zimmerman.

Hackett said heavily, "Get on the radio to Animal
Control. They'll take charge of it. Mr. Packer, we'd like
you to come in and make a statement about this." Not
that they would likely ever find out any more about it.

"Sure," said Packer crisply. "Just tell me where to go.
I'll be glad to. If I could help you catch up to the Goddamned black bastards—"

Hackett told him and got his full name, Nelson Packer;
he was the manager of a big chain market in Hollywood. Hackett waited with Zimmerman until the Animal Control van came and took the dog away, and then
he sent Zimmerman back on tour and drove out to Cedars-Sinai.

At the first nurses' station in Emergency an efficient
middle-aged nurse looked at the badge and said, "Oh,
yes, the one just brought in about forty minutes ago."

"Was there identification on him?"

"Yes, he's a Charles Colby. There was an emergency number to call, we got hold of his mother and she just got here a few minutes ago. The doctor's with him now, you'll have to wait if you want to see him. That's Mrs. Colby over there."

She was sitting upright on the padded bench against the wall in the corridor, nobody else here but doctors and nurses passing. He went over and introduced himself. She was a nice-looking woman, probably no more than in the fifties, with hair still dark, a round face, bright blue eyes; she'd obviously come out in a hurry, wearing a cotton housedress under a coat. She said, "Oh, can you tell me what happened? The nurse just said Charles was hurt, and I drove right down—" He told her and she listened with an angry anxious expression. "Right on the street, in broad daylight—but, Sergeant, what happened to Belle? Is she all right? Where is she?"

"That's his dog?" He told her about the dog, and she hadn't cried yet for her son but she began to cry about the dog. He sat down beside her. Presently she sat up and wiped her eyes and blew her nose. She said, "I don't know how to tell him. If he's not going to die too. I just don't know. She was the most wonderful dog in the world. She gave Charles back his life." And she went on talking compulsively, waiting there to hear if her son was going to die, in this busy impersonal place with its own life humming all around them. "He was only twenty-eight when he lost his sight, you know, it was glaucoma and they couldn't do anything about it. I thought he was going to die. He was engaged to be married, and she seemed like a nice girl but she just couldn't face life with a blind man, she went away and that nearly killed him. You see, he'd been a photographer. Since he was just a youngster he'd been interested in photography, and he was saving money to open his own studio. He was working at a camera store in Hollywood—we live in West Hollywood, my husband and I bought the house thirty years ago. It had been terrible losing him, just the year before—Walter, I mean—he was nearly twenty years older than I am. And I thought Charles was going to die, he was so depressed and despondent. He's only thirty-five now, you know. And I was afraid he'd kill himself—saying there was nothing left for him, nothing to do with his life. The doctor talked about a guide dog, but he wasn't interested at first. It was the doctor really bullied him into it, he found a male nurse to help Charles on the plane—he had to go back to New Jersey to take the training, how to handle her. And Belle gave him back his life. She'd have given her life for him—and that's what she did do, didn't she?—she'd have protected him, attacked those men, and that's why they killed her. Where is she?''

He told her and she was distressed. ''Oh, I wish you hadn't done that—I'd like to have her buried in a pet cemetery, with a headstone. She gave Charles back his whole life. He could go anywhere with her, do nearly anything. He was himself again. He'd already been studying Braille and he got very good at it, and he started taking interest in helping other blind people. That's why he was down there this afternoon, you know. He taught at a Braille workshop for children on Sixth Street, three afternoons a week. He'd have been on his way to get the bus on Wilshire, on his way home.''

A sandy-haired young intern came up and said, ''Mrs. Colby?''

''Yes—'' She started up. ''How is he?''

''Not too bad,'' said the intern cheerfully. ''He'll be quite okay in a few days—he had a bad knock on the

head but there's no concussion, and a few knife slashes.
He's lost a little blood, but he's going to be all right. You
can see him for just a few minutes."

"Oh, thank you—oh, thank God—" But she looked
almost fearfully at Hackett and put a hand to her mouth.
"I don't know how to tell him about Belle. I don't like to
lie to him, but I think I'd better tell him she's all right—
until he comes home—and then I'll have to tell him."

"Mrs. Colby, would you look over his clothes, his
billfold, and try to tell me what was stolen? Did he wear
any jewelry? They probably won't let you stay long—I'll
wait."

"He only had a little money with him, five or six dollars and change for the bus. All right."

When she came back ten minutes later she was crying
again. "The first thing he asked—about Belle. Oh, I
didn't like to lie to him—and I don't know what he'll do
without Belle—she was the center of our whole lives, I
loved her as much as he did." She sobbed, and caught
herself, and said, "You wanted to know—his billfold's
empty, and his ring's gone."

"Could you describe it?"

"It belonged to his father, it's a five-dollar gold piece
dated eighteen ninety-three set in yellow gold, and it's got
my husband's initials engraved inside, W.J.C. I never
dreaded anything in my life more than telling him about
Belle."

HACKETT WAS late getting home; he hadn't left the hospital until after six. When he came into the kitchen Angel
said, "I was beginning to worry about you."

"I got held up."

The children came running to meet him, with the huge
ungainly mongrel Laddie bounding after them. And

when Laddie had saddled himself on them Angel had said he was a useless mutt, because he loved everybody—even the handsome Persian Silver Boy, who regarded him with proper disdain—but he adored the children, and Hackett had the notion that he'd protect them vociferously if any danger threatened.

"Sometimes," he said to Angel, "I wonder why I picked this damned dirty job."

On Friday morning Horder called Mendoza about eleven o'clock. "This corpse that turned up behind the Japanese restaurant. You still don't know who she is, we've run her prints through and she's not on file with us. I sent them to the Feds, could be they'll have her on record."

"And maybe not," said Mendoza.

Hackett was in court at the arraignment of Danny Fielding, and it was Galeano's day off. The night watch had left them another heist, and most of the witnesses from that market heist were coming in to make statements; they'd be busy. He went out to lend a hand on that, and typing up the statements kept Palliser and Grace busy until midafternoon. Mendoza talked to the other victim in to make a statement, the attendant at the all-night gas station. He was a student at LACC and his name was Randy Sills, and he was still furious.

"That Goddamned bastard," he said. "And when he drove in I thought he looked like a nice guy! I hadn't had a customer in a couple of hours. He was about my age, he acted friendly—well, all I can say is, he was about my size, five ten, a hundred and sixty, and he had dark blond hair. It was a Ford four-door about five years old. He says to fill it up, and it'd be cash, and of course at night the register's in the garage, I never gave it a thought when he got out of the car and followed me back there. And then he sticks a gun in my chest and says, hand over the loot, buddy—and I was so damned surprised—and then he says with a funny kind of grin, now take it all off, he says, and I said what, and he says, come on, strip, buddy—I didn't believe it, he made me strip right down to the skin—Goddamn it, I'd bought that coat just two days before, ninety bucks! Naturally I don't usually wear good clothes on the job, but I hadn't had time to go home and change after the date with Jean—''

This was all probably a waste of time, reflected Mendoza. There were no leads, it was unlikely they'd ever lay hands on Jack the Stripper.

''—But I tell you, he was getting the hell of a kick out of it, he was laughing like crazy when he tossed my clothes in the back of the Ford and took off. And my God, it was damned cold, I was freezing by the time the squad car got there, it's just lucky there's a phone in the garage—and of course Mother was out at her bridge club and I couldn't get hold of her till midnight—sitting there naked—by the grace of God I didn't have any more customers. My God, it's a wonder I'm not in the hospital with pneumonia.'' He was still swearing as he signed the statement.

It was Friday afternoon before Wanda could get a brief appointment to talk to Dr. Felicia Baxter. Dr. Baxter had a busy practice and a high reputation, and they were duly grateful for the time she donated to the inmates of Juvenile Hall. She was a big handsome woman with short-cropped iron-gray hair and shrewd dark eyes. She looked at Wanda across her neat desk and said, ''That's a queer patient you've handed me, Miss Larsen. That girl—she's like a blank slate. I think she's got a good brain, potentially, but she's as ignorant and inexperienced as a two-year-old. What you told me about the case—there must be a special place in hell for women like that. The poor little soul doesn't know anything except how to clean toilets and cook a few simple things, she's never seen a book or a copy of the alphabet—you said apparently she'd been kept a prisoner in that house—"

"We knew that. It could have been as long as seven years, it probably was."

"My God. Since she was around five. It's unbelievable, only the unbelievable things do happen. Well," said Dr. Baxter abruptly, "you asked me to try to get something more out of her, any relevant facts you can use to find out who she is, how she came to be with the Polachek woman. That's a funny one, how she comes out automatically with that little recitation, the name and address. My guess would be that she was taught that a long time back, and it got fixed in her unconscious mind. It could very well be all she remembers of her early background."

"And what do you think about Louise?"

Dr. Baxter smiled. "I'd have to work with her a good deal longer before I'd have a guess about that. Beginnings of a multiple personality?" She shook her head. "But I got one little thing, I think. I don't know how useful it might be. You gave me a clue when you said she hadn't known she was in Los Angeles, or in California, and she said she only knew New York and another place with a funny name. I tried to get her to remember what that was, and she came right out with it. She said it was a place named Philly. She remembered the man named Billy saying he sure wished he was back in Philly."

"Philadelphia," said Wanda. "Good Lord. Well, that's interesting but I don't know how useful it might be, that's another big town."

"She'll have a lot of catching up to do," said Dr. Baxter thoughtfully. "I'd say she's twelve or thirteen, but she's as ignorant of the whole world as a babe in arms. The things people do to each other. I'd like to see her again. What's going to happen to her?"

"Nothing much. She'll be put on probation and stay at Juvenile Hall or some minimum-security place until she's eighteen."

"And we don't know when that will be. And turn her loose to earn a living? She wouldn't be fit for it any more than a four-year-old. I presume she'd get some teaching?"

"I suppose they'd try. It's a queer case all right. I wish we could see just where to get any further on it. Well, thanks."

"I'll see her again," said Dr. Baxter. "She's really quite a nice child, Miss Larsen. Or she could be. In time we may find out more about her."

Wanda was to get her wish sooner than she had expected. She'd just got back to the office when Mark came in and looked pleased to see her. "Say," he said, "I'm sorry as hell about this, we don't often goof up but we've been busy. You're on that homicide where the kid knifed that woman, aren't you? You turned us onto that place last Monday—Geneva Street."

"Yes, what did you turn up?"

He spread his hands. "Nothing much. The place hadn't had a thorough cleaning in years, and there wasn't much furniture. We picked up a lot of confused smudges, the only few clear prints belong to the corpse. There wasn't much there except clothes, some food in the refrigerator and freezer, a couple of bottles of bourbon and gin in the kitchen. But we poked around, and I came across this in an old suitcase in the front closet—tucked into a side pocket. I meant to pass it on to you, but it got buried on my desk and I just came across it fifteen minutes ago. I'm sorry as hell." He handed her a limp envelope.

"As long as it came to light," said Wanda. She sat down at her desk and looked at it. It was a small cheap envelope with its top roughly torn open, and it had a blurred postmark. With a stirring of excitement she saw that it was addressed to Katherine Polachek at an address in Philadelphia. There was a return address scrawled in the left-hand corner: Mrs. James Anderson, Edgewood Drive in South Pasadena. And there was a letter in it. She drew it out, a single sheet torn from a cheap tablet covered with rather sprawly handwriting in ball-point. The first thing she noticed, incredibly, was the date at the top—a date of nearly seven and a half years ago.

Dear Kathy, I'm sorry you're down on your luck, but I'm afraid we can't help you out right now, Jim isn't earning much yet on the new job and I'm expecting another baby in September. I wish you would break off with Billy Seay, he's no good and you say you've given him money. I don't think it's such a hot idea about your taking foster kids, I know the state pays pretty well but you don't know much about kids or like them, and they can be a lot of work. Well, I wish you best of luck anyway. Gloria.

Wanda said excitedly, "Henry." This old letter, put carelessly away instead of being destroyed, surfacing after all these years—and, foster kids.

Glasser read it and said, "For God's sake. But it's a long while back. People move."

Wanda already had the right phone book open. "But they didn't," she said softly. "Here it is—James Anderson, Edgewood Drive."

"It's a common name. I'll be damned," said Glasser.

Wanda dialed and on the third ring a woman answered. "Mrs. Anderson? May I ask if you know a Katherine Polachek?"

"Why, yes, she's my sister. Who is this?"

"I'm afraid we have some bad news for you, Mrs. Anderson. This is the police, LAPD. Can we come and see you now?"

"Well, I guess so—but what is it about Kathy?"

"We'll be with you in half an hour," said Wanda. "Come on, Henry. Talk about breaks—and we might have had it last Monday—"

On the way to South Pasadena on the freeway, Glasser driving, she glanced at his blunt profile and wondered irrelevantly if he'd ever get round to asking her to marry him. Probably not. They'd been out together a few times, and Henry was a good man to work with but she didn't know that she'd want to spend the rest of her life with him by any means.

The house in South Pasadena was an old California bungalow. The door was opened by a woman about thirty-five, a rather pretty woman with light-brown hair and friendly blue eyes. She looked at Glasser's badge, at Wanda. "You're the one called. Police. Something about Kathy?"

"I'm afraid we've got to tell you that your sister's dead, Mrs. Anderson."

"Oh, I'm sorry to hear that," but she didn't sound too upset. She said, "You'd better come in. You'll have to excuse the mess, I've been sewing for my little girl." The combination living-dining room was neat enough except for the sewing spread out on the couch, the open sewing machine on one wall. She sat down on the couch. "Sit down, won't you? I ought to explain, we hadn't seen Kathy in years, I'm afraid she'd got pretty far down, Jim wouldn't have her in the house."

"Did you know she was in California?"

She nodded. "We came out here when we got married ten years ago. The rest of the family was still back in Philly, Mama and Dad and Kathy. But Kathy'd started to drink and take up with men when she was still in high school, and Dad threw her out when we saw she wasn't going to straighten up. She was brought up right, I don't know why she went wrong—we've always been honest respectable people. Of course she married Pete Polachek, and he wasn't much good, and then he left her. She ran around with different men, I guess—she used to keep in touch with Mama, as long as Mama'd hand her money. It was a real grief to Mama, I guess you can see. I hadn't seen her in years."

"She was living with a Billy Seay at one time?" asked Glasser.

"Say, how'd you know that?" Wanda showed her the letter. She looked at it wonderingly. "I'd forgot writing this. All that time ago. It was the first time I'd heard from her in years. She was five years older than me—was she still living with him? He was a real no-goodnik, we knew the family from the neighborhood—riffraff."

"When did you see her last? You said you knew she was here."

"That's right. She showed up here one day with him, it must be almost seven years back, Marcy was only about three. She looked terrible, she'd bleached her hair and they were both a little drunk, and Jim ordered them out of the house and told her never to bother us again. I hadn't laid eyes on her since, nor wanted to, and Mama hasn't heard from her in years. It's an awful thing to say about my own sister, we've always been respectable but—"

"What about this mention of her keeping foster children?" asked Wanda.

"She had the idea back then, it'd be an easy way to make money, but like I wrote her in that letter, she didn't like kids. No, I don't know if she ever tried that."

"There wasn't a child with her that time?"

"Golly, no, and she didn't say anything about that. They were both drunk like I say." She looked from Wanda to Glasser, and now she was embarrassed. "I don't know just how to say it, but—well, if you were looking for relatives to pay for her funeral, I don't think Jim would go for that at all. Or me. I suppose it was an accident—well, like I say, none of the family had seen her in years, we'd cut her off because she'd gone the way she did, and whatever happened to her was her own fault."

They left without telling her how Katherine Polachek had died, and she didn't ask, accepting it as her own invented accident.

"But," said Wanda in the car, "I'll bet that's just how she got hold of Linda. And now we've got a place to look. She'd offered the foster home."

"That flashy hooker?"

"Yes, I know they do check up, try to be sure it's a fit home, but also they're always desperate for decent foster homes in most cities. And it was seven years ago—if she'd fixed herself up and put on a good front, she'd have had the sense to do that—''

"But why in the name of God did she keep the kid, if that's so? One of the kids? Technically it'd be a charge of kidnapping, all the way from Philadelphia, across state lines—why the hell? And the Linda kid would only have been about five then.''

Wanda said grimly, "We can guess. Billy liked the little girls to play with. And she wanted to please Billy. And after he left her, whenever that was, she got the bright idea of turning Linda into a slavey to do what work was done in the house. Of all the damnable things—but maybe we can trace Linda back now.''

"We don't know she ever was in Philly. She just remembered the man talking about it.''

"Oh, don't drag your heels, Henry. It's the likeliest thing—the woman was living there then. Wherever she got the girl, and it could be a couple of different social-service agencies—''

"You do realize, don't you," said Glasser, "that it is now after eight P.M. in Philadelphia, and Friday. We won't be able to contact any of those places before Monday now.''

"Oh, damn,'' said Wanda.

ON SATURDAY morning Mendoza had just come in and was talking to Hackett and Higgins about the anonymous body—they hadn't had a kickback from the Feds on her prints. "I had a look at her in the morgue, and she doesn't look like a drifter, somebody who wouldn't be missed. She was wearing good-quality clothes, nothing expensive but good. She'd had a manicure lately.''

"Somebody may report her missing sooner or later," said Hackett, not much interested.

"I checked with Carey in Missing Persons. He hasn't got her on his list yet, and it's nearly four days ago." The phone buzzed on his desk and he picked it up. "Yes, Jimmy?"

"I've got a long-distance call for you from Newark."

"¡Siga adelante!"

The rough elderly voice of Sergeant Durand said, "Mendoza? I know this is pretty damned quick service, but you sort of aroused my curiosity. I rummaged around in the basement, had quite a hunt but I finally found that file for you on Gilbert Kramer."

"And we're very much obliged. What did it tell you?"

"Well, when I read it over I remembered it clearer—it came back to me halfway. I'd just made rank then and got into plain clothes, and I was in on part of it. God, that's a long time ago. I was just a young punk, eager beaver to be the great big important detective, and here I am with corns and false teeth and fixing to claim my pension next year, and God, it seems like yesterday I pinned on the badge. Sorry, I guess it just hits all of us when we get to this stage in life. This Kramer—"

"Yes?" said Mendoza patiently.

"He worked with a partner, we charged them both at the same time. They were running a bucket shop out of a hole of an office downtown. You know, the cats and dogs—the fancy printed stock certificates not worth the paper under the printing—"

"Say that again," said Mendoza, and punched the amplifier. Durand's voice came booming out into the office as he obligingly said it again. "—Been taking some nice loot from the trusting old ladies and the rest of the suckers. Sometimes it's damned near impossible to prove fraud on a deal like that, even reputable brokers can give you wrong advice, but the stuff they were peddling wasn't bona fide stock, just made-up company names on paper. We'd had some complaints. And we nailed them right away on fraud. They both did some time in the joint for that—"

"And who was the partner?" asked Mendoza.

"A fellow about Kramer's age, let's see, Kramer was twenty-nine then. The other one was Archie Kershaw. And a couple of years later we busted them again, that time they were selling stock in a nonexistent gold mine. They only got probation that time. You said later on Kramer got charged with mail fraud—that's the Feds' business, we wouldn't know anything about that."

"Have you by any chance," asked Mendoza mildly, "got a description of this pretty pair?"

"I've got mug shots and particulars right in front of me, I didn't know how much you'd want. But my God, Mendoza, it's twenty-four years back, Kramer might look a lot different now."

"Let's hear what it says."

"Well, Kramer's described as Caucasian, six one, a hundred and seventy, brown and blue, no marks. He was a good-looking bastard then, by the mug shot."

"What about Kershaw?"

"Caucasian, five eight, a hundred and sixty, brown and blue."

"Durand," said Mendoza, "thanks much. You've been a big help."

"Have to cooperate," said Durand amiably. "Glad we could lend you a hand."

Mendoza put the phone down and cocked his head at Hackett and Higgins. "Always so gratifying when a little light shows through the crack in the door. It's beautiful—*¡Queé maravilla!* I really should have put two and two together and remembered how the wife told us he used to sell Indian good-luck charms by mail."

Hackett said blankly, "Maulden was Kershaw? But there's no evidence he'd been working with anybody, Kramer or whoever, on any kind of job crooked or straight, in years."

"No, maybe they parted company all those years back. I wonder if Kershaw was in the federal pen with him." Mendoza took up the phone again and got the lab. "I hope you've still got the prints on that recent corpse—one Robert Maulden, Valentine Street last week. If you've tossed them out as dead matter—*apologia*, I didn't intend the pun—we'll have to dig up the body to get them all over again."

"They should be here somewhere," said Scarne.

"*Muy bien*. Will you kindly send them back to the Feds for a make."

"Sure."

"But, Luis," said Higgins. "You're making the hell of a long jump here."

"Not that long, George. There were Kramer's prints on that bottle of bourbon. Which is funny in a way, because he'd know they're on file and you'd have thought he'd be more careful. But con men—do I know the con men—very seldom have any violence in them, and he might well have been a little nervous, committing a murder."

"But how had they got back in touch, and why the hell should Kramer murder him?" asked Hackett.

"You can read it a dozen ways, but it fits. It fits." Mendoza barked a laugh. "Oh, that cute old con man— Archie Kershaw—getting older, developing the crippling arthritis, and shopping around for a nice motherly woman to take care of him and believe anything he said!

No Social Security because of the niggardly parents—and the little grocery store back in Illinois!''

"You know, if you're right," said Higgins suddenly, "they could have been in contact all along, even if they haven't been working together. Went their separate ways maybe, but they'd been friends—partners. The wife wouldn't have known if he got personal mail, she said that. Even if they weren't on a caper together, they might have kept in touch."

"They might have." Mendoza brooded over his steepled hands. "And then there's that cash. Why should Kramer want to murder his old partner after all this time? There's never much honor among thieves, boys, and say they had kept in touch, and Kramer had prospered where Kershaw hadn't—say Kramer was on some successful caper and Kershaw said, spare a little for an old pal, and Kramer sent him a little present and then had second thoughts."

Hackett gave a skeptical snort. "You don't know that Maulden was Kershaw."

"I'd lay a bet. It's the only logical answer. And that could say something else, Arturo. Kramer's vulnerable in some way. If Kershaw knew about some lay he's on, and said, share some loot or I'll blow the whistle, there must be somebody to blow the whistle at. It could be that Kramer's picked up a wealthy wife who'd cast him off if she knew about his record. It could be—anything could be. But I think we've got a long step on in the offbeat mystery."

"I'll wait to do any speculating until we hear from the Feds," said Hackett.

As WELL as distributing all the copies of the mug shots to lawmen, they had got the willing cooperation of the press, and for a couple of days at the first of the week photographs of Alvarez and Camacho had appeared in the *Times* and the *Herald*. On Sunday morning Patrolman Finnegan of the Santa Monica force was peacefully cruising down San Vicente Boulevard on his regular tour when a young woman stepped off the curb and frantically beckoned him. Finnegan pulled in and she ran around the squad to peer in the window. She was a pretty blonde, and very excited.

"It's him!" she said. "I recognized him right away— it's that man in the paper! One of the armed robbers who escaped—it said his name's Alvarez—I just saw him—"

"Now calm down, miss," said Finnegan, but he felt a little excited himself. For half a second he had a vision of headlines—LOCAL OFFICER CAPTURES ARMED DESPERADO. "Where did you see him?"

"Right across the street back there—the car-wash place—he's getting his car washed—I recognized him right away, I know it's him—"

Well, stranger things had happened, and Finnegan made all the right decisions. Alvarez was known to be armed and dangerous. Finnegan called in for a backup. Three squads descended on the Acme Car Wash lot, pulling in at different angles, and Finnegan and two of his colleagues, guns out, canvassed the lot and spotted the suspect in thirty seconds. They surrounded him with barked commands and Finnegan got the cuffs on him.

"What the hell do you think you're doing?" demanded the prisoner. "Say, I'll sue you guys to hell and back if you try to pin anything on me—" He looked quite a bit like Tony Alvarez, but he turned out to be Carlos Romero, an honest citizen and a security guard at a local national bank.

THE NIGHT watch left them two new heists. Mendoza had said various things about the Feds, wandering around the office on Sunday afternoon. It wasn't until Monday morning that they got the kickback from Washington. Maulden's prints identified him as Archibald Kershaw, record appended.

"I told you so," said Mendoza happily.

"Very interesting," said Hackett, "but it doesn't give us any lead to Kramer."

Mendoza slouched down in his desk chair and regarded his two senior sergeants, emitting a long stream of smoke, and he said dreamily, "Rental cars."

SEVEN

"ARE YOU out of your mind, Luis?" asked Hackett. "Even if Hoffman's right about that, we said it would be hopeless to track down. And it's over a week ago."

Mendoza said, "Yes, it's a hell of a long chance and it'll be one hell of a job, but I think we'll give it a try. I have a hunch that Mr. Hoffman's specialized knowledge is right on the ball. It all feels just too smooth not to be true. Kramer was in that rental car, and he came to see his old pal Kershaw with the spiked whiskey. You see by the record they were in Leavenworth together on that mail fraud. They'd been tried separately, and Kramer got released a couple of months before Kershaw. We don't know what the hell might be behind this, but we know Kramer's the one who fed Kershaw the whiskey because of the prints. And anything else can wait until we lay hands on Kramer." He was rereading the teletype.

"Through the Hertz car? You're daydreaming, Luis," said Higgins. "My God, there'd be hundreds of rental cars all over the county any day of the week, and we don't know what name Kramer may be using now."

"*Claro está,*" said Mendoza. "Hoffman said, and I'll believe he knows what he was talking about, that car hadn't been out of the garage long, probably rented that day or the previous day. A big outfit like Hertz will have the computers. They can tell us the names of everybody in possession of one of their cars that day."

"And just where would that take us?" asked Hackett.

"It always come back to the legwork, Arturo. The Feds will be slightly more up-to-date with Kramer's mug shot—"

"Twenty years old?" said Hackett.

"Unfortunately. But there'll be the general features, and I think he'd be recognizable. *Dios,* legwork is no word for it, but it's the best chance I see."

"Go all around and look at them with the mug shot in hand? My God Almighty, they won't all be here! Why does anybody rent a car?—because they haven't got one handy, usually because they're in strange territory away from home. Business executives traveling on business, relatives on a visit to relatives or friends. Oh, you might rent a car a couple of days while yours was in the garage, but most people here driving Hertz cars would be from out of town, just in the nature of things."

Mendoza said lazily, "And we haven't any idea where Kramer might have been all this time, where he's based now. But they'd kept in touch, that we can guess. It doesn't matter a damn what the motive was, Art, skip that. They've been in contact, Kramer back in Newark or Chicago or Tucson or wherever the hell, and for some reason he wanted Kershaw out of the way. He landed here and acquired the car, under whatever name he's using now, and after he's dealt with Kershaw he turns it in and goes back home. Or he could be based right around here somewhere, and rented the car because his was in the garage. Whyever he rented it, we know he did."

"You're putting a lot of faith in Hoffman," said Higgins.

"I think he knows what he's talking about. So we get Hertz to give us a list of everybody who rented a car here that day or the day before, and there'll be home addresses, and we go and look at all the ones living around here, and we pass the mug shot on to every force where the rest hail from and ask them to look.''

"My God, the ideas you do get," said Hackett. "Even granting that Kramer would be recognizable from that old photo—and he might have got fat or bald or lost all his teeth—that'd be asking a lot of a lot of lawmen all over the country. I see it, I see it. But it's one hell of a long chance. So, John Smith in Kalamazoo was driving a Hertz car here those couple of days, and Joe Brown of the Kalamazoo force goes to ask about it and thinks he looks like Kramer, Smith says chance resemblance, and there's no legal reason to take his prints to find out for sure. And every force everywhere is damned busy these days, would all of them cooperate that far and really use any imagination on it?'

"But I think we'll take a stab at it, Art. I'll talk to the Feds and get the mug shot sent out. Give the lab something to do, make up copies. And meanwhile we'll contact Hertz. *¡Condenación!* They must have a central office somewhere where all the records are kept—we'll find out.''

"And I can hear what they'll say when we ask for that list," said Higgins. "It's just worth a try, but it'll be the hell of a lot of work. For us and everybody else. My God, in any given day, how many rental cars all over the damned county?''

"I wouldn't even guess." Mendoza picked up the central telephone book. "First thing, find out who to talk to at Hertz.''

That was a big, efficiently run outfit, and by two o'clock Mendoza and Hackett were talking to a Stanley Eggers in a well-appointed office on the top floor of a high-rise building out at Century City. There were Hertz agencies scattered all over the county, but there had to be a central business office to collate all the records, a local general manager to keep tabs on all those, and Eggers seemed to be it. He was a big bald man in the fifties, and he listened to them and said, "My God, you don't want much, do you? Well, I suppose we have to cooperate with the police. Sure we've got computers, you can't run a business without computers these days."

"Would you have a rough guess how long the list might run?" asked Hackett.

Eggers turned both hands palm upward. "God knows. Five or six hundred? It does fluctuate, and I will say business isn't quite as heavy at this time of year. You're just interested in those two dates?"

"That's right. Everybody who rented a car either of those two days." Which was, Hackett thought, putting the hell of a lot of faith in Floyd Hoffman.

"Well, I'll get work started on it, I suppose we can have something under way by tomorrow or the next day. I don't know one damn thing about computers myself, I'm just the front-office man who oversees all the records and hands out the orders. But it'll be a little job. I'll see what I can do and probably let you know by tomorrow how soon you can expect a list."

"That's fine," said Hackett. They wouldn't get that mug shot from the Feds until tomorrow anyway.

But in the car he said to Mendoza, "This is going to be a hell of a lot of legwork for nothing, if you ask me. It's too far up in the air."

"Preserve the optimistic thoughts." Mendoza switched on the ignition. "I'm very damn curious about what's behind this, Art. I'd like to know just what the hell Kramer's motive for that homicide was. And sometimes we get lucky. Kershaw may not have been much loss to the world, but I'd like to know the ins and outs of this damn queer thing. One like Kramer showing up after all these years—I wonder what he's been doing since he got out of Leavenworth. That kind doesn't reform. Whatever, he hasn't been picked up for anything since.''

''Or Kershaw,'' said Hackett. ''Him and his Indian good-luck pieces. Probably both of them mixed up in various con games, just lucky not to be caught again. At any rate, after the collision with Uncle Sam over the fraudulent mail-ad racket, they were smart enough not to risk that again. Kershaw was safe enough advertising the good-luck pieces, customers sell themselves on that kind of thing and it's not illegal. But I can see this job taking a hell of a long time and a lot of chasing around, and getting us nowhere in the end.''

''Time will tell,'' said Mendoza.

ON SECOND thought, Wanda had realized there was something else she could do on Saturday. The foster children sent to the foster homes could come from any of several places: the various social-service agencies, Aid to Dependent Children or whatever it was called now, and others, even the general welfare office, and also from Juvenile Hall, which would come under police jurisdiction or at least the police would be in contact, and police forces didn't take weekends off. She had called the central desk in Philadelphia on Saturday morning, got the number, and talked to one of the matrons of Juvenile Hall there, passed on the request for information. The matron said doubtfully, ''Seven years—I don't know whether we'd have records that far back. We have quite a turnover, you know. And we get the children for all sorts of reasons. It wasn't a police case?''

"I shouldn't think so." It was likelier that the children were sent to the foster homes from one of the social-service agencies.

"Well, I'll ask the office and see if we can find anything. What was the name again?"

Wanda wasn't surprised that nobody had called her back by Monday. On Monday morning she talked to quite a few people in Philadelphia, at all those various agencies. It had occurred to her belatedly, as it had occurred to Glasser, that if this was the way Polachek had acquired Linda, there must have been quite a little fuss about it at the time in Philadelphia. Some of the children sent to the foster homes were orphans, without any relatives, but not all of them, and it was usually a temporary arrangement. Whatever agency was involved, if one of their foster children vanished away from their jurisdiction, there must have been questions asked, somebody would have taken some action, and it would be sufficiently unusual that somebody ought to remember it. But nobody she talked to recognized Linda's name. And seven years ago—there might be all new personnel at those offices now, but there ought to be records, if somebody would go looking. Several people promised cooperation, said they'd get back to her if they found out anything relevant in the records. But with all the faceless unfortunates and derelicts they had to deal with, day in day out, adults and children, would anybody remember an individual case after all this time? She felt frustrated, putting the phone down for the last time. The big impersonal welfare agencies—but there must be some records. A five-year-old couldn't just disappear without anybody noticing.

And then she thought, sitting back and lighting a new cigarette, staring out the window at the gray sky, yes, one could. A child, say, without any relatives, parceled out to the foster home by the social-service office. With the foster home duly approved, it might not be inspected again for months. The checks to the foster mother returned to sender, after Polachek left town—she'd have had sense enough not to try to get those from another state—it might be a long time before news that the child was missing filtered down to any agency, and anybody tried to check up. The child would be just a name to the agency, and there was always so much red tape and passing the buck.

There were ways Linda could have got lost in the shuffle, so the speak, she thought angrily. Would they ever find out anything at all? At the moment she wasn't taking any bets.

BILL MOSS, riding a squad on night watch, was drifting down Fourth Street in Boyle Heights about eleven o'clock, now and then taking a look around the side streets. He'd just turned down Chicago Avenue when the headlights picked up a man lying against the curb in the street. Drunk or hit-run, thought Moss, and stopped the squad and got out. In the beam of the flashlight he saw the man was young and not bad-looking; he had on brown pants and jacket, a tan shirt. He didn't look exactly like a bum. He tried to sit up as Moss bent over him. "Goddamned bastards," he muttered thickly, and Moss realized that he was drunk all right, he could smell the whiskey on him. He'd better be ferried into the tank. Moss reached to heave him up, see if he could stand, and the man was suddenly and violently sick into the gutter. "Goddamned bastards," he said. "Le' me alone. Where's Al?"

"Come on, buddy," said Moss, and then as the man staggered against him he saw the bloody bruises on his face, and thought, he's been in a fight. There were bars close around, and maybe he lived somewhere here, was trying to get home. Street fights were no novelty down here, and the vagaries of drunks weren't Moss's business. He heaved the man into the squad, hoping he wouldn't be sick again, took him downtown to the drunk tank, and went back on tour.

PALLISER HAD just come in on Tuesday morning, and Mendoza hadn't showed up yet, when a call came in from the jail. "Say, we had a guy brought into the tank last night, nobody paid much attention to him until just now. A couple of us went along to see which men were sobered up, to weed them out, and Carl noticed that this one wasn't breathing just right. He should have been sobered up by now, he was looking pretty stinko when Traffic brought him in, and he'd been in a fight. We took a closer look at him and by God, I think he's been stabbed. He's got a little hole in his chest and blood all over his shirt."

"Is he dead?" asked Palliser.

"Naw, we just sent him to Emergency."

Palliser thought that somebody would have to follow that up, try to find out who the man was and if possible what had happened to him. Another unimportant little thing making more paperwork, no hurry about it. They were still hunting the possible heisters from Records and he joined up with Galeano at that. They'd all heard about Mendoza's brainstorm on Kramer, and when they got that list it was going to occupy a lot of time and involve a lot of running around; they agreed with Hackett that it would probably all be for nothing. He passed on the news about the drunk to Lake and went out on the never-ending legwork.

Just after Mendoza came in the D.A.'s office called, having now seen the reports on Polachek, and wanted to talk about Linda. Mendoza discussed it back and forth with the assistant D.A. and looked over the reports on his desk, and presently went out to an early lunch. He was on the phone again at two o'clock talking to Eggers, Eggers slightly more hopeful that he'd get the list out sooner than he'd thought. As soon as Mendoza was off the phone Lake buzzed him. "Emergency just called about that drunk, only it seems he wasn't as drunk as everybody thought. You know, the jail found he'd been stabbed and sent him over to the hospital. He's sitting up yelling for cops, says he's been attacked and robbed and his pal might have been killed."

"What next?" said Mendoza. "All right, I'll go and see what it's all about." He got his hat and went out, drove up to Cedars-Sinai. As he went into the Emergency wing he thought about that blind man and his dog, that poor devil probably released by now. He asked questions at the nursing station, and a sandy young intern lounging there straightened and said, "Well, maybe now he'll shut up. He's been raising the hell of a fuss ever since he came to after we fixed him up. He had a couple of stab wounds in his chest and cuts on his face, but he'll be okay. He's a sailor."

"What?" said Mendoza.

"Or whatever you call it now, he's off a ship docked at San Pedro, and he says this is the damndest burg he's ever been in and he's got to talk to cops."

"He was stabbed?"

"Not very efficiently, it missed his lung," said the intern. "He's taken a beating, he's got a pretty black eye,

but he's a young healthy specimen and he can leave anytime. He's down this way." He led Mendoza down a cross
corridor and opened a door. "Here's your cop, Gleason."

Only one of the three beds was occupied, by a man
about thirty, a wiry rather handsome man with reddish-
brown hair and bright blue eyes. "Thank God," he said,
and then, "You're a cop?" He looked at the elegant tailored Mendoza with some doubt but seemed reassured by
the badge. "Listen, you got to find out what's happened
to Al! Find out what those bastards did to him—I think
maybe they killed him, I was nearly out myself but they
both had knives, and I saw him tangling with the other
guy—"

"Calm down and let's hear the story. What's your
name?"

"Jim Gleason, I'm one of the engineers on the *Sco-
laris,* she's docked at San Pedro, we just got here from a
run to Argentina, it's the first time we made the West
Coast since Al and I've been on her. Al Newman, he's
one of the engineers too. Neither of us ever been in this
burg before, we've been on Atlantic runs the last three-
four years. I've seen the hell of lot of towns since I
shipped out, and Goddamn, I thought I knew how to
take care of myself." He accepted a cigarette. "Goddamn, I hope Al's all right. Like I say, we docked yesterday and she'll be a few days unloading cargo, and Al and
I headed up here to have a look at L.A. We're both from
New York, see. Well, you know how it is, we'd been on
that long Atlantic run, through the Canal, awhile at sea.
We had dinner someplace, and roamed around looking
at the town—it's quite a town—and had a few drinks.
And then we picked up these two girls in a bar—I don't
know the town, don't know where it was. We went back

to their pad with them, and we was having a couple more drinks, but Goddamn, neither of us was drunk—and Al, like a damned fool he's flashing his roll—we just got paid off and he had the whole bundle on him. That's about the last I remember before the fight, all of a sudden there's two other guys there trying to roll us, and I see one of them going after Al with a knife, and then I guess the other one knocked me out. Next thing I know I'm here with a damn doctor putting a bandage on me, and no sign of Al."

"Were the girl hookers?" asked Mendoza.

"Damn right, what else? And if Al had had the sense to leave most of his money on board everything would have been okay, but when they saw he had that roll—I only had about fifty on me, but they got that and my watch."

"Would you recognize the girls?"

"I sure would, the one making up to me was a Latin type, her name was Maria, a real cute girl, I'd know her anywhere. The other one was Sandra."

"I think they're ready to let you out of here," said Mendoza. "Do you feel up to coming in to headquarter and looking at some mug shots?"

"Your damn right I will. I'd sure like to know what those bastards did to Al. He hasn't shown up anywhere that the cops know?"

"Not that we've heard."

"Well, I'd sure like to help you nab those damned hookers. I'll look at your pictures and then, by God, I'm going back to the ship. I've seen all of L.A. I want. And I'm just as damn glad we're heading back to New York next week. I don't like your L.A. worth a dime. Say, my clothes don't look so good, all bloody, but I suppose they'll do till I get back to the ship."

The hospital released him and Mendoza drove him down to Parker Center, settled him at a table with one of the big books of mug shots, a collection of known prostitutes. It was barely half an hour before he stabbed a finger at the book and said, "Goddamn, that's her. Maria. You got her down as Maria Cabrillo."

Mendoza looked at the terse particulars under the mug shot, and the last line said: *See Chavez, Manuel; Chavez, Juan.* He said, "I'll get a squad to take you back to San Pedro."

"Well, I'd be obliged, thanks, I've still got a headache. I sure hope you can find out what happened to Al."

AT FIVE PAST four Lake got an urgent call from a squad, the report of at least one body and some general mayhem down at Eighth and Hill. Palliser and Higgins were the only ones in, and they started out to see what it was all about.

When they got there they found two squads in the narrow old street, and one of the uniformed men was Armstrong. "It was a heist at one of these jewelry marts, Sergeant, there was some kind of running gunfight, and there are a lot of witnesses—"

The jewelry marts had been occupying most of this block for the last ten years, and of course they were a prime target for heisters, but there hadn't been as much trouble as might have been expected. They all dealt in gold and silver as well as the jewelry, loose gemstones. Now most of them were lodged in one big building for better security, and there were security guards on every floor. In the ground-floor corridor, which had shop fronts down both sides, at least thirty people were gathered in a little crowd with the other Traffic men keeping them away from the body. The body lay not far from the front entrance, just down from the second shop on this side. The door was labeled Goldstein and Wolfe. There was a big heavy man leaning in that doorway staring at the body. It was the body of a darkly handsome young man in a neat gray suit and white shirt, and he'd been shot through the forehead. The big man looked at Higgins and Palliser as they came up, and he said in a dull voice, "He was going to be married tomorrow. That's why he was leaving early, some of his pals were giving a stag party for him, and he left early to go home and get cleaned up for it. I'll have to call Rachel and Joe. But he's only twenty-four. A good boy, he's my nephew, his name's Bernie Wolfe."

"Can you tell us anything about this?" asked Higgins. "You were held up?"

"Not us—Manny Abrahams. Bernie was just about to leave when we heard the shots up the hall, close, and we both ran out, they're just coming, running out of Manny's place—three of them—they all had guns—and Bernie, quick as a flash he tackled the big one, he knocked him down and almost got his gun, but he got up and Bernie was just getting up when he shot him. He put the gun at his head and shot him—Manny and Frank Goldfarb were just coming out—and the guard shooting from the end of the hall—I'll have to call Rachel and Joe." He went on staring at the body.

The security guard had come up behind them. He was a hefty youngish man in a blue uniform. "I got one of them," he said. "I know I winged one of them just as they were running out." He was still excited, breathing heavily. "I was up at the other end of the hall when it started, at Abrahams and Goldfarb. I heard the shots— they came running out of the store, and it was the damndest thing, it was just Goddamn bad luck we didn't get the bastards—because when I got out to the front, by God, their getaway car's hemmed in, there's a Brink's van double-parked and this old Chevy in the loading zone—it must have been their getaway car, there's a guy at the wheel and he comes belting out of it and the big guy shouts something, I couldn't hear what, and they all take off up Hill Street—and by God, there must have been a dozen of us chasing them—''

"All right," said Palliser, "let's take you one at a time. Mr. Abrahams?''

A little thin dark man stepped out of the crowd as they edged over there away from the body. "I'm Abrahams, this is my partner, Frank Goldfarb." He had big sorrowful-looking dark eyes and a narrow face. "Business had been slow all day, there wasn't a customer in when they came in and started asking about Krugerrands. That looked like a big sale, they were talking about a couple of rolls, forty pieces, maybe forty grand. I got some out of the safe, they wanted to see they were uncirculated—and then they wanted to look at some sovereigns. The big one asked will I take a certified check. I tell him that's okay if it's on a local bank, and that's when he pulled the gun.''

"I was keeping an eye out from the other counter,'' said Goldfarb, "not that I suspected anything wrong, but it was a big sale." He laughed without humor. "These bastards think we're in big dealing like this and we're little lambs, back off from the gun and watch them walk out with the gelt? With half a million of the real value stashed around, we don't rely all the way on Ricky here out in the hall. I saw Manny duck behind the counter after his gun, and I went for mine. I got off two shots over their heads before they fired back—they only hit the wall—I got the idea they were damned surprised we'd have guns and put up a fight—and we both chased after them, shooting all the way—"

"They got away with the gold," said Abrahams. "The big one scooped it into his pocket when Frank got off the first shot."

"They got away on foot?" asked Higgins.

"Goddamn the luck, they did," said the guard savagely. "I saw young Wolfe shot, and I winged one of them, I know I did. The big one in the light-colored raincoat. Abrahams and Goldfarb were right behind me after them, and Mr. Wolfe joined up, and some others out of the stores opposite—they're fast slick pros, they saw the car was no good to them and the driver jumped out and they all took off up Hill. We all chased after them, but naturally we couldn't use guns with all the crowds in the street, and they had a head start. But we were close enough behind that we all saw them, all four of them, dive into the Ascot Building up the block. They could go right through the building to the rear door and out to the parking lot behind and be in the middle of the crowd over on Broadway in thirty seconds. And Goddamn it, that's just what they did, by the time we got up there, no sign of them, and if they just mingled with the crowds and acted casual, who could spot them?"

"Would any of you recognize them again?" asked Palliser. "Could you describe them?"

Abrahams said wryly, "I've got to say no. They were in the place about seven minutes, and part of the time I was getting the gold out of the safe. It was the tall one did all the talking, and I couldn't say I'd recognize him. He was about six feet, thin, a light complexion. He had on a hat so I couldn't say about his hair. The other two were shorter, they had on dark coats. They were all pretty young, twenties, thirties." His dark eyes were sad. "They got away with two rolls of Krugerrands and one of British sovereigns—call it forty-five grand—and my God, I'd let it go if that would bring Bernie Wolfe back to life. He was a fine boy. We'd been in business next to Sam Wolfe for ten years, I saw that kid grow up, and he was learning the business quick like the smart boy he was.'' His eyes were on the body.

Wolfe said numbly, "I'll have to call Rachel and Joe, and there's Bernie's girl—Rosalie. They were getting married tomorrow.''

At first glance there wouldn't be any work for the lab on this; and then they thought twice. Abrahams said they hadn't touched the counter. But it was better to be safe than sorry. The slug was still in Wolfe's head, no exit wound; the lab would tell them about that later. Palliser called the morgue wagon from one of the squads, and then they had a look at the abandoned car. The Brink's van was still there, but the two men in charge of it had been up on the second floor and hadn't seen any of the action, only heard the shots. Hearing about the heist, they'd left the van where it was to keep the car hemmed in. It was an old four-door Chevy, and there was registration in the glove compartment made out to Richard J. Toomey of an address in Hollywood. But Armstrong called in on it, and in three minutes the want on it came back; it had been stolen from a public parking lot on Vine Street that morning.

Higgins grunted. "Even the pros slip up. Tow it in and see if they left any prints in it.'' They called the police garage and set that up.

Then they followed the guard up Hill Street, through the new crowds who didn't know that anything had happened here forty minutes ago, to the tall new building in the middle of the block. It housed mostly professional offices. They asked questions at every office on the ground floor, but nobody had been out in the corridor to see four men running through. They went out the rear door and there was the big parking lot with its rows of cars, and Broadway on the other side of it, with more crowds there.

It was Palliser who spotted the raincoat. It had been thrown down in a wadded-up heap on the blacktop of the lot, just inside an exit out to Broadway; a man's off-white poplin raincoat. Palliser picked it up and held it up at full length, and said, "Look at this, George."

On the upper left shoulder of the raincoat was a moderately big blood stain, just beginning to dry.

"By God, I knew I winged him!" said the guard.

"He knew that would show, on that light color," said Higgins, "so he got rid of it on the run. He probably had a dark suit on under it, and the blood wouldn't show on that." Palliser was feeling in the pockets. "He wouldn't have tossed it away if there was anything important in it. Let the lab go over it."

But Palliser had felt a little something in the bottom of the left-hand pocket, and brought it out. It was a little strip of thin paper about two by four inches. It had some printing on it in light blue. REMINDER OF YOUR NEXT AP-POINTMENT, with blanks for P.M., A.M., and DOCTOR'S NAME. It was a familiar homely little thing they'd all seen counterparts of: the little slip the office nurse handed you when you left the doctor's office. In ball-point pen two of the blanks were filled in. A date: the twenty-fourth of next month, two P.M., and a name: Dr. Peterson.

"IT'S A VERY nice little clue," said Mendoza, looking at that on Wednesday morning. "Straight out of a detective story. And it's going to give us some more hard work. Of course, it won't involve any running around at first.''

Palliser sighed, his long legs stretched out in front of him where he sat in one of the chairs beside Mendoza's desk. They had all gotten home late last night, but today was Higgins' day off. And today, and tomorrow, and probably the next day, depending on when they could find time to come in, all those witnesses would be trooping in to make the formal statements. Hackett shifted his bulk in the other chair and said, ''Well, the lab—''

''Mmh, yes, if the fast slick pros were careless enough to leave any prints in that car, or in the shop, we won't have to go the long way around. But it's a queer thing— as all of us are aware—how relatively seldom it is that the lab boys pick up any really useful prints. Kramer—that's very much the exception. You can see what we can do with this.''

''Oh, we saw it, we saw it,'' said Palliser. ''It would be a name like Peterson. How many Dr. Petersons do you suppose there are in the county? And it could be a dentist, any kind of specialist, it could be a private office or a clinic—''

''I wouldn't have a guess,'' said Mendoza. ''So often we do end up doing things the hard way, *compadres*. But there's no point in starting the spadework on this until we know definitely from the lab that there aren't any prints to give us the shortcut to the fast slick pros. They'll tell us sometime tomorrow. Then we rope in all the help we can muster and start phoning.''

''Yes, yes,'' said Palliser.

''We go down the list of every Dr. Peterson in the county, whatever kind of doctors they are, and get the names of all their patients who have an appointment scheduled at this date and time. And,'' said Mendoza, blowing smoke at the ceiling, "it'll probably be a damned difficult job to do that, because doctors can be very touchy about the privacy of their patients. We'll have to prove that we really are police and have a valid reason for wanting to know, and"—he considered his cigarette—"it could be that I just told you a lie, that it can be done on the phone. We might get quicker results calling on the doctors in person."

Hackett shut his eyes. "Thousand Oaks to Santa Ana," he said hollowly. "Santa Monica to La Cañada. Why the hell did we ever pick this job? It's the same sort of deal as those rental cars, and it'd take us a month of Sundays, Luis. And neither of the victims could identify him."

"Nada Más," said Mendoza. "It doesn't matter. There's the bloodstain on the coat, and I'd take a bet he's listed in Records when we get his name. This was, as John says, a pro job. And at the moment we've got another job on our hands which may not take as much work to clear up, but of course you never know." He told them about Gleason and Al Newman and the two hookers. "The brothers Chavez are a pair of pimps, they've both got little pedigrees. They're usually running a few girls—it's no big wholesale deal, no ties to the Syndicate, nothing as superior as that. Maria Cabrillo is one of them. I had a look through our collection of pretty pictures after Gleason had started back to his ship, and found that one Sandra Cook is another they're running. It's been a while since either of them or the Chavezes have been charged, and that kind don't stay in one place long, the last known address is probably out of date. But we'd better go looking for them."

"You needn't spell it out," said Hackett. "The pair of sailors came up to the big town for a little spree, and when one of them flashed the roll in front of the hookers the girls decided both of them were loaded and they'd come by a nice windfall. But why call the pimps in to help, if the sailors were on the way to being drunk?''

"Gleason claims he wasn't that drunk, and neither was Al. They'd just had a few, and I'd guess they're both experienced drinkers. They were out for a good time with the hookers, they wouldn't go getting falling-down drunk. One of the girls phoned the pimps and said, come see what we've found. It's another stupid damned thing, but God knows that kind are never very smart."

"Could Gleason say where their pad was?"

"Not a clue. He doesn't know this town. The squad picked him up on Chicago Avenue in Boyle Heights. One thing I will say, it's a likely area for the Chavezes. You might start with the last known address and ask around."

It was the tiresome kind of street legwork that they often got let in for, which didn't make them like it any better. They started out on it glumly, and Hackett said, "At least it's nice cool weather to be pounding the streets."

"If it doesn't start to rain again," said Palliser.

The last known address was Houston Street. On general principles at least some of the residents of this area didn't care much for police, and they didn't get much cooperation at first. If anybody they talked to knew where the Chavezes had gone, they weren't saying. But at getting on for noon, they ran across an old lady in the neighborhood market where they were questioning the proprietor. She overheard the questions, and said triumphantly, "You cops! You want these guys for doin' somethin' bad maybe? Manuel and Juan Chavez. I told Catalina, I told her they were bad men!"

"Do you know them?" asked Palliser.

"No, no, I don't know or want to know! But Catalina, she's my granddaughter, she just moves to a new place and these men live next apartment, she says she's scared of. They look at her funny, they ask her to come drink wine, but Catalina's a good girl. I told her lock her door good, they don't come after her! Better she should move back to old place, but the rent goes up. Better also she find a good husband to protect her, but she's too particular."

"Where does she live?"

"It's Winter Street," and after cudgeling her brain she produced the address.

"Well, praise be for a little luck," said Palliser. They found a parking place half a block away and walked back. The Chavezes lived on the second floor, and Juan opened the door to them. He recognized them for what they were at a glance, and backed away looking sullen. He was short and thin with a pockmarked face. "We're clean," he said. "You got nothing on us, dirty cops."

Manuel was lying on the ancient couch leafing through a girlie magazine. He didn't say anything, but his expression said it for him. "Come on," said Hackett, "you're coming in to headquarters to answer some questions."

"We don't know no answers to give you. You got nothing on us."

"Not so far," said Palliser. They took them back to the office and stashed them in an interrogation room. "For God's sake, Art, let's take a break for lunch before we start to grill them. I'm beat."

"I wonder if anybody's got a line on the girls yet." Galeano and Landers had gone out looking for Maria and Sandra. Lake said neither of them had called in and everything was quiet, but Abrahams and Goldfarb were coming in about two o'clock to make statements. Glasser and Grace were both in to sit in on that.

They went up to the canteen for a hasty lunch, came back and started pounding at the Chavezes. They got nowhere; neither of them would open their mouths. They were both feeling frustrated when Landers tapped on the door and looked in. They went out to the narrow corridor.

"I think Nick and I have found a shortcut," said Landers amusedly. "We just picked up the two girls. We got the address right off from a neighborhood variety-store owner, Chicago Avenue, but they've been uptown shopping. The sailors' money burning holes in their pockets. The reason the store owner steered us onto them, one of them had tried to pay for something with an Argentine bank note yesterday." Hackett began to laugh.

The two girls huddled together at one side of the little table, and Landers told them paternally that the cops knew all about it, and proceeded to outline the scenario, the enticing of the two sailors, calling up the Chavezes, the fight. Maria was dark and pretty, Sandra Cook blond and not so pretty, and both of them were scared stiff. They might be pro hookers but the idea of anything worse was something else.

"Nobody meant to kill nobody!" whimpered Sandra. "It was an accident, that's all, Juan didn't mean to kill that guy—"

"So how did it happen?" asked Hackett interestedly.

"They weren't so very drunk like we thought—and they started to put up the hell of a fight when Juan and Manuel showed up," said Maria in a shaking voice. "Juan and Manuel had to put them out someway, and it was just an accident Juan stabbed that one too deep, kind of. We didn't know what to do when we saw he was dead, it was awful—"

"So what did you do?" asked Palliser.

"Juan and Manuel, they did it—we put the other one out in the street down the block, and I dunno what Manuel and Juan did with the dead one. They just took him away. Nobody meant to kill him, it was just an accident—"

They went back to the other room and asked the Chavezes what they had done with it. When they knew the girls had told the tale, the Chavezes began to swear. "Damn stupid girls have to open their mouths," said Juan. "But it was just an accident like they said, nobody meant to kill the guy."

"What did you do with the body?" asked Palliser loudly.

"Oh, for God's sake, we took it and put it over the wall in that cemetery out Whittier Boulevard. It was all we could think of to do with it.

It was no wonder that headquarters hadn't heard anything about Al Newman. That was in county territory and in the sheriff's jurisdiction. Wordlessly Hackett went out to his desk and called the sheriff's department. The deputy he finally talked to was relieved to have a mystery cleared up. One of the groundkeepers at the cemetery had found the body yesterday morning; there wasn't any identification on it, and the sheriff's boys had been doing some wondering about it.

They would take the four of them over to the jail before starting the red tape on the warrants. There hadn't been a sign of Mendoza, and Hackett asked, "Where's the boss, Jimmy?"

"Up at Hollywood Division. I guess something broke, on that body at the Japanese restaurant."

"Well, surprise, surprise," said Hackett.

SERGEANT BREWER up in Hollywood had called Mendoza an hour ago. "I've got an informant in I think you may be interested to listen to, Lieutenant. When she mentioned the locality I thought I'd better check. Would you have an unidentified body on your beat, found somewhere around Little Tokyo?"

Mendoza said, "*Más vale tarde que nunca*—Better late then never! We do indeed. What do you know about it?"

"Come to Papa and hear," said Brewer.

Up at the sprawling one-story building that housed Hollywood Division, Brewer was waiting for him, a solid beefy man with sandy hair. "This girl walked in off the street," he said. "I don't think she's got the brains to be telling lies. Her name's Linda Lindstrom."

As he led the way up the corridor from the lobby and stopped at a door, Mendoza said, "You've got Barth's old office."

"That's right, you know him? Good man, we miss him, but he'd put in forty years and he's happy as a clam drawing the pension. He's taken up golf, of all things." Brewer opened the door.

She was a conventionally pretty girl, with a lot of blond hair, a peaches-and-cream complexion, nicely dressed in a navy pantsuit. Brewer introduced Mendoza. "First off, let's give the man the particulars about you, Miss Lindstrom."

She said in a low voice, "If you want. There isn't much to say about me, I work at the RCA building, I'm a receptionist." She was obviously very distressed; she said, "I was awake all last night making up my mind to come in here. I don't like to do it, but—but I guess you could say I've got a conscience. All right, I'll tell it all over.

About three months ago I met this fellow, he works for one of our distributors, the wholesale distributors, his name's Don Faulkner, he seemed like a nice fellow, and when he asked me for a date I went out with him. We've been dating regular, I—I thought he was going to ask me to marry him. I didn't know if I'd say yes. And we had a date—last Wednesday night—we were going to dinner at that Japanese place down in Little Tokyo. And when we got there, Don parked in the lot and we got out—and all of a sudden there was this woman—and she came up and—and she said—she said she was his wife. She said to me, did you know he was married or don't you care? I couldn't say anything. She said she'd suspected he was two-timing her, but she wasn't sure—until that restaurant had called to confirm the reservation—and she wanted to see what kind of floozy he'd picked up—'' She looked at them a little wildly. ''I'd never have gone out with him if I knew he was married! I'm not that kind of girl—and she said she'd taken a cab down there to catch him—and they started to argue, and I—well, and then he hit her, and she fell right down, and he said we'd better go. We'd go somewhere else for dinner—and he said the woman was crazy, she was just some woman he knew and of course he wasn't married, she was just crazy— I didn't know what to think—I was just terribly upset about it, I trusted him, I liked him a lot, but when he hit her—and later on in the other restaurant when he paid the bill I saw he'd taken her purse, it was dark in the lot and I hadn't seen him do that, it was just a little clutch purse, he didn't mean to let me see it but it came out with his billfold—and I couldn't help worrying about it, thinking about it— he laughed and said she was just a nut, but when he hit her, all of a sudden I was scared of him—and then—and then—there was a little thing in the *Times,* it said a woman's body found right there—in that parking lot—right where we'd been—and I kept wondering—'' She drew a long breath and sat up straighter. "He called to ask me for a date last night, and I turned him down— He sounded—queer. And I couldn't sleep, thinking about it, I thought I'd better come in and tell the police."

EIGHT

THE AUTOPSY report on that body had come in this morning; the woman had died of a fractured skull. It would add up to another charge of murder two. Faulkner was in the phone book, at an address in Hollywood. Mendoza got his plate number from Sacramento and put out an A.P.B. on the car when they couldn't raise anybody at the apartment, a middle-class apartment on Fernwood Avenue. The woman at the apartment next door confirmed that he and his wife lived there, but didn't know anything about them. Sometime Faulkner would be picked up. The stupidities, said Mendoza to himself on the way back downtown. And he'd no sooner got into the office than he had a call from Eggers. "I've got the beginnings of that list for you, Lieutenant, I thought you might want to start work on it as soon as you had some names. We probably won't get to the end of it until tomorrow or next day." Palliser had just got back from the jail, and said he'd chase out to Century City to pick that up.

Kramer's mug shot had come in from the Feds yesterday and the lab had already run off some copies. Now Hackett picked one up from Mendoza's desk and said reflectively, looking at it, "Maybe you had a useful idea after all. I will say it's not a face that might change much over the years." It was a distinctive face, a handsome face with a high-bridged straight nose, wide-set eyes under sharply arched brows, an expressive mobile mouth, a smooth thick head of dark hair. "Even if he's gained weight or something—he'd be around fifty or a bit more now—but what a job. And now we've got the reports to type on these damn hookers.''

Another day had somehow passed, and the paper-work was piling up as always, and what with Kramer and all the Dr. Petersons they could see the tedious mounds of work ahead of them.

When Palliser came back with the beginning of the list of rental cars they looked at it in dismay. It contained about a hundred names, and only a few here and there had a local address attached. The rest of them were from all over, New York, Chicago, Indianapolis, Miami, and all points between. It was too late to start calling all those forces, wire the mug shots. They were ready to call it a day, but as Mendoza was leaving, a messenger came in with a manila envelope and he took time to look at the contents. It was the autopsy report on Mabel Green. She had been dead about six or seven weeks, and she'd died of a coronary. Tomorrow he would be talking to the D.A.'s office about that; they'd have to decide what to do with Ed Filer, if anything. After they knew the answers, had the guilty ones in custody, there was always the on-going machinery of the law, the mounds of paperwork. He landed at the elevator with the rest of the men, on the way home. Tomorrow was also a day.

ON THURSDAY morning, with Hackett off, they forgot about everything else and started phoning all those other forces. The list got split up among Galeano, Grace, Landers, Higgins, and Wanda Larsen, and they spent all morning talking to other officers in all those places, explaining enough of the story on Kramer to provide the background for asking cooperation. All the officers they talked to were interested, ready to take on the extraneous job. The mug shots started going out on the wire. At least the night watch hadn't left them anything new to work.

About eleven forty-five Scarne called Mendoza and said, "You wanted to hear as soon as we knew. We just finished going over that car—the Chevy on the jewelry-mart job—and it's clean, no latents at all. Or in the store that got heisted."

"There you are," said Mendoza to Higgins and Palliser, "we said we'd be doing it the hard way. After we've got through the list on Kramer we start in on the damned doctors. And I've just had the D.A.'s office at me about Hernandez, they want to set up the arraignment. We'll have to check with the hospital, see if he's fit to transfer to jail and appear in court. Let's take off for lunch, we all need a break."

WANDA CAME back to her desk at one-thirty, feeling stale and tired. She still had eighteen or twenty names to call on her share of the list, and they were all in the eastern time zone and by three o'clock it would be six there and too late to talk to detectives on day watch. She was just reaching for the phone to call Dallas when Lake buzzed her and said, "You've got a call from Philadelphia." Wanda waited, feeling suddenly more alert, and a deep contralto voice asked, "Miss Larsen? This is Sergeant Doris Holland, Juvenile Bureau, Philadelphia. I just had a call from Juvenile Hall, they'd dithered around on this like the idiots they sometimes are. You called awhile ago asking for information about a Linda Kent?"

"That's right, we're trying to trace her back, get some background."

After a moment Doris Holland asked, "Why?"

"Well, we're looking for any possible relatives, and she can't give us any information—"

There was a long pause at the other end and then Sergeant Holland asked, "You've got her? You know where she is?"

"She's in our Juvenile Hall."

"Well," said Sergeant Holland, "I will be damned. I don't believe it. I don't believe it. Just like that. I suppose somebody in your Juvenile Bureau there remembered the fliers and put you onto us. We sent them out to every Juvenile Bureau in the country at the time."

"I'm not Juvenile," said Wanda. "I'm Robbery-Homicide."

"Robbery-Hom—you'd better tell me why you're asking about Linda Kent."

"You've got some record, where she came from?"

"Suppose you tell me your end of the story first," said Sergeant Holland equably, "and then I'll fill in."

Obediently Wanda told her the whole sordid tangled little story, and it took a while. "You can see how it left us up in the air, Sergeant. She'll probably be charged with manslaughter in one degree or another, and be held in protective custody until she's of age, but we've got no background for her at all. What that poor child's been through with that Polachek woman—"

Sergeant Holland said in a rather hollow voice, "Oh, yes, the Polachek woman. My God. I'll tell you, Miss Larsen, I'm not sure what I believe about the world in general, if something's managing things or it's all blind chance, but this shakes me. My God in heaven. If there is one, and I sometimes wonder. This reminds me of something in the Bible—'the one shall be taken and the other left'." There was another little silence and then she said, "I've got a story to tell you too. It goes back a little more than seven years."

"For goodness' sake, tell me what you know," said Wanda.

"Well, it goes back to Brian Kent and his wife Margaret. He was a junior executive with Eastern Oil, they lived on Long Island. He got transferred to their office in Philadelphia, and they put their house up for sale and moved here, the whole family. They didn't know anybody here, he didn't know any of the people in the new office, and never got a chance to. They'd rented a place in one of the suburbs and stored their furniture, until they sold the house. We only found out all this later on, I'm just giving it to you the way it happened. They'd only been here two days when the house caught fire in the middle of the night, it was a short circuit of some kind, the fire department said afterward. It got quite a hold before it was discovered, and we don't know who called in the alarm, Mr. or Mrs. Kent—but by the time the fire department got there it was too late to save the house. Evidently Kent had got the children out and went back for his wife and couldn't get out again. They were both burned to death."

Wanda said, "Good Lord. Terrible. You said children?"

Sergeant Holland said, "That's right. Twin girls. Linda and Louise. Five years old."

"Oh, my dear heaven," said Wanda. "Louise! And we thought—yes, never mind, I'll tell you later. Go on."

"Well, you can appreciate the problem it gave the police. Nobody knew who they were, they'd just got here, and all the papers in the place had gone up in smoke. The garage was attached and the car was burned out, we couldn't trace them through that. All the children could tell us was the last name, Kent, but it was through the kids we finally did trace them. They'd been put in Juvenile Hall, and eventually one of them came out with something."

Wanda said, "My name is Linda Kent and I live at Thirty-four Holly Road in Hempstead."

Surprised, Doris Holland said, "And how did you hear that? That was it. We tried a couple of Hempsteads before we found the right one on Long Island. And then we came to another dead end. Neither of the Kents had any parents living but people in his office and a couple of neighbors could tell us that he had a brother named Gregory, he was an engineer of some kind and working on some construction project in the Middle East. And of course we were looking for a Gregory Kent, we didn't know he was a half brother and his name was Harrison. Kent usually spoke of him as Gregory or my brother. We didn't find out for over a month, until the realty company on Long Island where the house was up for sale reported there was mail being left, and we had to get a court order to get hold of it. The Kents had moved in something of a hurry, and as it turned out, the Harrisons hadn't any new address for them, and got worried when they didn't hear."

"The twins were in Juvenile Hall all this time," said Wanda.

Sergeant Holland said grimly, "Until the week before we found the Harrisons. At any given time we get a few street kids in, and the little girls were only five. There are never enough decent foster homes, as I expect you know, but it seemed the best solution until we found out about any relatives. Of course they should have been placed together, they're identical twins and the poor mites were bewildered and scared. But there was a stupid mix-up, there was some new staff at Juvenile Hall then, and they were placed out separately. Louise went to a nice couple named Klein—"

"And Linda went to the Polachek woman," said Wanda.

"Oh, my God, did we go round and round on the Polachek woman! She'd just applied to take a foster child, she'd been officially inspected and accepted—"

"She put up a front to pass the inspection, she thought it was an easy way to make some money. And then you found the Harrisons."

"More than a month later. Nobody in Kent's company at either end had a new address for him, and he wasn't supposed to report on the job for a month. When they finally got worried they came to us. We were still looking for a Gregory Kent, it was Kent's immediate boss in New York put us straight. Then we got the letter from Harrison and things began to move. We located the Harrisons and broke the news and they flew straight back. They were the children's legal guardians, by Kent's will. They haven't any children of their own. They're very nice people, Miss Larsen. Marjorie Harrison and I have got to be pretty good friends through all this, I still hear from her regularly. We got Louise back from the Kleins but when we went to get Linda the Polachek woman had just disappeared."

"Of course, of course," said Wanda. "She and Billy decided to drive out West, and she didn't care a damn about Linda, she didn't like kids, but Billy liked the little girl to play with, so they took her along. Neither of them had the sense to realize it could be a kidnapping charge. Just doing what comes naturally. My God. And later on, after Billy had left, she kept Linda on, maybe not so much as the convenient slavey as somebody she could boss around absolutely. Completely in her power. I can see that would be quite an incentive to a certain kind of mind. I can just imagine how you went round on it.''

"There wasn't any way to follow her up," said Doris Holland. "The neighbors told us there was a man living there off and on, but we didn't know his name, and they'd taken off in his car—"

"The family knew who he was. I don't know her maiden name but she had parents living in Philadelphia.''

"Now you tell us," said Doris Holland. "We never came across them. But it was in the papers—not headlines, and maybe they don't read the papers. There was some fracas going on in the Middle East and the local TV news didn't have time to cover it, so they claimed. Naturally the Harrisons were frantic. They tried everything, even hired a private detective, but when we couldn't find the woman he hadn't a prayer. She might have gone anywhere. We sent out fliers to every juvenile bureau in the country, as I said, and the Harrisons put ads in every newspaper, offering a reward and no questions asked. They never gave up trying to find her for a couple of years, and they're still hoping.''

"They've got Louise," said Wanda.

"Yes, and she's such a nice kid, Miss Larsen, a bright kid and a good kid, she's very talented musically and she's had all sorts of special things done for her—dancing lessons and art and piano—and she's going to be such a pretty girl when she grows up. They passed through here on the way to Greg's new job last fall, and we had dinner together.''

Wanda thought of that lost waif over at their Juvenile Hall saying, you've been nice to me, and shut her eyes. She said, "The one taken and the other left. Dear God.

It does make you wonder if there's any reason in the universe at all. Where are the Harrisons now?''

"Up in Oregon, Greg's on the construction of a big new irrigation project for the state. They're not going to believe this any more than I did, and you can imagine how they'll feel. But what's the legal position going to be? I don't know your state laws.''

"They're her legal guardians," said Wanda, "and she's only twelve. I think in the circumstances she'd be released to them on probation. None of us holds any brief for the bleeding-heart judges handing out slaps on the wrists, but we really don't like to be vindictive either. I can't say how it might go, but there'll have to be a court hearing before she can leave Juvenile Hall.''

"Yes. Well, I'll wire Marjorie right away and she'll get down there as fast as she can. You know," said Sergeant Holland, "it's queer about twins. Louise has never forgotten Linda, and Marjorie says she'll say pretty often she was with Linda last night in a dream.''

"Yes, she would have been. Linda says the same thing. I'm afraid there may be some problems, you know—she's illiterate, she's never been to school and doesn't know a thing, but the psychiatrist says she's got a good mind, and given any chance, and patience—''

Doris Holland said gently, "And love, Miss Larsen. Which she will have. Even hearing what you've told me, I think in time Linda will be all right. I'll get a wire off to Marjorie.''

Wanda sat staring at the phone a minute before she looked up. She didn't quite believe this either. Everybody else in the big communal office was on the phone, working through that list. She got up and started for Mendoza's office. Mendoza always liked the offbeat ones, and he'd be interested in this. In the hall Lake was talking to three men; he said, "That Hill Street heist, they're in to make statements."

Wanda said, "Somebody ought to be off the phone in a few minutes, Jimmy. I want to talk to the lieutenant."

THE A.P.B. didn't turn up Don Faulkner until noon on Friday, when a squad spotted his car in a motel lot in Santa Monica. He was picked up in the motel room and brought in to headquarters, and Mendoza and Higgins talked to him. They didn't have to talk to him long. He was a boyishly handsome young man with wavy brown hair, a weak mouth, and restless eyes, and he came apart right away, anxious to explain himself, explain just how he couldn't be blamed.

Before they'd asked him three questions, he burst out at them, "I never knew she was dead! Edna. I never meant to kill her, for God's sake. I wouldn't kill anybody! It was just—I tell you how it was, she was always so damned jealous of me, she was always suspicious. In a selling job you've got to be friendly, mix with people, and she didn't understand that. She was always accusing me of stepping out on her—"

"Well, you were, weren't you?" said Higgins.

"There wasn't anything wrong in it. She didn't like to dance or go out to nice restaurants, she said it was a waste of money, she was all for saving every penny so we could buy a house and start a family—well, God, you're only young once and I didn't want to be tied down like that— so I dated some other girls, there wasn't anything wrong about it, it was just to go out and have a good time once in a while. I can't be blamed for that. Well, look, I'm just damned sorry it happened, but if she hadn't been so jealous—"

"Yes, it was bad luck that she took that call from the restaurant confirming your reservations," said Mendoza, "wasn't it? And you couldn't very well have said you were entertaining a business client, not the kind of place where you'd take a business client—"

"She never said a thing to me about it, damn it, never gave me the chance to throw her an excuse—I never knew a thing about it until she showed up there just as Linda and I got out of the car—" He was looking a little sullen now. "She started chewing me out, she called Linda a floozy, and I got mad—doing a thing like that, follow me around—I never hit a girl before, but I was just mad enough to belt her one, and I just thought she was knocked out. I didn't mean to kill her, for God's sake. I didn't know I had. And she dropped her purse, and I only took it because I thought it would serve her right, get stranded there without money for a bus or cab—she didn't have a car, she'd taken a cab down there, she said so. I never knew she was dead, I thought she'd just walked out on me when she didn't come home, I mean. I thought she'd probably gone to her sister's, she's got a sister in Burbank." He looked around the little room restlessly. "It just knocked me for a loop—Tuesday night—when I called Linda to ask her for a date, and she turned me down—and she said something about a piece in the paper, a woman's body found right there in that parking lot—where I'd knocked Edna down. She sounded scared of me, for God's sake, and I thought, well, it couldn't be Edna—but suppose it was? If she was dead, you'd say I killed her, and I never meant anything like that! It was just an accident, you could say, I guess she hit her head when she fell down. But I was worried about it, worried as hell—I couldn't go to work, and I was driving around last night thinking about it. I thought, well, you wouldn't know who she was, but sometime her family'd be asking where she was and naturally they'd ask me, they wouldn't believe she'd just taken off somewhere. And I didn't know what the hell to do. I was so tired, I'd just checked into that motel to get some sleep."

There really weren't any more questions to ask, and they were tired of him. Higgins typed a statement and he signed it readily. As he went out with Higgins on the way to jail he said, "You let me make a phone call, don't you? I've got to call Mom. She never liked Edna much, she'll understand how it was. Mom always understands me. She'll get me a good lawyer, and it was just an accident, I'll get off on manslaughter or something."

They had got the name of the sister from him, and Mendoza called her to break the bad news. Then he talked with the D.A.'s office; the hospital had said that Hernandez was in stable enough condition to be transferred to jail. The D.A.'s office had set up an arraignment, on murder two, for next Tuesday. Somebody would have to take him to jail tomorrow or next day, and be in court on Tuesday. In the outer office Grace and Hackett were taking statements from witnesses, and everybody else was on the phone at the long-distance calls to other police forces. And there'd be more of that list of the rental cars to come. And then all the Dr. Petersons.

Mendoza sat swiveled around in the desk chair looking out at an overcast sky, the view over the Hollywood hills not so clear today and possibly it was gearing up for more rain, when Scarne called him from the lab.

"I just thought you'd like to know, the morgue sent over the slug out of that Wolfe fellow. It's from a thirty-two Smith and Wesson revolver, it's not much damaged, if you ever pick up the gun we can match it."

"Gracias," said Mendoza. Idly he picked up one of the copies of Kramer's twenty-year-old shot and studied it. He wondered if this had been such a bright idea after all, but he was very curious about that one, what had triggered the murder of Kershaw. He was just starting down the hall to get a cup of coffee from the machine when his phone rang and he picked it up. It was Duffy again at the D.A.'s office.

"We just got this report you sent down, the autopsy on the Green woman."

"Oh, yes. Are you going to charge Filer with anything?"

Duffy said exasperatedly, "There's nothing in it, damn it. Concealing a body? Damnation, Mendoza, the courts are backlogged enough as it is. He'd only get probation. The woman died a natural death and we can't charge him with being stupid and greedy enough to cover it up."

"Let him go?" asked Mendoza.

"Let him go, damn it," said Duffy disgustedly.

Mendoza sighed and called the jail.

WANDA WAS just covering her typewriter at five-thirty on Friday afternoon when Lake ushered a woman in and said, "This is Miss Larsen, ma'am."

She was a tall, very pretty woman, probably in her early forties, with smooth dark hair in a smart cut, a frank attractive face with a fine complexion, bright dark eyes. She was rather elegantly dressed in a black wool suit with a crisp white blouse.

"Oh, Miss Larsen, I'm so glad to meet you. I'm Marjorie Harrison. I came down from Portland as soon as I could get a plane. When we got Doris's wire—well, we didn't know if we were on our head or our heels, we just couldn't believe this nightmare is all over and we've found Linda. I can't thank you enough for all you've done."

"I haven't done much really, Mrs. Harrison, but I hope Sergeant Holland warned you—I don't know if you know the whole story—"

"Oh, as soon as I got my senses back I phoned Doris—I knew she wouldn't mind that it was late—and we've heard all about it." Wanda offered her a chair and she sat down looking sober now. "It's a terrible story," she said. "When I think of Louise—what life's been for both of them—and that damnable wicked woman—when I told Greg—well, you can imagine how we both feel. It doesn't bear thinking about, only we have to think about it, don't we? To think what's best for Linda, how we'll handle it. If she's got as high an IQ as Louise, she'll learn quickly, with the right kind of help, and please God we can make it up to her as best we can, she'll have the happiest life we can make for her, and the rest is up to her, isn't it? Doris said you thought a judge might release her to us."

"I think that's probably what will happen, considering her age," said Wanda, "but we'll have to wait and see. It's hanging fire in the D.A.'s office at the moment, until we found out more. Now the lieutenant can talk it over with them on Monday, and they'll try to get a date set for a court hearing." She felt unaccountably warmed and reassured just to look at this warm generous attractive woman. Whatever problems and worries might be in store, she felt, poor lost waif Linda would be safe with Marjorie Harrison, and helped into the life she'd never had; and Louise would help too, she felt oddly sure of that.

"When can I see her?"

"It's nearly six, but if you don't mind that I could take you down to Juvenile Hall now—you couldn't stay long."

"But I'll be keeping you from your dinner—I'm sure you've had a long day—"

Wanda smiled at her. "I don't mind for once. We've all been interested in Linda, the lieutenant and the other detective who's worked on the case with me will want to meet you."

"That's very kind of you. Another thing, Greg said I should get her a lawyer. He was wild that he couldn't come down with me, but he can't get away until Monday, he's coming then, of course. Louise is staying with some friends of ours, their girl is just her age—oh, I do hope Linda will love Louise and be happy with us—" She went on talking on the ride down, but as they got out of the car she fell silent. "Oh, I can't help being nervous," she said apologetically. "Seven years—with that devilish woman—she's twelve—and when I think what she's lived through—"

"Don't worry," said Wanda. "You'll be fine."

She talked to the matron, who said, "Well, it's against regulations but just for a few minutes—" She warmed to Marjorie Harrison too, and led them down to the little cubicle. "We've just finished dinner, we always get that over with early."

On the narrow cot Linda was just sitting, looking at the opposite wall, and it suddenly struck Wanda forcibly how boring life must be for anyone who didn't know how to read. And Marjorie Harrison said involuntarily, "But you're exactly like Louise!—and isn't that the silliest thing to say, of course you're alike, you're identical twins—oh, Linda my dear, my dear!"

Linda looked at her in surprise. "Do you know Louise?" she asked in her thin little voice.

Marjorie put her arms around her and hugged her. "Of course I know Louise, I'm her Aunt Marjorie, and that makes me *your* Aunt Marjorie too. My darling, we've been looking for you for seven years, ever since you were lost, and I prayed so hard that you were safe—thank God we've found you!"

"Was I—lost?" asked Linda slowly. "Why are you crying?"

"Because I'm so thankful we've found you, darling. You're never to worry about anything again, or if you do just tell me and we'll straighten it out. Everything's going to be all right from now on, darling. You've got an uncle too, you didn't know that—Uncle Greg, and I hope you'll love him the way Louise does. I think I can promise you that you won't have to stay here long, and we'll all go home together to Louise."

Linda stared at her incredulously, and a new expression showed in her eyes, a dawning shy adoration. "To Louise?" she said. "Home? Where's that?"

"It's wherever we're all together, darling. Everything's going to be all right."

But ten minutes later when she got into the car beside Wanda she was crying again. "She's so thin—and too pale—she's like a lost soul. But we'll try to make it up to her—oh, when I think of that woman I'd like to believe in hell!"

"I'll take you back to wherever you're staying," said Wanda sympathetically.

"It's the Holiday Inn in Hollywood. And I've got to call Greg—but Miss Larsen, won't you stay and have dinner with me? You've been so kind—"

Somewhat to her own surprise, Wanda said, "Thank you, I'd like that, Mrs. Harrison."

IT WAS PIGGOTT'S night off. Conway and Schenke came in and settled down with the radio on to police frequency in the background. They didn't get a call until eight-fifty, and they were sitting playing gin on Higgins' desk when that came in. Communications just said, a body, and added the address: Naud Street.

"I thought I knew this town," said Schenke. He reached for the County Guide and looked it up. "Over by the freight yards. That'll be a classy area all right. Sometimes I wonder what it'd feel like to be a cop some place like Beverly Hills."

"Damn boring, I should think," said Conway. "At least down here we do run into the characters on occasion, Bob. The drunks and the dopies and the thugs, so all right, just what's the difference between a stupid damned idiot high on cocaine driving a Porsche and living in a twelve-room pad in Beverly, and the same stupid idiot mainlining H on skid row? Neither of them knows any better, but theoretically the idiot in the Porsche ought to."

"One way to look at it," said Schenke.

"I'd bet if you'd ask anybody on the Beverly Hills force, they'd tell you it's a dirtier scene than the Central beat. Because," said Conway, warming to impromptu philosophy, "there's the facade. Down here we don't expect anything but the derelicts and drifters and dopies and mindless muggers—the whole damn dirty scene. Up there, with all the show-business money floating around and the designer clothes and the Mercedes and Rollses and all the rest of it, it's just all the dirtier. Those hookers Tom brought in—my God, they may be cheap hookers but they aren't pretending to be ladies. Like these gussied-up tramps who get their names in the *TV Guide*." He lit a cigarette as Schenke caught the light at Los Angeles and Temple. "I can't watch the tube these days. When it isn't soft porn—and I never did think sex was a spectator sport—it's just inane." Schenke made an inarticulate grunt of agreement.

Naud Street must be one of the oldest in this oldest part of the city. It wasn't very long, a narrow winding little street just this side of the great freight yards. They spotted the address by the squad in front. It was a ramshackle ancient two-story house looking as if it was about to fall down. It sat on a narrow lot with one-story frame houses on each side, of the same vintage. Schenke parked and they went up the crumbling strip of cement that was supposed to be a walk to the front porch, where the uniformed man was waiting for them. "What have we got?" asked Schenke.

The patrolman was Bill Moss. "A body," he said laconically. "This is Mr. Frost."

The other man on the old wooden porch was scrawny and elderly. The feeble gleam of a low-watt bulb over the front door revealed him as incredibly wrinkled, bald, clad in shapeless pants and a ragged shirt and sweater. He said querulously, "If I could sell the place for anything I would. Go back to New Hampshire. I never did see why folks go so crazy about California. But Martha, nothin' would do but we had to come way out here to see the nice house her old great-aunt left her, and look at it. She's bound to live in the city for a change—" He spat over the porch rail. "And look what it did for her—she gets this cancer and dies the next year. I'm not so good myself these days, only eighty next June and my Dad lived to be ninety-nine, but I got the rheumatism."

"This body," said Conway.

Moss was leaning on the front porch rail smoking and grinning.

"Make a fine rooming house, she says, fourteen rooms. Put a sign up and they'll come flocking around. Let 'em take care of their own rooms, no trouble, she says. And here I am stuck with the dadburned place, and Martha gone, and the dadburned Social Security don't go so far even when you're careful. Hadn't been here six months before I wanted to turn around and go home again, but I had to let the farm go for back taxes and what with the rheumatism I don't rightly know where I could go back there."

"The body," said Conway.

He gave them a leisurely look. "Bunch of drunks and bums," he said. "Comin' and goin'. Ten bucks a week, and if they don't pay up on the dot out they go. But they're all bums and drunks—who else'd be comin' to a place like this? You fellers more police, good, you come to do somethin' about the corpse." He turned to the door and led them into a narrow hall, still grumbling. "Dadburn it, bad enough they throw up on the floor and come in all hours of the night without goin' and dyin' in the place."

It was an incredibly ancient place, with doors in unexpected places and cracks in the walls. Another low-watt bulb lit, barely, a stairway that creaked under their combined weight. At the top, Frost went down a narrow hall to a half-open door at the left side. "He's in there. A dadburned corpse. I wouldn't never have found him but I come up here to see if the roof's leakin'." It had started to rain again about an hour ago. Schenke and Conway went into the room. It was about eight by eight, with an old iron cot and a rickety chest of drawers the only fur-

niture. The body was on the floor beside the cot, the body
of an elderly man with a fat stomach. He was wearing
ancient gray slacks and a grimy blue shirt, and there was
dark dried blood on one side of his head, several deep
wounds which had bled freely.

"What's his name?" asked Schenke.

Frost shrugged. "I dunno any of their names. They
come and go, they pay me the ten bucks or they don't
stay." The dim bulb in the one fixture was no help at all,
and Schenke sent Moss out for a flashlight. In the
stronger gleam they could see the little trail of blood on
the floor leading to the door. Bent over, they followed it
like bloodhounds, a spot here and another there, four
feet across the hall to a door on the opposite side of the
hall. Schenke rapped on that with the flashlight. "Who
lives here?" he asked Frost.

"Another one of the bums. I dunno their names."

The door opened and a man peered out at them. He
was another elderly man, but a thin one, with about a
week's growth of gray beard on his chin. He was wearing shorts and an undershirt, and he was halfway drunk.
He spotted Frost and said thickly, "I give you the damn
money—"

Schenke aimed the flashlight again and leaned over.
There was a dried clot of blood just inside the door, and
another a foot away. "No facade," he said to Conway,
who laughed. A third clot of blood was in front of the
little unpainted chest of drawers, and on top of that was
a hammer with its handle wrapped with black tape. There
was blood on its head, dried some time ago.

"No facade," said Conway.

"What's your name?" asked Schenke.

The man squinted up at him. There was a bottle of
cheap bourbon beside the hammer, and he reached for it

and took a swallow. He said with the elaborate gravity of the drunk, "The name's John J. Rafferty. Who wants to know?"

"Do you know the man across the hall?"

"He's a Goddamned thief, he is." Rafferty took another drink and hiccuped. "When I come back from the john he's stealin' my whiskey. I let him have it. Goddamn thief. Whiskey costs a lot of money."

"Oh, for the love of God," said Schenke. He turned to Moss. "There's no damned point in hauling out the lab on a thing like this. Go and call up the morgue wagon and we'll stash this old lush in jail."

Rafferty had no objection to a ride, but he was annoyed that they wouldn't let him take the bottle along. They'd have to write a report on it, but they'd let the day watch take it from here. It would give them a little paperwork.

On Saturday morning, with Landers off and Sergeant Farrell sitting at the switchboard in Lake's place, the rest of them had a glance at Schenke's report and Mendoza said resignedly, "And it doesn't matter a damn but we do have to abide by the regulations. Somebody had better go through their various belongings, find out if there are any relatives to notify and just for the record, better get some pictures of the bloodstains, not that any of the bright boys in the public defender's office is going to waste much time on it."

Galeano started out to do that, which left them more shorthanded. There would be more names coming in on the list of rental cars, and on Monday they'd be embarking on more phone calls to all the Dr. Petersons. And there were still the heisters to look for.

There hadn't been a smell of Alvarez and Camacho since the heist pulled out in the valley.

They drifted out for an early lunch, and went in a body up to Federico's on North Broadway. It was sprinkling very slightly, and the forecast was for more rain; it might turn out to be a wet winter after all. They had just got back to the office and Hackett was reaching for the phone when a woman came in, hesitated in the doorway, and walked over to his desk. He glanced up. At first he didn't know her, a middle-aged woman with a drawn tired face and red-rimmed eyes, and then he said in surprise, "Mrs. Colby." He got up and pulled a chair forward.

She sat down on it, moving as if she was a much older woman, and she said, "You were kind—the other day at the hospital. I could see—you minded—about Belle. I thought you ought to know."

"Know what, Mrs. Colby?"

"Charles killed himself, Sergeant Hackett. He killed himself on Thursday, I found him when I came home from the market. He cut his wrists in the bathtub and it was too late to save him."

Hackett said quietly, "I'm very sorry to hear that, Mrs. Colby."

She opened her handbag. "I want to show you what he wrote. He'd learned to use the typewriter, you know, he was quite good at it. He'd just started going to another school for the blind, for blind children, teaching that. He earned a little something for the teaching, but the main thing was that it made him feel useful, that he was accomplishing something. He used to enjoy it, going out like that—with Belle. Knowing he could go anywhere and do anything on his own. I want you to see what he wrote, the note he left for me. There has to be some sort of—

inquest I think they called it—and the police took it for evidence. But I made a copy of it. And I wanted you to see it—you were kind." She handed the slip of paper to him and he took it silently.

For some reason his vision was a little blurred and he had to hold it close to make it out.

Dearest Mother, I'm sorry to cause you any more grief. But I just can't go on without Belle. There could never be another dog like her and I wouldn't insult her memory by trying to put another in her place. I think God will understand, and if He is as good as they say, I will meet Belle again and some-day we will all be together. Please don't grieve for me, this is best for all of us. Charles.

Hackett handed it back to her, feeling a little lump in his throat. "I'm very sorry," he said again.

She looked at him with her new haggard, ravaged expression. "There were just the two of us," she said. "That doesn't matter, I'm all right, and I know Charles is all right. But I'll pray every day of my life that you find those men and punish them. They killed Charles. Oh, I know, not by what the law says, but morally they killed him. Belle gave him back his life, and when they killed her they killed him all over again. I'll pray that you find them and they'll be punished somehow."

There wasn't anything to say to her. Hackett said, feeling it to be an insult, "You know we'll do our best, Mrs. Colby." And that probably wouldn't be good enough. "There's nothing to say—except that I'm so sorry."

"I thought you'd want to know. You were kind." She got up and went out without another word.

EGGERS CALLED late that afternoon to say he had the rest of the list, and Palliser drove over to pick it up. On Sunday, with Wanda off and Mendoza not in until later, they divided those names up and started to call some other forces. Fortunately, some of the names overlapped, as it were: There were a number of men who'd rented cars from Hertz those two days who lived in New York or Pittsburgh or Chicago. But they weren't going to get through the list today, even by talking to detectives on the night watch in those cities after three o'clock here.

The night watch had left another heist at a liquor store. Mendoza came in at one o'clock and lent a hand with the phone calls. "And after we finish this job," he said in an interval, "we make up a list of the car renters with local addresses and go and have a look at them."

They were all rather annoyed when the two witnesses to the heist showed up to make statements and look at some mug shots. Palliser took them down to R. and I., and everybody had more or less forgotten them when one of the policewomen down there called to say they'd picked out a photo. Palliser went down to look, and they were positive he was the heister. He had the record for it; his name was Ricardo Espinoza, and he'd just been released from Susanville four months ago after serving a three-to-five on armed robbery. He was still on parole. Another stupid bastard, thought Palliser. There wasn't any point in going to look for him now; his parole officer would know where he was living, they'd contact him tomorrow.

When there was a general exodus at ten minutes of six, Lake was just shutting down the switchboard; Communications would relay any calls to the night watch. They all said automatically, "Good night, Jimmy," and headed for the elevators together. When they got outside it had started to rain harder.

LAKE WAS sitting behind the wheel with the windshield wipers going, at the parking-lot exit, waiting to turn out onto Los Angeles Street, when he reached into his side pocket and said, "Oh, hell." He'd left his cigarettes up there on his desk. For a moment he debated about going back, but it was too much trouble. He had a little drive ahead of him, on the freeway up to Pasadena. When the lane was clear he turned up Los Angeles to Temple. Just before the entrance to the Pasadena freeway there was a drugstore, at the corner of Temple and Olive. There was a parking slot right on the street in front of it. He parked and went in to buy a pack of cigarettes.

THE NIGHT watch hadn't had time to settle down before they got a call to a heist. It was raining steadily outside. They tossed a coin for it and Conway lost. He swore, got into his raincoat again, and went down to the parking lot. The address was on Temple, the squad angled into the curb. He parked and went in; it was a drugstore. The uniformed man was up at the counter at the back of the store, talking presumably to witnesses. But the first thing Conway saw was the body on its back on the floor, a body in a navy-blue uniform, and he took two strides up to it and he said in naked astonishment, "Sweet Jesus Christ, it's Jimmy Lake!"

NINE

THE PATROLMAN came down the aisle, a man Conway didn't know, and said, "I've called an ambulance." Conway said stupidly, "He's dead." The patrolman said, "But the other one isn't. I don't know who the uniformed man is but he winged the heister—" Conway saw that Lake's gun was lying beside his right hand—it was regulation to carry the gun. He looked up the store. A man in a white smock was leaning on the counter, that would be the pharmacist, and another figure was huddled up on the floor in front of the counter.

"He's just a punk kid," said the patrolman, "just a punk kid. Our man must have walked in on the heist—"

"Oh, my God," said Conway. There was a great stain of wet blood on the front of Lake's uniform, only you couldn't see the color of it. The ambulance pulled up in the street outside.

Conway walked up the store and looked at the heister. He was a kid in the late teens with long black hair and he was lying there on the dirty floor with tears pouring down his cheeks. His left thigh was bleeding freely and he was clutching at it. He was whimpering, "Why? Why did he have to shoot me? I didn't aim at him, the gun just went off."

The pharmacist, an elderly man, was looking pale; he leaned on the counter shaking. "He'd just pulled the gun on me when the officer came in, he shouted to this one to drop the gun, and then the kid just turned and fired at him—"

There was an automatic on the floor beside the counter. Conway's training took over and he did all the right things automatically. He searched the kid's pockets and found a billfold with a student-body card from Roosevelt High School in it. His name was Allen Goebel and he lived on Union Street. The ambulance took him away, and Conway got the pharmacist's name, and he asked for a paper bag and dropped the automatic into it. He went behind the counter to the telephone and called in to Piggott and Schenke. "You'd better call the lieutenant," he said.

"Oh, my God," said Schenke. "Yes. You need any backup?"

"No backup. It's all finished, Bob."

The patrolman had gone to call the morgue wagon. Conway went back up the aisle and looked down at Lake, lying there staring up at the ceiling with expressionless eyes. He thought numbly, things were queer. Lake sitting there in the Robbery-Homicide office all those years, handling the switchboard, while other men in uniform roamed the streets of the city jungle, and in the end it was Lake who ran into the slugs from the heister's gun. It wasn't until the morgue wagon came that he thought of the word *ironic*.

He went back to the counter, looked around on the floor, and found the shell casings from the automatic, three of them. And he thought, the same kid had pulled those other heists and by all they had heard he was an amateur with a gun. It would have been just blind chance that he hit Lake at all. The morgue wagon came, and he sent the patrolman back on tour and headed back for the office in the driving rain.

Half an hour later everybody knew about it; Schenke and Piggott had been on the phone. Mendoza called

Hackett and they both headed up for Lake's address in Pasadena. Hackett got there first, not having so far to drive, and sat waiting for Mendoza. It was an old sprawling stucco house on a quiet block, a strip of lawn on each side of the front walk. Mendoza pushed the bell and the door opened immediately. She would already have been worried; by then he was overdue getting home by over an hour, but there were always hang-ups on the freeway. But she knew, the moment she saw them there on the porch, though she'd never met either of them. It was never easy to break the bad news. And strangely Mendoza was remembering the last time he'd had to break the bad news to one of their own, and that had been a long time ago. He remembered going with George Higgins to tell Mary Dwyer that Bert had been killed. There had been a lot of water under the bridge since then.

She sat on the couch and wept. And the children were there, tall nice-looking Jim junior and the pretty eighteen-year-old girl. Mendoza and Hackett couldn't say much to her. But after a while she said shakily, "It's so queer, you know, so queer. When we were first married and Jimmy on Traffic patrol, I used to worry. I was so relieved when he got assigned to an inside job. I never worried after that. He wasn't out on the street dealing with all the thugs. I never worried at all, and now it had to be just chance that he ran up against one of the thugs after all. He was only forty-seven." The girl was sitting beside her, still crying, and the boy on her other side with a protective arm around her. "He used to complain about the job sometimes, he always had to worry about his weight and it was the kind of job where he didn't get any exercise. And it doesn't seem fair—only forty-seven— just chance he was somewhere at the wrong time."

There wasn't much they could do or say. But they said all there was to say. "We'll be all right," she said, and thanked them for coming.

"If there's anything we can do—" said Hackett.

"You'll let me know—so we can arrange for the funeral."

They walked down to the street where the Ferrari and Monte Carlo were parked. It had stopped raining. Hackett said, "It'll seem damn queer without Jimmy in the office."

Mendoza said, "He'd been sitting in that office before I was transferred up from Vice. It'll seem damn queer." They stood there in the cold night air, and a cloud sailed over the moon. A little over three hours ago, Lake had been shutting down the switchboard for the night, getting ready to drive home.

"And just the chance—the wrong place at the wrong time," said Mendoza.

"She'll have the pension. And the kids are nearly grown up."

"Yes, we always have to think about money," said Mendoza remotely. "The pattern changes. I was just thinking about Bert. And George."

Hackett sighed. "I suppose the funeral will be Wednesday or Thursday."

"And the work piling up at the office. I wonder who we'll get to handle the switchboard. Administration will be doing some shuffling around."

"I wish there was more we could do for her."

Mendoza tossed his cigarette into the gutter. "Chance," he said, and laughed. "I wonder. It'd be nice to think there's some reason to the way things happen, and maybe there is if we only knew what it is. Good night, Art. We won't be getting much work done tomorrow, but it can wait." He got into the Ferrari.

The moon went under and it began to rain again as he drove home, and he was tired when he passed the tall gates and drove up the hill. The big house was silent and mostly dark, but the garage lights had been left on for him. He went in the back door and climbed the stairs to the big master-bedroom suite. Alison was sitting up in bed reading, surrounded by the four cats, Cedric stretched out on the floor beside the bed.

"I thought you might be later."

"There's not much we can do for her, *cariña*. She's a nice woman."

"I'm so sorry, Luis. You'd worked with him a long time, I know."

"He was a year younger than I am," said Mendoza. "Just fate he walked in there on the heister? I wish I knew."

Alison said, "You're tired to death, you'd better come to bed."

"I think I'll have a drink first."

Hackett had got home before that, having not so far to go. Angel gave him a practiced look and asked, "Do you want to talk about it?"

He said heavily, "No, not specially, my Angel. There's nothing to say about it, is there? It happened. No, I don't want to talk about it, but I don't think I'll sleep much. And tomorrow we'll have to talk to the damn punk who did it, and by what Rich Conway said he may be a juvenile, and they'll put him on probation and turn him loose, or at most he'll spend a few years inside. No, I don't want to talk about it."

NOTHING MUCH got done at the office on Monday. It was supposed to be Palliser's day off but he came in. There wasn't anybody on the switchboard, and Grace and Galeano took turns sitting on it. After a while, when they'd said all there was to say, Palliser suddenly remembered that heister, Ricardo Espinoza. They couldn't just let everything go, because one man had died. He called Welfare and Rehab, got the name of Espinoza's P.A. officer, and talked to him.

"Well, I never expected he'd straighten up and fly right," said the P.A. man, "but the damn fool might have waited to get off parole. He's living in one room at a place on Twentieth, supposed to be working at a gas station on Beverly. You might let me know when you pick him up." Palliser didn't feel inclined to go out hunting Espinoza right away, and it was still raining. They all sat around smoking too much, and at least they didn't get any new calls.

Mendoza checked with the hospital at intervals, and about noon the hospital said the kid could be talked to. In one way they all wanted to do that, and in another nobody wanted to, but somebody had to see him. Mendoza and Hackett went over to the hospital.

His name was Allen Goebel and he'd just turned eighteen. He had a broken thigh, and he was looking very sorry for himself in the narrow hospital bed. It was a three-bed room, but the curtains were drawn around his bed. He wasn't very big, a weedy undersized kid, and he had a slight case of acne: just a nondescript young punk. The nurse had told them that his mother had been there. They had called her last night; the phone number was on his student-body card.

Mendoza asked him, "Where did you get the gun?"

He said weakly, "I never meant to shoot that cop. It just went off. I never knew a gun could go off so easy. I'm sorry, I hope he isn't hurt bad."

"You've been pulling some heists lately, haven't you?" asked Hackett. "We've heard about you."

"I guess it wasn't a very smart thing to do," he said ingenuously, "but damn everything, I never had no bread. Mom's just got that cruddy job at the dress factory, and she's always bitchin' about the rent and how much the grocery bill is, she never gives me no bread, and it's a drag—the other kids get to take girls out and have some fun, I never did, what girl's gonna go anywheres with a guy can't even buy her a hamburger? I just wanted to get hold of some bread so's I could have some fun sometimes—and now Ma's cryin' all over me sayin' I'm a disgrace and she don't know how she'll pay the hospital bill." He looked resentful.

"Where did you get the gun?" asked Mendoza. This one wasn't even the expectable street tough, the gang member; just an immature greedy kid.

"Oh, hell, that was what give me the idea, I knew where to get the gun. Old man Brodsky just died last month, they lived across the hall from us. Mom's friends with old lady Brodsky, and I knew he had a gun, he was afraid of burglars. And I heard Mis' Brodsky tell Mom she was scared of it, she'd hid it on the closet shelf. And she's away at work all day like Mom, and I got in the window easy from the fire escape and got it. There were bullets for it too, I didn't know how to load it but I found a book at the liberry showed me." Mendoza and Hackett didn't look at each other. "But it went off so easy—I was kinda nervous those first couple of times and it just went off. Like it did last night. I never meant to shoot it, it just went off—that guy in the drugstore was just goin' to hand over the bread to me when that other guy, the cop, come in and yelled at me, and it scared me and the damn gun just went off. And he shot me, he hadn't no call to shoot me, and my leg hurts somethin' awful."

In the corridor Hackett said, "Just at random like that. It makes you tired, Luis."

They went back to the office and started the machinery on the warrant. At least he was eighteen and he'd be tried as an adult. But they all knew how it would go: it would get called involuntary manslaughter, and he might go up for a couple of years, or he might just get probation.

AT FOUR O'CLOCK a call came in from a squad, and Higgins took it. Like Mendoza, he'd been thinking back all that while, to the day he'd gone with Mendoza to tell Mary Dwyer that Bert had been shot and killed; it was that day he'd fallen in love with her, lovely Mary with her gray eyes, and he'd never thought she'd marry him, but she had, a long while later. Bert's kids were good kids, Steve and Laura, and now there was their own Margaret Emily patting him and calling him George, and they were a family. Things happened, and things changed.

The address was Magnolia Avenue. The Traffic man said, "It's that fellow again, the one that offers to carry parcels for the old ladies, but he got scared off this time."

It was the usual old apartment building, and down here the tenants would all be black. In the minute lobby there were two women talking volubly, one little and one big. The little one was very black, very thin and scrawny, in her sixties or older. She said, "You're another cop." Nobody could ever mistake Higgins for anything but a cop. "I hope you catch that thievin' yeller boy, but he didn't get my money! Nossir, it takes somebody bigger'n him to get money from Rosie Miller!'' She told the familiar tale, she'd been walking home after getting off the bus up on Adams, and the nice polite young man had offered to carry her bag of groceries and then when they got inside the apartment he knocked her down and tried to grab her handbag. ''But I wasn't about to let no thievin' yeller boy get my money, I hung onto my bag tight and he was still tryin' to get it away from me when Mis' Bedloe here come down the stairs, and he was scared and run off. But I still got my money, and my groceries too!''

Higgins asked, ''He had his hands on the bag?'' It was a big plastic bag, bright red.

''He sure did, but I hung on tight—''

''We'd like to take it in and see if there are any finger-prints on it, Mrs. Miller.'' She was suspicious and reluc-tant but finally agreed, as long as she could have the money out of it. He handled it gingerly, trying to touch only the clasp, gave her the wallet with the money in it, and carried the bag by its handle back to the car. At headquarters he took it up to the lab.

''It's the kind of surface to take prints just dandy,'' said Scarne. ''We'll let you know.''

PALLISER AND LANDERS didn't pick up Ricardo Espi-noza until Tuesday afternoon; he hadn't showed up at his one room or on the job Monday afternoon. When they found him in his room he was recovering from a hang-over and called them a lot of names on the way to jail. There wasn't any point in talking to him; they booked him in. The warrant had come through that morning. Palliser called his P.A. officer. The night watch had left them nothing to work, but there was work to do. This morning Communications had sent up a policewoman to handle the switchboard, a pretty dark girl named Rita Putnam. She seemed to be efficient.

Mendoza was roaming around the office, and Grace and Galeano were on the phones. What with the overlapping of the names of car renters who lived in the same places, they would finish up that job today, and start phoning all the Dr. Petersons.

Mendoza told Palliser, "Wanda's over at the D.A.'s office, she wants to get the court hearing set up for that Kent girl as soon as they'll do it."

"That was a queer one," said Higgins.

"And there's that homicide from Saturday night—I don't think anybody's done much on it. The old drunk Rafferty. Who was the dead man?"

Palliser said, "I had a look at the place on Sunday morning. God, what a place, it must be one of the oldest houses in the city. His name was Burkhart by a driver's license ten years out of date, Edward Burkhart. There was an address in Hollywood but of course nobody there knew him. Just another drifter ending up down here, probably panhandling for the room rent and the occasional meal."

"And stealing Mr. Rafferty's whiskey," said Mendoza.

The D.A.'s office called to say that Don Faulkner would be arraigned on Thursday. Hackett started to go through the list of car renters to weed out the locals. There were more than they might have expected, and of course their home addresses were all over the place, Santa Monica to La Cañada and points east and west.

The Chief's secretary called Mendoza to say that Lake's funeral was scheduled for Thursday at Forest Lawn. The funeral director wanted to know about pallbearers. Mendoza called the funeral home and arranged about that; there were enough Robbery-Homicide men to perform that little service.

And there was still work to be done, but they drifted out early before the end of shift.

For one thing, Palliser thought on the way home, a thing like this made cops' wives a little nervous, and he was anxious about Roberta with the baby due so soon. But when he came in the back door, to be greeted politely by Trina, he found Roberta serenely taking a cake out of the oven while Davy was sprawled out on the floor over a coloring book. He kissed her and said, "Nobody feels much like doing the damn routine, we all got away early. Are you feeling all right?"

Roberta said calmly, "I read you like a book, John. You're worrying that I'm worrying. Having been reminded that cops can get killed on the job. Don't fuss. It's a hazard all cops' wives accept when they say 'I do.' Worrying never does any good, and just as you said, it was only bad luck—he wasn't a street cop apt to run into the thugs in the jungle. You look tired."

"For no good reason," said Palliser moodily.

"Well, you'd better sit down and relax and have a drink before dinner."

THERE WAS a new heist to work on Wednesday, and Grace, Galeano, Landers, and Glasser started in to call all the Dr. Petersons but soon gave up, discovering that most doctors took Wednesdays off. A couple of witnesses came in to make statements. As if the criminal element was respecting feelings for once, nothing new went down, and in the afternoon Higgins and Palliser went out to make the first cast looking at the local car renters. They sorted out addresses in the same general area, to save time and trouble. They would tell the car renters that they were a survey team checking on the efficiency of the Hertz service; there wasn't any need to flash the badges, all they wanted was a look at them to see if any of them could possibly be Gilbert Kramer grown twenty years older than his mug shot. Higgins got a look at four of them in the beach area and none of them could be Kramer by any stretch of the imagination. Palliser contacted another five in the valley area, and drew blank, none of those was as tall as Kramer. They came back in at five-thirty and for the first time since Saturday night saw everybody in the office laughing. "What's been going on?" asked Higgins.

"Oh, wait till you hear, George," said Mendoza.

IT WAS HACKETT'S day off, and Mendoza had been sitting at Hackett's desk in the outer office talking desultorily to Landers when Rita passed on a call. They both went to see what it was; the squad had just reported an attempted heist. It was out on Wilshire, and when Mendoza slid the Ferrari into a red zone they saw an interested little crowd up the block where the squad car was double-parked. They walked back, and found the patrolman talking to a girl. He had moved the handful of people back against the building, and they were just staring; more people were giving the scene a wide-berth and hurrying past, leery of involvement with a drunk or an accident. The store front there had shiny plate-glass windows with an attractive display of fancy bottles, and the sign said GOLDEN STATE LIQUORS. On the sidewalk in front of the entrance was a huge sprawled body.

Mendoza took one look and said, *"¡Por el amor de Dios!* The ape-man!" The man was enormous and very black; he had coarse primitive features, a low brow and thick lips, and his eyes were rolling wildly. The patrolman had got cuffs on him.

"Well, now, isn't that a pretty sight," said Landers. There was a big Colt revolver on the sidewalk beside the ape-man. "How'd you come by this?"

The patrolman was having trouble keeping a straight face. He said, "Don't congratulate me, he was out of commission before I got here."

There was another man in the doorway, a spare middle-aged man in tailored sports clothing holding a wet towel to his head.

"You needn't have put the cuffs on him," said the girl dispassionately. "His arm's broken, and he probably has some damage to his neck." She was a very pretty girl with a mop of black hair and green eyes. She wasn't more than five feet two, and had a nice slim figure. She was wearing a dark skirt and sweater and high-heeled patent-leather pumps. "Are you detectives?" She looked at them with interest. "I got him for you. I didn't really plan to, I just lost my temper. I've got a perfectly terrible temper. My name's Molly O'Donoghue, by the way."

"*You* got him?" said Landers. "How do you mean?"

"Well, I just lost my temper when he hit Uncle Ben. That's Uncle Ben," and she indicated the man in the doorway. "Mr. O'Donoghue. It's his store. I go to LACC, but I don't have any classes in the afternoon except for trigonometry and that's a snap, I don't have to do much studying for that, and I've been helping Uncle Ben in the store because his clerk's in the hospital with appendicitis. And there weren't any customers in when that big gorilla came in and held us up. My goodness, he is a big one, isn't he? And Uncle Ben, of course, thought of protecting me first, he tried to push me down behind the counter, and I guess the gorilla thought he was going after a gun, and he leaned over the counter and clouted Uncle Ben, knocked him back against all the fancy liqueurs, and what a mess that's going to be to clean up—and he came around and opened the register and scooped out all the cash and ran out. And when I saw Uncle Ben's head was bleeding I got mad and ran after him and caught him on the sidewalk.''

"But—" said Landers.

"Oh, well, you see, I want to join the police as soon as I'm twenty-one next year, and I've been studying jujitsu for years—when you're not very big you've got to give yourself an edge, you know. Those big clumsy brutes are never very fast. I tackled him from behind and used a few basic holds, and I heard his arm snap and then I got his legs out from under him and down he went. So I gave him a good hard belt on one temple with the heel of my shoe to put him out. Uncle Ben was calling the police by then.''

Mendoza started to laugh. "*¡Vaya por Dios!* Just like that?''

"There's nothing to it really, it's just knowing where to apply pressure.''

"Miss O'Donoghue, my congratulations. You're going to be an asset to the force when you get around to joining us, we'll look forward to having you." The ape-man was moaning horribly and rolling his eyes again. "Let's get him into the squad, and you'd better take him over to Emergency to see how much damage Miss O'Donoghue's inflicted on him.''

They were both laughing as they started to follow the squad. "What a girl," said Landers.

"And one damned good-looking girl," said Mendoza.

"Yes, but who in hell would marry one like that? With the combination of the temper and the jujitsu, my God, if you were fifteen minutes late for dinner or forgot her birthday, she'd land you in Emergency.''

Mendoza was still chuckling. "My red-haired Scotch-Irish girl's bad enough. But what a woman. She'll make a good policewoman if she can learn to control her temper."

The doctor in Emergency said the ape-man had a broken arm and a bang on the head, nothing else wrong with him. All he would tell them was his name, which was Joshua Slocum, and he hadn't anything on him but the loot from the liquor store and a half-empty bottle of cheap rye. The Colt was unloaded, which set Mendoza laughing again. "Those witnesses at the market—oh, it's beautiful, Tom! *¡Me gusta!*" When his arm had been set they took him over to the jail and booked him in.

NOTHING MUCH, of course, got done on Thursday. The funeral was scheduled for one o'clock at the Church of the Recessional, and as there wouldn't be the long ride from church to cemetery there wasn't the usual motorcycle escort. The Chief was there, and quite a few LAPD men who hadn't known Lake personally but turned out in respect, and all the Robbery-Homicide men and Wanda. After the graveside ceremony the Chief folded the flag from the casket and gave it to Caroline Lake. The three of them were looking a little lonely there, the nice-looking dark-haired woman, the fresh-faced young man and his pretty sister flanking her. The Chief said some nice things about Lake, and they all went up to speak to her, and then the Lakes got into the limousine and were driven away, and it was all over.

Hackett had taken an hour this morning to cover Faulkner's arraignment. They went back to the office at four o'clock, with the exception of the men on night watch, more by habit than inclination. But there was always work to be done. They hadn't got to first base on calling all the doctors, and something new might go down anytime.

WHAT NEXT went down was for the night watch, and it came in at nine-forty. The report was assault with intent, and Schenke went out on it.

The squad was in front of an old duplex on Kensington Drive and the patrolman had a girl in the backseat. "I've called an ambulance, she's in pretty bad shape. She came staggering up to this house here half an hour ago, and the people were afraid to let her in but they finally called us when she kept asking. She says she's been raped and beaten up."

There were bruises on the girl's face and arms, and she had a badly cut lip. Her clothes were half ripped off, and she was clutching the remains of a coat around her.

"Please," she said, "you've got to go and find Suzy—they hurt her too, I think they hurt her terribly—grabbed us in the parking lot at college—it was in the park down there they did it—and after they went away I knew—had to get help—I couldn't make Suzy answer me, and I could hardly move—but I knew had to get help—please go and find Suzy and help her, she's still down there in the park—"

The ambulance came and took her off, and Schenke said angrily, "That damned pair of rapists again!" They took the Traffic man and drove the block down to Echo Park, the strip of green in the middle of the city with its little lake and boathouses, and started to look with flashlights. They found her in five minutes, lying in a crumpled heap on the grass inside the entrance to the park. She looked very small in the dancing gleam of the flashlights. She was a pretty Japanese girl, unconscious and nearly naked.

"Goddamn these bastards," said Schenke savagely. They called in for another ambulance.

THERE HAD to be priorities, and in this office that was Homicide. They all got busy on Friday calling the doctors. Mendoza had been pessimistic about the doctors' cooperation but most of them were reasonable. Assured that they were talking to police who had a reason for asking, all of those they reached turned them over to office nurses to provide the information, and they began to get all the names, the men who had scheduled appointments with all the Dr. Petersons at the time and date indicated on that little slip of paper from the bloodstained raincoat. As they collected the names they phoned them down to R. and I. to see if they showed in Records. By the middle of the afternoon they had drawn blank on twenty-seven names; but they had expected this to be a long job.

Mendoza had talked to the hospital this morning, and at four o'clock the hospital had called back to say that he could talk to one of the girls beaten and raped last night.

Her name was June Rendell and the doctor said she had been savagely and forcibly raped and beaten; she had broken ribs, a broken wrist, bruises all over her. She was obviously in some pain but anxious to talk to police. It was hard to say whether she'd be a pretty girl normally; she had a grossly swollen cut lip and two black eyes, and she was half propped up against pillows in the narrow hospital bed.

He introduced himself, and she burst out at him at once, "Did they find Suzy? Is she all right? The nurse won't tell me anything—I'm afraid she was terribly hurt, I heard her scream—''

"We'll be finding out," said Mendoza. "Has your family been contacted, do you know?"

"Oh, heavens, they'll be wild—I suppose somebody had better call them—it's James Rendell in Fresno," and she gave him a number.

"And who is Suzy?" asked Mendoza.

"Oh, you don't know! Didn't they find her? Her name's Masako Suzuki, but everybody calls her Suzy—she's such a dear wonderful girl—all her family's in Japan, she came here to go to college, we're both at USC—yes, I'll tell you what happened, it was just terrible." She sobbed once, and touched her lip gingerly with Kleenex. "We'd heard about the rapist picking girls up off the campus, but we thought with two of us together it'd be safe enough, and it wasn't late, it was only five-thirty when we left the college library—Suzy doesn't drive. She's got an apartment on Eleventh Street and she usually takes the bus in the morning but lots of people drove her home at different times and took her other places—everybody likes Suzy—and I was going to take her home last night, my place is up in Hollywood. There weren't many cars in the lot, and just as we got to my car there these two men came out at us from behind a car in the other aisle and just sort of fell on us—I heard Suzy scream, and I tried to fight, but he was just too strong—and then he knocked me out." She touched the bruise on her jaw. "When I came to we were in a car, and I could hear Suzy crying and trying to fight with the other man in the backseat. They took us to that park—of course it was all empty at that time of night, in January—and dragged us out of the car—and I don't know how long they were there with us—it was just a nightmare—and when they finally went away I—I couldn't make Suzy answer me, I was afraid she was dead—and I knew we had to have help, I had to try—"

"You did just fine, Miss Rendell."

"I couldn't tell you what they looked like at all, they had these horrible ski masks on, but they were both awfully big—"

Mendoza came out to the corridor and he thought, another dead end. No descriptions and no leads. He asked questions and located the doctor who would know about the other girl. He was an older man with tired eyes, and he said, "You can't see her yet. She's not so good, Lieutenant, and I'm afraid she won't be. She's got a bad concussion and some broken ribs, but aside from that— she's a very small, thin girl and in the course of the beating I'm inclined to think that one of the men deliberately jumped on her—what's called a stomping, isn't it?—her spine is fractured, there's excessive damage, I'm afraid, and it's possible she'll be paralyzed."

"*Por Dios*—these bastards—when might we talk to her?" Not that she could tell them anything.

The doctor shrugged. "Possibly in a few days. Of course, when we can make a more extensive examination, the prognosis might be better. There's a lot being done in spinal surgery these days. I just can't say right now. We'll let you know when you can talk to her."

Mendoza went back to June Rendell and got the address of Suzy's apartment. He drove up there and got the manager to let him in. In the old building dating from the twenties, Suzy's apartment was refreshingly neat and clean, with a couple of interesting Oriental panels on the walls. There was an address book, and he found the name of Senji Suzuki, an address in Tokyo. He went back to the office and sent off a cable.

HIGGINS WAS about to go out for lunch on Saturday when the phone rang on his desk. He was the sole occupant of the office; the doctors couldn't be reached on Saturday and everybody else was out, even Wanda, driving all over to take a look at the car renters. He had stayed in to see the witness to a heist, but it was all a handful of nothing, the witness admitted he wouldn't recognize the man. It was Higgins' private opinion that the rental car business was a handful of nothing too. Luis Rodolfo Vicente Mendoza had the occasional flashes of brilliance but Higgins didn't think this was one of them.

He picked up the phone and said his name. "Oh, good, you're in," said Scarne. "You know that handbag you brought in the other day—I didn't get to it right away, but I finally did this morning, and it has some beautiful clear latents on it. Six of them. Lovely. I just got the word on them from R. and I."

"They're in our files? Good. Who is he?"

"His name's Clyde Anderson. He's got a little pedigree of possession, selling, one charge of pimping."

"Thank you so much," said Higgins. He changed his mind about a leisurely lunch and went up to the canteen for a sandwich, and then drove to R. and I. to see if they had a recent address for Anderson. The last known one was nearly three years out of date, and the ones like Anderson tended to move around, but he went out to look anyway. It was Bonnie Brae Street in the Westlake area, and it turned out to be an old duplex. He pushed the bell and after an interval the door opened and a woman peered out at him. She was more yellow than black, a combination of Negro and some Oriental. "I'm looking for Clyde Anderson, does he still live here?" asked Higgins.

"Oh, you want Clyde? You got to excuse me, I don't see too good, my eyes goin' bad on me and the light hurts 'em, you step in so I can shut the door. You want Clyde? Is it about that job in Gardena? He'd sure like to get that job, he's been out of work awhile."

"That's right," said Higgins. "Do you know where I can find him? Are you his mother?"

She gave a shrill cackle. "Grandmother's more like it. I 'spect you might find him at that pool hall over on Alvarado, Andy's it's named. Clyde's a good boy generally but he just can't leave them ivories alone, and they mostly got a crap game goin' in the back room over there."

"Thanks," said Higgins. "I'll have a look." He didn't think he'd trouble to call any backup; but he rather wished he had a pair of cuffs on him. Then on second thought he reflected that he might as well have COP tattooed on his forehead, and anybody running a crap game in back would kindly let Clyde know that the law was asking for him. He stopped at a public phone and called up a squad, and was pleased to find it had Dave Turner in it. Turner was a good man. "We're going fox hunting," he said.

"Is that a fact?" said Turner, his black face deadpan.

"It's kind of unsporting. Before they set the dogs on the fox they fill up all the foxholes. Of course it's a pity you're in uniform but it can't be helped. First of all I'll look and see if there's a convenient alley behind this pool hall." There was, so he told Turner to leave the squad in the street and saunter down there. "If he's there, he should come sliding out the back door as soon as he hears I'm asking for him." He gave Turner three minutes, walked into the pool hall, and flashed the badge at the proprietor. "I'm looking for Clyde Anderson, would he be here?"

"Never heard of him," said the proprietor. He glanced over at a fancily dressed young fellow sipping a beer at a makeshift bar, and the young fellow slid off the stool and started toward the rear. Higgins asked a few more questions, and went out and up the side street to the alley entrance.

"Here's your fox, Sergeant," said Turner blandly. "Clockwork. He came slithering right out into my arms." He had Anderson in cuffs.

Higgins regarded him with warm satisfaction. The old ladies had given an accurate description. Nobody would be frightened of Anderson at first sight; he was only middle height and thin, with a mild-looking face, and he was nattily dressed in good-looking sports clothes. "You've got nothin' on me," said Anderson. He was still looking in surprise at the handcuffs.

"That's what you think," said Higgins.

ALL THE REST of them had got out and about on Saturday, except Landers; it was his day off. They had divided up the list of the local car renters, and there were fifty-nine of them still to take a look at, with addresses all over the county. Of all the people living in the Los Angeles area who had rented a Hertz car on one of those two days, only a few had been women. It entailed a lot of driving, but the freeways were slightly less heavily trafficked on a weekend. With all the driving, they managed to contact only twelve of them on Saturday; the drawback about the weekend was that a good many people were away from home, and they'd have to come back to those. A majority of them, of course, had jobs, with the home address all Robbery-Homicide had, so most contacts involved a double trip. Nobody any of them laid eyes on looked remotely like Gilbert Kramer, by that old mug shot, and of course it was possible that some obliging detective in New York or Miami, dutifully cooperating with other lawmen, was even now looking at Kramer and recognizing him.

Sunday was just a replay of Saturday.

On Monday morning Glasser, Grace, and Landers started calling the Dr. Petersons again, and as they were given names relayed them down to R. and I. They hadn't counted the number of Dr. Petersons there were in all six phone books.

The D.A.'s office called Mendoza to say that the earliest date they could set up the court hearing on Linda Kent was the twentieth of the next month. The courts were always busy. And before Mendoza started out on the legwork, looking at the car renters, he had a call from the hospital. He could, the hospital told him, talk to Miss Suzuki now.

She looked very small and frail lying flat in the hospital bed, smiling faintly up at him. She was a pretty girl with the rather flat face of the Oriental, very black eyes and very long black hair braided in a pigtail; perhaps she'd usually wear it in a smooth coiled knob. He wondered if they had told her about the possibility of paralysis. "I won't bother you long," he told her gently. "We'd just like to know if you can tell us anything about those two men, if they called each other by any name, if you noticed anything about the car."

She said in an unexpectedly firm clear voice, "Yes, I can tell you something, Lieutenant." Her English was nearly unaccented. "It's when they are pulling June and me out of the car, it was on the street beside the park, there was a streetlight—and when the door of the car opened the light came on in the roof of the car, you know how it does. I was trying to fight the man holding me, I

was trying to bite him, and"—she gave a little laugh—"I
have very strong teeth! He was very strong, and still I go
on trying, and then I felt the sleeve of his jacket tear
where I had bitten it—and just one little second his sleeve
pulls up and I see his bare arm—just above his wrist—
and there is a tattoo mark. I can still see it in my mind."
Her eyes widened in remembered terror. "The light fell
on it, so I am very sure what it looked like. It was a tattoo mark of a naked woman, and above that there were
the words *Lady Killer.*"

Mendoza said softly, "*¡No me diga!* Jackpot."

"I am very sure of it," she said firmly.

"Thank you so very much, Miss Suzuki. You may like
to know, I have cabled your family in Tokyo."

"That was kind." She smiled again. "Yes, there is a
cable from my father, and he is coming—He will perhaps tell the first airplane it must push all the passengers
off if necessary and send the airplane to Los Angeles instead of New York perhaps—that is my father! He has a
big export business, you see, and he's used to giving orders—quick, Senji Suzuki says it must be done, and it is
done. He was not very happy that I came here alone, but
I'd always wanted to see America. Now he will come and
say, I told you so."

Mendoza started back for headquarters, cursing at the
traffic that slowed him down, and when he got there he
went straight down to R. and I. They had the computers
there, and among the records were the lists of nick-
names, known marks, other little peculiarities. If God
was good that tattooed rapist was somewhere in their
records.

AT ABOUT THE same time, Hackett was out in Orange
County looking for an address and thinking what a

damned waste of time all this would probably turn out to be. The car renter he was looking for now, and he might as well skip this one, was a minister yet, and the address was a church. But you had to be thorough at any job.

The church was called the Tabernacle of God, and it was a handsome new-looking church with a steeple and bell, on the corner of a broad landscaped street in Santa Ana. He wondered if the minister would be here on a weekday, but the double front doors were open and he went in, leaving the car a quarter block away. There was a willowy blond young man up by the pulpit, just going into the rear of the church, and Hackett hailed him.

"Is the Reverend Thurlow here?" He had a dim recollection that he'd heard the name before.

"Oh, the Reverend hardly ever sees anyone without an appointment, sir, he's a very busy man, you know."

Hackett was in a hurry to get this over and go on to the next name, and he pulled out the badge.

"Oh," said the youth, "it'll be about the security arrangements for his lecture at the college next week." He led Hackett down a hall behind the main body of the church, to an open door giving on a large square office. "I'm sorry to interrupt you, Reverend, but this police officer—"

The man behind the desk was distinguished-looking, with a thick crop of wavy silver-gray hair, and a handsome regular-featured face. He stood up and gave Hackett a genial warm smile. "Anything we can do for the law, of course. Do come in."

And Hackett said, "It's nice to meet you at last, Mr. Kramer."

TEN

NOBODY COULD have mistaken him who'd seen that mug shot. He hadn't aged much; the major change was the silver-gray hair, and that just made him look more distinguished. And Hackett saw the instant flare of alarm in the fine dark eyes before the man said easily, "I'm afraid you're mistaking me for someone else."

"I don't think so," said Hackett. "Fingerprints don't lie, Mr. Kramer, and you left yours on that bottle of bourbon. We're rather curious to know why you murdered Archie Kershaw."

The blond youth uttered a faint bleat. "The prints, of course, told us that you were the one who slipped him the spiked whiskey. Kershaw, Maulden, whatever he was calling himself. That's cut and dried, and nice clear solid evidence. It'd be interesting to know why."

He sat back in the padded chair, the very handsome prototype of the popular man of God with his tailored black suit and clerical collar, and for a long moment he just looked at Hackett. Then he said in an expressionless voice, "Prints."

"That's right," said Hackett. "Four nice clear prints of your right hand, Mr. Kramer. And of course they were on file with the Feds on account of that mail fraud all those years back."

Kramer said again, and his voice had dropped, "Prints." And then, startling both his listeners, he came out with a colorful string of obscenities. "Prints!" he said violently.

The willowy youth looked ready to faint.

"I'll have to ask you to come downtown. You're under arrest, Mr. Kramer, and the charge will probably be murder one. I'll use your phone if you don't mind."

Kramer said, and his voice was expressionless again, "Claude, you'd better lock the church after me and give the keys to Mr. Adams. Call him and explain."

The youth gave a little yelp. "But Reverend— But Reverend, I don't understand—" Kramer reached into his pocket and handed him a bunch of keys, ignoring Hackett on the phone. He got up and stood by the window looking out. After a wild look at him the willowy youth bolted.

Hackett said, "There'll be a squad coming to take you in to jail. I don't suppose, while we wait for it, you'd care to tell me the motive for that murder?"

Kramer didn't say a word. Hackett, who was still feeling astonished at this totally unexpected thing, looked at the man interestedly. He was a fine figure of a man, not looking his age, and Hackett suddenly remembered seeing his name in the *TV Guide,* in newspapers, in newspaper items on the religious page.

Kramer said distinctly, "Go to hell."

Hackett said, "I don't think it'll be necessary to put the cuffs on you for the ride in, will it? There's no way you can get away from those fingerprints."

And Kramer said again, as if it were a dirty word, "Prints!" This time his voice was almost agonized. He stood looking out the window, and Hackett realized he was watching everything he had going up in smoke—the beautiful reputation following everything else. All because of the simple little scientific fact, four fingerprints lifted from a paper label. In a way it was an interesting sight.

Neither of them said anything again until Hackett said, "We'll go out front and wait for the squad."

Kramer walked ahead of him to the front steps of the church in rigid silence. When the squad from the Central beat pulled up, the driver was Armstrong, and he looked completely dumbfounded when Hackett told him to deliver Kramer to the jail. "You won't be giving us any trouble, will you? It'd be a little futile."

Kramer said again, "Go to hell," and bent his elegant tall figure to enter the backseat of the squad car. "I'll be right behind you," said Hackett.

When they got to the jail forty minutes later he booked Kramer in, and the booking jailer looked astonished. Hackett called the office; Mendoza was out and he got Higgins. Higgins listened to the news with various comments, and asked, "Do you think we'd get anything out of him now?"

"I don't know, he's had a little time to get accustomed to the idea that we caught up to him. I'll tell you, George, when I walked in there and recognized him, I thought for a minute I was seeing things. It's a beautiful front, he looks so damn noble. We can prod at him some and see if we get anything."

When Higgins walked into the lobby of the jail he said, "On the way over I remembered the name. My God, Art, this fellow's a famous TV personality, he's got the hell of a following—a lot of people go for that kind of thing."

"Yes, when you think about it, it must be a damned profitable racket, George. Not that I ever listen to sermons on TV, but I gather there are always the pleas for contributions, build a new church, convert the heathen, and with the appearance he puts up I'll bet he's been raking it in. And all tax free. But, my God, I thought I was imagining things when I first laid eyes on him."

They talked to Kramer in one of the tiny interrogation rooms. He hadn't yet got issued the tan jail uniform, and he looked incredibly handsome and utterly respectable in his elegant tailoring, with the crest of silver hair and well-shaped manicured hands. But he wouldn't talk to them. He would know, of course, that with two of them there there'd be a witness to anything he said. He only said distinctly, "I'm not answering any questions until I talk to a lawyer. That's my privilege, isn't it?"

"Certainly, Mr. Kramer, that's your privilege."

"WHENEVER WE get one break sometimes we get another," said Mendoza. He was slouched in his desk chair smoking, and he looked a little excited. "*Vaya,* I like our Mr. Kramer—and it's a natural racket for the con man to get into, isn't it?"

Hackett said, "And don't say it, we dragged our heels on your brain wave, Luis, but it looked so damned far-fetched—and, oh, my God, now we'll have to make more phone calls and call all those other forces off—"

Mendoza laughed. "To tell you the truth, I had doubts myself that anything would come of it, Art. But it was an indicated place to look. And now we've got a lead on the rapists. The Japanese girl spotted a tattoo mark." He told them about that. "I've got R. and I. setting the computers going looking back in Records for anybody with a mark like that."

Higgins said, "If he is in Records— Neither of them will necessarily have pedigrees. Oh, it's a place to look. Sometimes we get the breaks." And neat trim Rita Putnam brought in a teletype and a manila envelope.

Mendoza glanced at the teletype and said in exasperation, "The Feds. At long last they get around to passing on more details about Kramer, and it tells us nothing we don't already know." He slid the contents of the envelope out on his desk blotter, a single short sheet, a report from the lab. It confirmed that the slugs that had killed Lake had been fired from the S. and W. .32; and that they had known, but the court liked the scientific evidence. At least now everybody could be called off the car renters and get back to other routine; there had been two new heists over the weekend, witnesses to come in, and usually the new things were coming along. There had been another mugging in a parking lot on Wilshire last night, not that there was much to do about that.

Landers and Grace came in looking weary and heard the news and said in one voice, "Thank God." "As if I didn't have enough driving to do, just getting back and forth to the job," said Landers. "And the baby's turned out to be a night owl, she sleeps peacefully all day and then yells all night. But what a damned queer thing, that TV preacher—I've heard this and that about him, he's very hot stuff, thousands of people thinking he's got a direct line to God."

Grace grinned, brushing at his moustache in unconscious imitation of Mendoza. "Matt Piggott isn't going to like it one little bit, him the earnest fundamentalist. I wouldn't doubt he's one of the Reverend's admirers."

"And I don't think the D.A.'s office is going to like it very much either," said Mendoza. "If he's all that popular and well known this may be making quite a few headlines, boys."

It was getting on for six and they were ready to leave when his phone rang, and it was R. and I. "We sorted out your tattoo mark," said one of the policewomen down there. She didn't sound too excited about it, but that kind of thing was routine to R. and I. "It's listed for a Robert Drake, there's a little package on him, do you want it?"

"Pronto," said Mendoza, and they all stayed a few minutes overtime to wait for that. It came up five minutes later and they took an interested look at it. Robert Drake was Caucasian, six three, a hundred and ninety, black and blue, and the other mark was appended to the description. He'd be twenty-nine now. He had a pedigree of rape, assault with intent, and armed robbery, all committed in Hollywood and the charges made by Hollywood Division. He had served his latest term, a one-to-three for armed robbery, and had been released last May. The last known address was in Hollywood.

Mendoza said, "Night watch is usually slow at the beginning of the week. Let Matt and Bob see if they can pick him up." It was Conway's night off.

PIGGOTT AND SCHENKE tried the Hollywood address for Drake, but he wasn't known there; that wasn't too surprising, it was an apartment and he'd gone to prison from there twenty months ago. The people living there now had never heard of him. They went back to the office and stopped at Communications to ask Sacramento what he was driving, as Mendoza had asked them. The word came back in five minutes. There was a car registered to him, a five-year-old Plymouth, plate number thus and such. They put out an A.P.B. on it. Traffic wouldn't be briefed on that probably until the day shift came on at eight o'clock; and they didn't get another call all the long hours of the night watch.

DUFFY AT THE D.A.'s office called Mendoza that morning. "You aren't going to like it," he said uneasily, "but this Goebel kid. The one who shot your sergeant. He's got no record as a juvenile, and he's just turned eighteen. We can't go for anything but involuntary manslaughter.''

''Did you think that'd surprise us?'' asked Mendoza. ''Of course I don't like it worth a damn, but I can see your position too.''

''One of the public defenders has been to see him,'' said Duffy. ''The hearing will probably be sometime next month or on into March.''

Mendoza said equably, ''And I don't think you're going to like something new we've got for you—you'll get a report tomorrow.'' He told Duffy about Kramer. Duffy was astonished and annoyed.

''For the Lord's sweet sake,'' he said, ''my wife's mother thinks that guy's right next to God. He's got one hell of a following, Mendoza, this is going to make a big stink and plenty of headlines. You're absolutely sure of the evidence?''

''The nice fingerprints. I haven't the foggiest idea what the motive was, but you can't get away from the prints.''

''Damn it,'' said Duffy, ''you don't have to show motive in law, but I'd be happier if you knew something more.''

Mendoza was swiveled around looking out the window. ''I'll tell you, Duffy, some homicides I can get excited about, I'd like to drop on these rapists, but I don't think it matters much in the scheme of things that Archie Kershaw's dead. I can't say I'd lose any sleep if Kramer gets acquitted in a jury trial. But just to satisfy my private curiosity, I'd like to know what the hell was behind it. I can read it up to a point, but beyond that—''

Duffy said dismally, ''And I can just see that happening. You can talk about the nice scientific evidence to hell and back, but I've seen that slick talker on TV sometimes, at my mother-in-law's. He's handsome enough for a movie star and he's one hell of a charmer. And if all the reports are true he'll have money enough to hire a top attorney. Goddamn it, you and I both know what he'll do. He'll stand up there looking all noble and righteous and tell the court he was bringing religious consolation to a poor sick fellow who'd asked him for help, and of course he doesn't approve of drinking alcohol but it seemed to give the poor fellow some comfort and he'd just poured him a little drink, which is how his finger-prints got on the bottle. And of course he had no idea that the misguided man had already added the sleeping pills to the whiskey, meaning to commit suicide. And the defense attorney will have seen to it that there are plenty of females on the jury, and they'll love him and believe every word he says.''

Mendoza laughed. "I can see that happening too. Damn it, I'd like to know why he took such a hell of a risk. We can deduce that Kershaw was blackmailing him, there was that cash, but why just then did he decide on murder? And Kershaw as Maulden, and his wife, were living pretty close to the bone. He hadn't been getting money from Kramer right along. And Kramer as the Reverend Thurlow has been on this racket for a long time, hasn't he?''

"Ten or twelve years at least, I think, he'd been on TV that long anyway.''

"There are still things we don't know. If they'd been in contact since they both got out of Leavenworth, why hadn't he cut Kershaw in on the racket as a secretary or something? What the hell did trigger that murder?''

Duffy said, "Even if we knew, when I think about it, it wouldn't help us to get a conviction. I don't like this one damn bit, Mendoza. But we'll have to go through the motions.''

THEY HADN'T got through the entire list of Dr. Petersons yet, and it was a tedious slow job. The A.P.B. hadn't turned up Drake.

Higgins had a halfway bright idea on Wednesday morning and called Welfare and Rehab to ask if Drake had ever been on parole. He had, from his first term in six years ago, and Higgins talked to his former parole officer, whose name was Peavey. ''What does he do when he does hold a job, if he ever does?''

Peavey said, ''If he's the one I remember, he hasn't much education, he'd worked as a painter, at gas stations. I couldn't give you any lead on where to locate him, Sergeant, but the DMV should have a current address—''

Annoyed, Higgins said, ''They're supposed to, of course.'' That had come down to the night watch on Monday night, part of the car registration, but it was out-of-date, it was another address in Hollywood and Drake had moved six months ago.

''Oh,'' said Peavey. ''Well, that's all I can tell you.''

Higgins swore at the phone. They now had three more heisters to look for, the ape-man Slocum was being arraigned tomorrow and the old drunk Rafferty the next day, and probably Clyde Anderson next Monday, and time in court was wasted time.

ON WEDNESDAY morning Landers was talking to another Dr. Peterson. This one was an allergy specialist in Westwood, the fourth doctor Landers had called this morning. He was a careful methodical man and it was a few minutes before Landers convinced him that he ought

to cooperate. Then he turned Landers over to his office
nurse with instructions to pass on the information. She
told him that a Howard Boyer had an appointment at
that time on that date, and Landers thanked her, phoned
the name down to R. and I., and sat back and lit a cigarette, massaging the back of his neck. He felt as if he
hadn't had enough sleep in days, and if he wasn't careful he'd fall asleep at the wheel on the way home and
leave Phil to raise a fatherless child. Of course they would
be stuck with that house in Azusa for God knew how
long.

Wanda and Glasser were talking to other Dr. Petersons. He still had about a dozen to call. He was reluc-
tant to pick up the phone again, and was just reaching for
it when it rang. The policewoman down in R. and I. said
impersonally, "There's a package on a Howard Boyer,
shall I send it up?"

"Yes, please," said Landers, and to the others, "Hold
everything, we may be getting somewhere." When the
package came up they looked at it interestedly, and
Glasser said suddenly, "Hell, I remember this guy. I arrested him the last time, for God's sake."

The pedigree consisted of two counts of armed robbery, and Boyer was just a year out of Folsom and off
parole. The description said he was six two, a hundred
and ninety, and he could very well be the big man in the
light raincoat who had robbed Abrahams and shot Bernie Wolfe.

"By God, I think we've got something here," said
Landers. The address was out-of-date but it would be a
starting point. Landers and Glasser went out to look.

It was an address in Westwood, an apartment, and
there wasn't anyone at home so they talked to the only
neighbor they found in, an old lady watching a soap op-

era on TV, and she said, Oh, Miss Boyer worked at that big stationery store in Santa Monica, Rogers Stationers, they could find her there. At the stationers', they found Harriet Boyer just leaving to have lunch, a rather homely girl with a big nose. She listened to the question and said quietly, "You're police, aren't you? And Howard's been up to something again and you're after him. I'll never know why he turned out to be a crook, we were all raised right, my other brother's a schoolteacher. Yes, he lived with me for a while when he was broke—before he did another robbery."

"Do you know where we might find him now?" asked Glasser.

"He calls Mother once in a while, he's got an apartment somewhere around here with a friend of his. Mother's got the phone number, I think." She called her mother and got it for them. Landers talked to a supervisor at the phone company and after she'd verified his name with headquarters she gave them the address, Rochester Avenue.

It was a new apartment building, and Boyer-Fisher were listed in an apartment in an upstairs front unit. Glasser pushed the bell and the door was opened by a wiry young fellow in expensive sports clothes. "Is Mr. Boyer here?" asked Glasser.

"Yeah, you just caught him. Hey, Howie—some guys asking for you."

He came out of the bedroom, a tall dark nearly handsome man. He had on dark slacks and was just putting a shirt on over his naked chest. And on his left shoulder was the not quite healed scar, still red and puckered, where the security guard's slug had struck him that day.

They pulled out the badges, and Glasser said, "We're taking you in, Boyer. And you too," to the other man.

"There were four of you on that caper—were you one of them, Fisher?"

They were taken completely by surprise. Fisher said stupidly, "My God, Howie, how'd they drop on us? We got away clean—"

"You'll never know," said Landers. They both began to bluster then, but Glasser called up a squad and they were packed off to jail. Glasser and Landers went back to base and applied for a search warrant. It came through at four o'clock, and they went back there and looked around. They found most of Mr. Abrahams' Krugerrands and sovereigns neatly stacked on the closet shelf; evidently Boyer had been selling them one at a time as he needed the money. They also found two S. and W. revolvers. They dropped those off at the lab. The lab could match one of them to the slug out of Bernie Wolfe, and there were witnesses to the fact that it had been the tall man in the light raincoat who had shot Wolfe. The endless routine got boring but sometimes it paid off in the end.

THE A.P.B. on Drake's car had been out for nearly a week before it was spotted. A squad man riding a beat in Central Hollywood on Sunday afternoon noticed it parked in a carport under one of the gimcrack apartments along Fountain Avenue, and called it in. Mendoza and Hackett were both in the office and got there half an hour later. No Drake was listed in the row of mailboxes; there was a manager on the premises and they showed the badges and asked which unit the carport belonged to.

"Why, Mr. Burns in number three at the end of the hall, but police—Mr. Burns wouldn't be in trouble with the police, he's a nice quiet young fellow, he works at a bank.''

Burns was at home. He was a stocky young man with friendly eyes, and he looked at the badges and heard the questions and said in dismay, "Oh, Lord, is something wrong about it? Don't tell me that car's hot?"

"Where'd you get it?" asked Hackett.

"I just bought it couple of weeks ago, the heap I was driving wasn't worth fixing up and I've got to have transportation."

"Who'd you buy it from? Where?"

"A fellow at a car wash down on Vermont. It was a week ago Tuesday, I'd had to borrow my mother's car to get to work, and I was going to look around some used lots that night, but I stopped in this place to get the car cleaned up for her and there was the Plymouth with the for-sale sign on it. It seemed to be in pretty good condition, and I drove it around the block, it seemed fine. The fellow was only asking six fifty for it so I clinched the deal. He's supposed to send in the change of registration, and I haven't got it yet but you know the DMV."

"Which car wash was it?" asked Hackett, and he told them.

They went down there to see if it was open on Sunday and it was. The manager said, "Drake? He's the big guy over there waxing the Chrysler."

Sometimes they had to go a long way around, but they had got there in the end. They put the arm on Drake and took him in, questioned him at the jail. He was a brawny fellow with heavy coarse features, and when Hackett pushed up his right sleeve there was the tattoo mark Suzy had described.

"The girl will swear to that," Mendoza told him, "and we'll nail you for the other girls—and the dead one—on the M.O., Drake. Will you take the rap alone or ring in your pal?''

He growled at them; he wasn't very bright. After a while he decided to tell them; the pal was one Gordon Estes and they shared a pad on Barton Avenue in Hollywood. They found Estes at home and booked him in too. There was still the endless routine going on, a couple of new heists and a yet unidentified body in an old hotel on Figueroa, but they were glad to have this one cleared up. There would be no more girls abducted from the USC campus.

AT TEN O'CLOCK on Wednesday morning the Central desk rang Mendoza and the Sergeant said, ''I just had a woman come in off the street, she said she wanted to talk to somebody important about Tony Alvarez. I sent her up to you.''

''What the hell?'' said Mendoza. ''Did she say why?''

''No, just that it was about Alvarez. There hasn't been a smell of that pair, they'll be long gone by now.''

''I wonder,'' said Mendoza. ''Thanks.'' The woman came into the anteroom alongside the switchboard a few minutes later and he was waiting for her. She was a dark, rather handsome woman in her thirties, if she carried a little too much weight and was flashily dressed. She looked him up and down. ''Are you somebody high up?'' she asked forthrightly.

''Lieutenant Mendoza.''

''I guess that'll do,'' she said.

He took her into his office and gave her a chair and she sat down. ''I'm Elise Alvarez, I'm Tony's wife,'' she said bluntly. ''I can tell you where to pick him up, and Camacho too.''

Mendoza regarded her with interest. "You're blowing the whistle on them? We thought you knew where they were."

She said equably, "They planned that break ever since they'd been in jail waiting to go to court. They were going to pull some jobs to get a good stake and then we were going to head down into Mexico, it's cheaper to live there. We had it set up so we could phone them from my sister's place in case you had a tap on my phone or Rosa's—Camacho's girl. They've been at Juan Garcia's pad out in Burbank."

"And just why are you telling the tale on them?"

She said bitterly, "Because Tony's fixing to run out on me, damn him. He's been all lovey-dovey on the phone but Juan's wife called me last night because she figured I ought to know, they're fixing to take off tomorrow and Tony's taking this other girl instead of me, some blond tramp he's picked up on the side. I don't put up with that from that bastard. I'd rather have him back in the joint. I'll tell you where they are, it's Valley Street in Burbank," and she added an address. "That's all I wanted to say," and she got up.

Mendoza watched her out and grinned. As he reached for the phone, he quoted to himself, "'Nor hell a fury like a woman scorned—'" He called Valley Division and they set up the raid for this afternoon.

EVEN AS DUFFY had predicted, the press had been busy on Kramer. There had been headlines, and the citizens taking bitter sides with letters to the editors. Kramer had acquired a famous, and it was rumored an unscrupulous, attorney; the trial wouldn't be coming up for some time. And Mendoza was still curious about him.

Kramer had been sitting in jail for two week when purely on impulse Mendoza dropped in there on a Saturday morning to see him. Kramer was still the handsome and magnetic presence even in the tan jail uniform; Mendoza sat down across the tiny table from him in the interrogation room and said conversationally, "You know, Kramer, I'm like the Elephant's Child, I'm full of curiosity. I'd like to know just why you committed that murder. We both know you'll get off clear, and we both know how and why. I haven't got a witness with me, and there aren't any bugs planted. I'd be satisfied if you'd just tell me privately, one citizen to another."

Kramer studied him for a moment and then he laughed. It was a hard and cynical laugh. "Oh, I believe you," he said. "You boys have to be so damned careful these days, you don't dare use the underhand tactics. Surely to God I'll get clear of this, and without a stain— as they say—on my character. That smooth shyster will ask all the right questions in front of a jury. And he'd make mincemeat of you if you ever tried to testify to this little talk."

"I wouldn't dream of trying to, Mr. Kramer."

"Thurlow, please—I changed it legally, you know, and it's so much more euphonious. I may be tempting fate but I've got an impulse to tell you the truth. Just between citizens," and his deep smooth voice was sardonic. Suddenly he slapped one hand down on the table in petulant gesture. "Archie Kershaw!" he said contemptuously. "That damned little small-timer! He was never in my class at the rackets, he couldn't think big enough. We'd worked a few scams together, and it was all his damned carelessness brought the Feds down on us that time. Oh, he was bright enough to sucker the old ladies but that's about all. When I got out of Leavenworth, I was shut of him. I had my plans all made, everybody knows California's full of the suckers, especially for anything with a religious twist, but there's a religious revival going on all over. I wasn't about to put on a turban and peddle the mystic bit. Plain old-fashioned evangelism, that's the going thing. I had a good stake put away, never mind where," and he grinned at Mendoza. "I headed west and began to build my image. I bought some TV time, and by God, Lieutenant, if I do say it myself I preach the hell of a good sermon. I gathered in quite a following, and the money started to come in, all the suckers sending in their ten and twenty bucks a month all for the glory of God and to convert sinners. I built that church down there, I'm raking in high fees for outside lectures and, by God, I had it made for life when Archie Kershaw had to poke his nose in. I hadn't thought of him in years. How the hell should I know he was in California? Small-timer Archie, starting to get crippled up so he finds the obliging female to support him—maybe it was a kindness to put him out of his misery, by God. It was pure chance he saw me on TV, that wife of his had started to listen to me. Of course he knew me and he wrote me a letter—a very cute letter. He knew it might be seen by a secretary, so all he said was that he hoped I'd remember an old friend who'd known me before I got to be such a great man, and if I could find time he'd like to see me, and he gave a phone number. Well, naturally I read between the lines, he knew the press would eat up the story about my record."

"And won't they now?" asked Mendoza.

Kramer-Thurlow said, "Needs must when the devil drives, so they say. The shyster and I'll have to do our best with it. He'll try to keep it out of the trial record on technicalities, but if it gets out in detail, hell, I'm a hum-

ble reformed sinner who's seen the error of my ways and
all the better Christian for it. There's no limit to what the
suckers will believe, especially in the name of religion.
Well, I phoned him, and I sent him some money but the
more I thought about it the more worried I got. He told
me he'd already had one stroke, and he never did have
any judgment, he was so damned pleased at knowing a
great big important secret, he might have been tempted
to let it out to anybody just to sound important himself.
I decided the only safe way was to get rid of him. I got
hold of those sleeping pills from a doctor in my congre-
gation, told him I was having insomnia through worrying about money for the cause, and by God he doubled
his contribution last month. I put the whole batch into
that bottle of bourbon and sealed the bottle again. Archie had told me his wife was away all day. I picked that
rainy day to be less visible as it were, but of course I had
to rent the car under my own name because of my driver's license. My own car's a Mercedes and around that
squalid little neighborhood somebody might have noticed it. He was delighted when I showed up, thought I
wanted to talk over old times. I had to persuade him to
take the drinks, but it was always his favorite brand and
finally he did. But I was nervous, I didn't want to hang
around there any longer than I had to. I didn't want to
wait till he passed out, that might take a while. I thought
I'd been so damned careful handling that bottle! Offering to fix the drinks, pretending to have one with him! I
got out as soon as I could, he was acting a little drunk or
maybe it was the stuff coming on.'' He sat back and
laughed savagely. ''By God, when your man said you'd
picked up my prints, I damned near passed out myself!
And now you can go away and forget all about this,
Lieutenant. After you'd locked me in here, and I must

say it's a more comfortable jail than a couple I've known back east, I thought it over and knew I could beat this one. With all the loyal following I've got, and the kind of tale I can pitch—'' he laughed. ''I may lose a few of the faithful but there'll always be more coming along. And they'll always believe the corrupt cops tried to frame me.''

''I don't doubt it,'' said Mendoza.

Thurlow sat back and laughed again. ''You have to make the best of bad luck— Think of all the free publicity I'm getting. And this is the best Goddamned scam I've ever been in on, because it's absolutely legal.''

UNEXPECTEDLY, the next morning Rita ushered in a visitor to Mendoza's office. He was Japanese, tall for his race, immaculately tailored. He offered Mendoza a card and it said *Senji Suzuki*. ''I want to thank you for your kindness to my daughter, sir, and for letting me know what had happened.''

''It's nothing to what she did for us, Mr. Suzuki. It was the information she gave us that made it possible for us to arrest those two rapists.''

''That was good.''

''I hope your daughter is better.''

Suzuki said gravely, ''We hope she will be, in time to come. The doctors tell me there are specialists, operations, and most fortunately I can afford that.''

''It sounds ironic,'' said Mendoza, ''that she came all the way from Japan, to be here and able to give us that information.''

''And to be injured so. Yes. But it is, how might I express it, the law of the infinite. We are Buddhists, Lieutenant, and we are taught that there is order and reason in all the world. In the cycle of rebirths good deeds are rewarded and evil punished—it is the law of Karma—but not in the same incarnation always. What you call fate, destiny, it is but the law of Karma bringing judgment of past lives and preparing for new." He gave Mendoza a grave bow. "I will not intrude longer on your time. I am honored to have met you, sir."

HACKETT WAS typing a report in the middle of the afternoon on Thursday when Rita passed on a call. It was a homicide, and by the first report nothing very important, a brawl in a bar down on Temple with a man knifed. But there would have to be a report on it, and he went out. It was a hole-in-the-wall of a place, and in front of the bar the uniformed man had a civilian handcuffed.

The bartender, a fat man in a dirty white apron, was saying, "I never seen either of 'em before, don't know who they are, they been havin' a few beers and they go to arguin' about somethin', and first thing I know they've got knives out—"

The man in cuffs was young and black and sullen. He said, "That damn bastard, he was holdin' out on me, that last piece of loot we took—"

Hackett bent to look at the body, the body of another black man. He'd been stabbed in the back, and his right arm was flung out on the dirty floor. There was a ring on his middle finger; Hackett lifted the hand and tugged it off. "That's right," said the other man, "go to robbin' him when he's dead. Dirty cops! He hung on to that too, wouldn't hock it and share the bread." The yellow-gold shank bore a five-dollar gold piece dated 1893. Hackett turned it over, and in worn engraving on the inside of the shank made out the initials W.J.C.

Belle had been avenged.

MENDOZA GOT home early that afternoon; business was slow at the office. He drove up the hill and saw the twins on their ponies trotting around the fenced ring with Kearney supervising and Cedric bouncing along after them. He waved at them.

Nobody was in the kitchen and he went down the long hall to the big living room. Alison was sitting in her armchair with all four cats on her lap; she was staring moodily at the opposite wall and her red hair was a little tousled. Baby Luisa was staggering around the floor practising walking.

"Nice day, *querida?*"

"No," said Alison. She added, "You will be so impulsive."

Mendoza regarded her quizzically. "What have I done now?"

"Of course Mairí thinks it's just fine, but I think it's ridiculous. You'll be forty-eight on the last day of the month."

"Indubitably," said Mendoza. "Time marches on. What are you talking about?"

"We said three was enough. A nice family."

Mendoza stared at her. "*¡No me diga!* You don't tell me—"

"Well, I've been wondering—and after you left this morning I was sick as a dog, and I'll see the doctor this week but I know what he'll tell me—"

Mendoza started to laugh. He collapsed into the opposite armchair and laughed until his sides ached, and sat up and wiped his eyes. "*¡Es demasiado!* Didn't I say there was something catching going around the office!"

"Lively and appealing. Simonson deftly juggles a cozy modern suspense story with an up-to-date romance."

—*Publishers Weekly*

LARKSPUR

SHEILA SIMONSON

ODE TO A KILLER

Distinguished poet Dai Llewellyn was throwing his annual summer house party—with the cream of Northern California's literary crop in attendance. Lark Dailey, owner of Larkspur Books, knew four days of bookish chitchat could be tedious—but good for business.

But no sooner had the party come to life when the host died—sipping a glass of Campari laced with a lethal dose of larkspur. Evidently, the killer had a sense of humor. Lark wasn't laughing.

Many had reason to kill the aging poet, whose lauded verse belied a life of sordid affairs and family disharmony. He was also worth millions. Soon, a second, then a third victim appear in this inspired sonnet of death... composed by a clever killer.

First Time in Paperback

TED WOOD
A REID BENNETT MYSTERY
ON THE INSIDE

GOING UNDERCOVER WAS NO WAY TO SPEND A HONEYMOON

But the police commission needed a favor—badly—so Reid Bennett, his new wife and police dog, Sam, pack up for the Canadian mining town of Elliot, where Reid lands a job as a local cop to investigate rumors of police corruption.

Violence seems to be a way of life in the rough gold mining town...so do kickbacks, payoffs, extortion...and sudden death. The closer Bennett gets to the playing table, the deadlier the game becomes. A cop willing to talk suddenly dies; a hooker with a big mouth is strangled. Bennett receives a Molotov cocktail.

"Travis McGee may no longer be around, but Reid Bennett's here to take his place."
—UPI

MYSTERY **WORLDWIDE LIBRARY**
TM

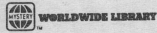

THE CRUEL MOTHER

A MEG HALLORAN MYSTERY

JANET LAPIERRE

WERE THEY CAPTIVES BECAUSE OF SOME MOUNTAIN MAN'S FANTASY? OR SOMETHING COMPLETELY UNCONNECTED?

Meg Halloran's romantic getaway with longtime love, policeman Vince Gutierrez looks less appealing when Vince reluctantly introduces the third member of their party, his spike-haired, foul-mouthed niece, Cass.

An accident with another car abruptly ends their plans. Then Meg and Cass are inexplicably abducted, held in a secluded wilderness cabin in Idaho's panhandle.

Meg desperately seeks answers—and a means of escape—unaware her fate lies with strangers: a terminally-ill sixties radical who recently confessed to murder; his wife, emerging from seclusion to reunite the dying man with their young daughter; and a lawyer, calculating one of the biggest scores of his circumspect career....

You'll flip . . . your pages won't!
Read paperbacks *hands-free* with

Book Mate · I

The perfect "mate" for all your romance paperbacks

**Traveling • Vacationing • At Work • In Bed • Studying
• Cooking • Eating**

Perfect size for all standard paperbacks, this wonderful invention makes reading a pure pleasure! Ingenious design holds paperback books OPEN and FLAT so even wind can't ruffle pages— leaves your hands free to do other things. Reinforced, wipe-clean vinyl-covered holder flexes to let you turn pages without undoing the strap . . . supports paperbacks so well, they have the strength of hardcovers!

Pages turn WITHOUT opening the strap.

SEE-THROUGH STRAP

Reinforced back stays flat.

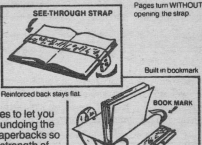

Built in bookmark

BOOK MARK

BACK COVER
HOLDING STRIP

10˝ x 7¼˝, opened.
Snaps closed for easy carrying, too.

Available now. Send your name, address, and zip code, along with a check or money order for just $5.95 + .75¢ for delivery (for a total of $6.70) payable to Reader Service to:

> Reader Service
> Bookmate Offer
> 3010 Walden Avenue
> P.O. Box 1396
> Buffalo, N.Y. 14269-1396

Offer not available in Canada
*New York residents add appropriate sales tax.

BM-GR